*The Penny Court Enquirers*

# *Deadly Spirit*
## *A Victorian Mystery*

**Raymond Buckland**

Queen Victoria Press

The Penny Court Enquirers Mysteries:

One Clue at a Time

The Noble Savage

Deadly Spirit

THE PENNY COURT ENQUIRERS:

DEADLY SPIRIT

Copyright © 2017  Raymond Buckland

ISBN 978-0-9794560-6-0

## Queen Victoria Press

P.O. Box 892, Wooster, OH 44691-0892

*www.raymondbucklandbooks.com*

For Tara and in memory of Tish

# *Deadly Spirit*

## London, 1886

## *Chapter One*

Ever since her attention had been diverted from the
medium's phenomena by the grumbling of a sitter's
stomach, Lady Marlborough had made it a point to
provide a small selection of snacks, together with a
glass of wine, before the start of her regular Friday
evening séances. With the gaseliers turned all the
way down, the sitters holding hands about the big
walnut table, and the medium breathing regularly
but heavily in the darkness, the last thing one
needed was to hear the growling and rumbling of
one's neighbor's empty stomach.

Her ladyship now sat with Professor Harry
Sedgeworth on her left and the medium, Prince
Honoré, on her right. Others about the table were
Dr. William Price, Captain Cyril Grimsby, Mr.

Maurice Austin, Miss Winifred Dobson and Miss Alice Bell. Together, the sitters made up what Lady Marlborough called her "Mystic Seven." All were now satisfactorily snacked, wined, and expectant of communication with the spirits.

Communicating with the spirits of the departed was all the rage in England, and especially so in a large city such as London. Mrs. Hayden, the wife of an American journalist, had brought the Spiritualist movement to England a little over thirty-five years ago and it had now progressed past the table-tipping and rapping phase to where talented mediums could produce actual materializations of the dear departed, right in one's living-room. Lady Constance Marlborough had immersed herself in such activities and considered herself one of the prime movers of this new society; not yet a religion but a fully-absorbing pastime. Certainly by the majority of people – the press in particular – it was assumed to have religious significance.

The medium moaned. It was a slight sound but sufficient for one of Lady Marlborough's sensibilities to know that some form of phenomenon was imminent. She found herself holding her breath and let it out as quietly as she could. The medium groaned again.

Prince Honoré was a phenomenon himself. Newly arrived in London, he was creating a stir among the spiritualist followers. Her ladyship was seen as honored in that she had so far been able to obtain exclusivity for his appearances. She glanced in his direction, though in the darkness she could see nothing. He was a dashing young man who stirred the hearts of many a woman – both young and the not so young. He wore a startlingly white turban with a large emerald jewel pinned just above the position of what Lady Marlborough had learned to be the "Third Eye" – one of the *chakras*, as the cognoscenti termed it. The prince was slightly tanned, with startlingly piercing green eyes and a thin mustache above his sensuous mouth. His teeth gleamed white and his voice, although somewhat high but never raised, reached all corners of the séance room.

"Winnie? Are you there, Winnie?"

Winifred Dobson gasped.

"Don't break the circle," murmured Lady Marlborough, in a low voice.

"No. No, of course not," came the response.

"Winnie!" The medium's voice came again. "We are all here. All here for you, my dear."

Lady Marlborough knew that Miss Dobson herself very much wanted to become a medium and was studying in that direction. But her ladyship didn't think that anyone else present knew of that desire.

"We will help you on your journey, my dear. We will smooth the path for you."

"Oh! Oh, thank you." Miss Dobson gave a little sob.

"Know that we love you."

"Thank you. Oh, thank you." Another sob.

There was silence for a moment, and then the voice of the medium took on a harsher note. "So it's *Captain* Cyril, is it?"

"W-what? Do you mean me?" Cyril Grimsby sounded surprised. Indeed, all of the Mystic Seven began to wonder at this sudden shift in tone. Prince Honoré had presided at a half dozen or more séances since initially taking the reins of the group but the spirits he had introduced had never been anything but friendly before. This one sounded undeniably antagonistic.

"*Captain* Grimsby! Hah! That's what you always wanted, is it not?"

"Who is this?"

"Never you mind who it is, Cyril. This is where it all ends."

"What . . . what do you mean?"

Lady Marlborough thought she heard a sudden gasp from Cyril Grimsby but she couldn't be sure. She was feeling slightly uncomfortable. Her séances were known for their professionalism. People frequently approached her, in the social scene, hoping to become one of her sitters. But she had once been told that seven was a "mystical number" of great power and she had determined to restrict her members to that number.

"Dr. Price, how goes your research?" The medium's voice changed again and everyone recognized the friendly tone of a spirit that had many times come through to speak with the doctor; a spirit claiming to be a past instructor of the doctor from many years before, when he was a student in medical school.

"Doctor Wilberforce!" acknowledged Price. "How nice to hear you again. Thank you, my work progresses well."

"I understand you have been having some difficulty obtaining suitable specimens?"

"Yes. Yes, I have. How did you . . . ?"

The voice chuckled. "Oh, we in the Spirit World know all that is going on there, William."

The exchanges continued for almost an hour, with every one of the sitters receiving a message; some short and some long but all seemingly significant. Miss Alice Bell heard from her recently deceased mother and even the skeptical journalist, Mr. Maurice Austin, got a message from his grandfather. Lady Marlborough was well pleased, despite the brief disquieting exchange between Captain Grimsby and the unknown spirit. She began to relax and prepared for the closing prayer which they always shared.

Prince Honoré's voice faded and he could be heard settling back in his chair. He let out a long, soft sigh, as he always did when the spirits left him. Her ladyship mentally counted to ten and then led the prayer.

"We thank the spirits who have blessed us with their presence.

May they know rest and repose, basking in the never-ending light

That fills their souls and refreshes their hearts.

May they come again, to pass through that veil which separates

The Summerland from the world of the physical;

Teaching us that what we term death is no more than a transition

From one reality to the next.

Amen."

"Amen," they all murmured.

"I will see to the light," said Professor Sedgeworth, the tallest of their number. His hand found the tap on the gaselier and turned it up. Bright light flooded the room and everyone blinked around at their neighbor.

Dr. Price stood and stretched. Winifred Dobson's and Alice Bell's heads came together as they excitedly exchanged thoughts on what they had just experienced.

"Come on Captain!" Maurice Austin, the journalist, reached over to shake the shoulder of Cyril Grimsby, who's head had fallen forward and was now slumped at the table.

"Is he all right?" asked Lady Marlborough. "I do hope that he was not too affected by that strange . . ."

"My God! Oh, your pardon, ladies." Austin had come to his feet and moved to stand beside the recumbent figure of Grimsby. "Doctor Price! I think we may need you here."

The doctor took up a hand of the slouched-over figure. He turned a serious face to his hostess. "It would appear that Captain Grimsby has transitioned to the other side, my lady. He is dead!"


The kitchen of number 27 Penny Court was the very heart of the house. Although dim of light and frequently odiferous with the smells of cooking, it was the head office for all the domestic activities and was the favorite gathering place for the residents and their close friends. It was the planning room for the wide variety of activities indulged in by the Penny Court Enquirers. The Enquirers were none other than Bertie Hawkins and his brother-in-law Arnold Middleton, with occasional input and financial control from Bertie's wife Nellie.

On being "let go" from his longtime job at *The Daily Chronicle* on the occasion of its absorption by *The Morning Post*, Bertie had decided to indulge in his dream of beating the detective police at their own game. For years he had read reports of Scotland Yard's ineptitude at solving cases of robbery and even murder, and in a few short months had already more than bettered the Yard's record. In the process, Bertie had managed to turn Police Detective Inspector Campbell Moss from a scornful critic into a firm friend. The good inspector was now a constant visitor to the kitchen – and the dining room – at Penny Court. It was no secret that Nellie's cooking had done much to cement the relationship.

The Hawkins's freckle-faced, ginger-haired, fifteen-year-old maid-of-all-work, Isobel, added her own unique flavor to the running of the house. When she could get her nose out of the Penny Dreadfuls she absorbed – aided and abetted by Arnold – she could be far more astute than her years and had many times surprised her master and mistress.

"This is a nice cup of tea, Nell," said Bertie, appreciatively, as he sat at the kitchen table and finished the job of waking up.

"You can thank Isobel for that," said Nellie, already planning her day. Breakfast had been made and if Bertie had let his kippers get cold, well, that was no fault of hers.

"Thank you Isobel," said Bertie dutifully. The little figure bent over the dishes in the sink nodded her carrot-red head and continued with what she was doing.

"Good kippers too," said Arnold. He did not live with the Hawkinses, insisting on not intruding on their "domestic bliss", as he put it. But he never failed to scurry around from his lodgings with old Mrs. Westbury on Fish Street, to join them for breakfast . . . or lunch, or dinner.

"Kippers," murmured Bertie, suddenly aware of them. "Mmm. Nice."

Arnold invariably had his head buried in a newspaper, no matter the time of day. He said that he liked to "keep up with things" though he seldom had any comments on what he was reading. This morning, however, was to be different.

"Did you see this?" Arnold asked of no one in particular. He stabbed at the item in the Saturday morning newspaper with the handle of his fish fork. There followed a pause while he extracted a kipper bone from between his teeth and placed it delicately on the edge of his plate. Meanwhile the others waited for him to elucidate.

"What is it?" Bertie could wait no longer.

"Fellow at one of them spirit see-ances, had a heart attack in the middle of things. I guess he was anxious to see how things looked from the other side."

Isobel laughed out loud and then tried to disguise it as coughing. Nellie looked at her sternly.

"What do you mean?" asked Bertie.

"Here!" Arnold tapped the paper with his fork again, then read the item to them "'At last evening's see . . . see-ance . . . that word . . . at Lady Constance Marlborough's Knightsbridge residence, the evening with the spirits ended when one of the regular sitters, Captain Cyril Grimsby, had an apparent heart attack. Lady Marlborough is well known among spiritists as a pioneer of the movement, hosting weekly gatherings, invitations to which are much sought after. Others at the evening's meeting included the well-known psychic investigator Professor Harry Sedgeworth and Harley Street specialist Dr. William Price.'"

"Quite a gathering," said Nellie.

"What do you think, Bertie?" asked Arnold. "Do you believe in these spirits?"

Bertie poured himself a second cup of tea and added milk and two lumps of sugar. "I don't know, Arnold. There seem to be many confusing sides to the question. Lots of fake mediums exposed but some who have been tried and tested and found to be genuine. At least that's what I have read about it so far."

"I'd like to see a ghost." Isobel's voice came from the sink. Everyone ignored her.

"Wasn't that Scottish man – Hume, was it? – wasn't he supposed to be the real thing?" asked Nellie.

"Daniel Dunglas Home," said Bertie, nodding. "Yes. He died just this year. They say he had never been caught out. But there aren't many like him."

"Don't think I'd fancy talking to dead people," said Arnold, pushing away his plate and then inspecting the toast in the hopes of finding a piece that Isobel had not burned.

There was a ring of the front door bell.

"That'll be Campbell," said Nellie, with a smile on her face. "He's becoming a regular for breakfast these days."

Isobel wiped her hands on her apron and ran off up the stairs to get the door. She soon returned accompanied by the tall, thin, police inspector. His pinched face and sharp nose presented a stern outward appearance, but seeing the breakfast on the kitchen table, and watching Isobel pull out a chair for him, caused a smile to break out under the scraggly grey mustache that echoed the bushy grey eyebrows above his nose. Like Arnold, the inspector, who was unmarried, had rooms that he rented and was always appreciative of home cooking.

"'ave you ever seen a ghost, Hinspector?" asked Isobel, as she returned to the sink.

"Isobel! You mind your place," said Nellie. Isobel sniffed. To the inspector Nellie said, "We were just talking about the man who had a heart attack at a spirit gathering in Knightsbridge, Campbell. Did you hear anything about that?"

The Scotsman scratched the bald spot on top of his head as his eyes ran around the table seeing what was offered. He quickly settled on the last of the kippers, to Bertie's slight annoyance.

"The one at Lady What's-her-name's place?"

"Yes."

Moss nodded. All eyes seemed to be on him now as he started his breakfast while the others finished theirs.

"That was just a heart attack though, wasn't it?" asked Bertie. "You wouldn't be called in for that, would you?"

"Normally, nay," agreed the policeman. "But as it happens, we *were* called in. It seems there is some suspicion regarding the circumstances." He had the attention of all of them, including the freckle-faced girl at the kitchen sink. "The man was in his thirties. Active – he was an army Captain – and outwardly fit. Nay the sort you'd expect to have a heart attack. Not while he was quietly sitting down with friends, at any rate."

"Per'aps they wasn't friends!" said Isobel, darkly.

"Isobel!" cried Nellie. "I've told you . . ."

"In fact, she may be right," said Moss. "That's something I have to follow up on. Were they all friends, or was there someone there who might have wished the man dead?"

"Well done, Isobel," murmured Arnold. The maid turned bright red and almost dipped her head into the water in the sink.

## Chapter Two

Bertie's mentor at the old *Daily Chronicle* had been the paper's senior editor, Evans "Taffy" Lloyd. Many years ago Taffy had got the orphaned Bertie a regular job at the newspaper after the boy had spent years selling papers on street corners. The Welshman had been fortunate enough to stay on when *The Morning Post* bought out *The Daily Chronicle* and Bertie looked up to him like a son to a father. In recent months Taffy had been able to provide Bertie with information vital to the cases he had worked on.

"I think I'll go and talk with Taffy," Bertie said to Nellie later that day. "See if he knows anything about these séances. Taffy always keeps his finger on the pulse. He has to, of course."

"You don't think Campbell and his Scotland Yard people can handle this one?" Nellie asked.

Bertie smiled. "You know I like Campbell, Nell, but we've already proven that the Penny Court Enquirers are superior to the Scotland Yard Detective Police. I don't think it will hurt to do a little enquiring about these séances. The Yard can always use all the help they can get."

He set off for Fleet Street and arrived at the junction of that street and Shoe Lane at lunch time, knowing that he'd find the Welshman lunching in *The Printer's Imp*, a hostelry popular with the newspapermen of the area.

"Bertie!" Taffy was at his usual corner table in the busy tavern and was delighted to see his old friend. "Come and sit down. Let me get you a porter."

He waved to the serving girl, who was balancing a tray full of tankards as she maneuvered around the closely packed tables. She gave Taffy a nod and Bertie a quick smile. Her name was Annie and she wasn't much older than Isobel, but had been serving at *The Printer's Imp* for several years.

"Do you want anything to eat, boy-o? This shepherd's pie is good."

"No thanks, Taffy. Just the porter will be fine."

When they were settled and had caught up on the latest newspaper business concerns, Bertie asked his old friend about Campbell's suspicions concerning the Knightsbridge séance death.

"Lady Constance Marlborough is a big proponent of this Spiritualism," said Taffy. "She's very well respected, you know? Lady Marlborough is the daughter of the late ninth Earl of Marlborough and is very proud of the family history. She must be devastated at the thought of a murder at one of her séances. But yes, Bertie. The word is that this Captain Grimsby had some help in making his transition to the Spirit World."

"Murdered, then?"

The Welshman nodded. "So goes the word on the Street." He looked up. "Ah! Now here's the man who can tell us. Is it not your friend Inspector Moss?"

Bertie swung around and was surprised to find the inspector squeezing through the tables to reach them.

"Campbell! What are you doing here?" he asked, as the policeman arrived and dropped down into a chair, his face red from the exertion of pushing through the crowded tavern. "Will you have a drink? Looks as though you could use one."

"I'm nay supposed to drink while on duty, you know that."

"Of course. Sorry."

"I'll have a porter, thank you."

Bertie suppressed a smile and signaled to Annie, who nodded her head and made for the bar.

"So what brings you here?" Bertie continued.

Moss nodded to Taffy. "Came to speak to your friend here. I know you always seek him out for that extra piece of information, so I thought I'd follow your lead."

"So it's adviser to Scotland Yard I'm to be now, is it?" Taffy didn't look too concerned about it.

"If you dinna' mind?"

"About this Knightsbridge séance of Lady Marlborough's?"

Moss nodded, and then took his beer from Annie and swallowed a mouthful.

"We were hoping to learn more about it from you, Campbell," said Bertie. "What does the Yard have to say?"

Moss took another drink and then put down the tankard on the table. "I went with my sergeant to the scene of the crime – it seems pretty certain that it was a crime – and we looked over the place. Very smartly appointed rooms, but then you'd expect that wouldn't you?"

"Knightsbridge is Knightsbridge," murmured Bertie.

"Nothing unusual," continued the policeman. "Or nothing obvious. The chairs were still all set around the table. Her ladyship said that nothing had been moved. Sergeant Gilmore made a sketch of who was sitting where. We had the names of all the sitters, of course."

"What was the cause of death?" asked Bertie.

"Stabbed."

"Stabbed?" echoed Taffy. "Was there much blood?"

"Nay. Very little, which is why they all thought it was a heart attack . . . or so they say."

"Why was there so little blood?"

"We're waiting on the coroner's report," said Moss, "but it seems it was a very thin instrument that was used."

"A dagger . . . a stiletto?" asked Taffy.

"We'll know soon enough."

"Suspects?" asked Bertie.

"Och! They're all suspects; even Lady Marlborough. But my money is on one or other of the two women who were there."

"Oh?" Taffy was interested.

"Aye. I believe it was one of them – perhaps jealous? – who had had a falling out with the gentleman."

"Why not one of the men?" asked Bertie.

"Aye. Well, as I say, they are all suspects." Moss returned to his drink.

"In other words, Campbell, you just don't know."

Moss frowned into his porter and said nothing.

"Do you have knowledge of the backgrounds of all these people?" asked Bertie.

"We took statements," said Moss defensively.

"But you don't know their full . . . ."

"We are just getting started on this case, Bertram," Moss snapped.

It seemed to Bertie that he had, perhaps, touched a nerve in that the inspector had not thought to discover the backgrounds of all the sitters. Taffy decided to step in.

"You said you came to see me," he said. "What was it you needed?"

"All you can tell me about this spirit business, and Lady Marlborough's little group in particular." Moss glanced at Bertie. "Some of this background information."

"I have already done some research on all of this," said Taffy, finishing off his shepherd's pie, pushing away the plate and wiping his mouth on a napkin. He took a brief drink of porter before continuing. "The Knightsbridge group has been holding regular weekly meetings at Kingston House for close on two years now. Their present medium – calls himself Prince Honoré, though I haven't been able to trace his origins – joined them about two months ago, at the beginning of August. I don't know how or where Lady Marlborough found him. The murdered man, Captain Cyril Grimsby, joined the others only two or three weeks back. It's a tight-knit group and Grimsby only got in when an elderly member had to move to the Continent for health reasons."

"There'll be a vacancy again now then," said the inspector, as much to himself as to the others.

"Who do you think will fill it?" asked Bertie, looking from one to the other of them.

Inspector Moss's eyes locked on to Bertie's. Bertie's stomach seemed to flip; he sensed that he wasn't going to like what his friend was about to say.

"I was thinking, maybe you, Bertram."

"Me?" Bertie had been about to take a drink but allowed his tankard of stout to sink back down to the table.

"Why Bertie?" asked Taffy, himself intrigued.

"I'd like to get someone into that little group; someone they willna' suspect and who can let the Yard know what they're saying and what's going on."

"You have men . . ." Bertie started to say.

"They'd spot a policeman before he even sat down in their circle!" snorted Moss. "I dinna' know what it is about us, but somehow it seems certain people can spot a policeman no matter how much he's disguised."

"Something about the boots, perhaps?" suggested Taffy, a twinkle in his eyes. Moss didn't smile.

"And dinna' forget that this is a group that is into all that psychic rigmarole," added Moss. "They can read your thoughts . . . or so I hear. No. I thought that if we could somehow get our Bertram as the new member of the group, no one would suspect him and he could be our eyes and ears at these séances."

Bertie picked up his porter again and took a long, steady drink.

"I can see that it could be useful," said Taffy, lifting his own tankard. "I might even be able to arrange an introduction. But what about the expense?"

"Expense?"

"Of course. My sources tell me that the sitters pay a guinea a meeting . . . and they meet every week."

"Well that lets me out," said Bertie, not unhappily. "There is no way I can afford that sort of money."

The inspector looked glum. "Nay. And I couldna' talk the Chief Inspector into coming up with that." He took a drink himself. "Maybe half of that, for a short time, but . . ."

"Scotland Yard would be willing to pay half?" asked Taffy, his dark brown eyes peering at the inspector from under his black eyebrows.

Moss pursed his lips and considered for a moment. Then he nodded his head. "Aye. I think I could get the DCI to agree to that, for a murder investigation. But that's only half of it."

"Well, I think I can commit *The Morning Post* to come up with the other half . . . on the understanding that I get the exclusive use of the information when you solve your murder."

Moss nodded. "Agreed."

"You think I should do it, then?" said Bertie to Taffy.

"Come on, Bertram," urged Moss. "You'd be perfect for it and you know it."

"I could certainly think of no one better," agreed Taffy, nodding his head.

Bertie put down his now empty tankard and looked around for Nancy. "I think perhaps I need another drink," he said.


"You said you'd do what?" Nellie's eyes were wide as she stared at her husband across the dinner table.

"Taffy thinks it's a good idea."

"You said you'd do what?" repeated Nellie.

"Campbell needs someone on the inside," he said desperately. "It would only be for a short time. And it could be very useful experience for the Penny Court Enquirers."

Nellie snorted in a most unladylike manner.

"All right," conceded Bertie. "It is experience that may not often be called upon, but this spirit business is really catching on. You just never know."

Nellie busied herself with the dormers, placing the fried, sausage-shaped mixture of minced lamb, rice and suet, onto each of their plates, along with carrots, peas and Brussels sprouts. She said nothing for a long time and Bertie shifted uncomfortably in his seat. Finally she poured gravy over the dish, handed him his food, and then spread her napkin across her lap.

"Is this dangerous, Bertie?"

"No!" He said it quickly, jumping on her words, feeling relief that she was at least willing to talk about it. "No, it's not dangerous, Nell. Quite the contrary. It's just sitting in the dark listening to – to – the spirits speak." Put like that it sounded a little ridiculous, even to himself, he thought.

"But the reason you can go is that one man has been murdered while 'sitting in the dark'," she said quietly.

"It's not like that's going to be happening every time," he said, and forced himself to laugh. She didn't join in. "Anyway, it's not yet certain that they will accept me into their circle. Taffy happens to know this Dr. William Price and he thinks he may be able to persuade the doctor to prevail upon Lady Marlborough to accept me. They do need seven people, it seems, so they have to find a replacement for Captain Grimsby."

"I wouldn't think people would be tripping over themselves to get into such a death circle!"

Bertie ignored that and stuck his fork into the dormer. Nellie was a wonderful cook and he always enjoyed whatever she decided to bake. The aroma of the lamb grabbed his attention and he ate appreciatively for a while.

"Where's Arnold?" he eventually asked.

"I sent him out with Isobel," said Nellie. "I needed her to pick up quite a few groceries and Arnold offered to help her carry them."

"He spoils that girl."

Nellie nodded. "Poor kid doesn't have much, with no family other than us. I don't mind if she gets a little bit of special attention once in a while. I don't think it's enough to spoil her."

"Most maids of all work have a really hard life," said Bertie, continuing to devour his food. "You don't see many of them with their own bedroom, even."

"I know." Nellie pushed away her now empty plate. "I don't think she knows how well off she is." She sighed. "Well, at least she eats well with us, and we do take care of her."

She got up and started clearing away the dishes. Bertie wiped his fork around his plate for the last time and licked it, savoring the meal.

"I have an appointment to see this Dr. Price tomorrow morning," he said. "He's a Harley Street man so I have to go there. All very formal."


Dr. William Price was a tall, distinguished-looking gentleman with silver-grey streaks gracing the sides of his macasa-shining black hair. He had a trim mustache and beard, with neatly combed sideboards that continued the silver-grey theme. His eyebrows were bushy, with deep grooves between them giving him the appearance of being perpetually puzzled. Sharp, steel-grey eyes peered out from under the brows. Bertie thought that the ruddy cast of his nose and upper cheeks might attest to his familiarity with the brandy bottle. He was dressed in an impeccable suit with black swallow-tail frock coat, silver-blue waistcoat and grey pin-stripe trousers. His cravat was maroon, held with a discreet small diamond pin. Spats peeked out from under the trouser bottoms, encasing gleaming black shoes of high quality. A solid gold watch chain stretched across his stomach, a gold Freemasonry symbol hanging as the fob. A pair of gold-framed, pince-nez spectacles sat astride his nose and he peered over the top of them at Bertie.

"So you are a budding Spiritualist, are you, Hawkins?"

Bertie stood on the Turkey carpet that covered the floor of the doctor's office. The room was dominated by a carved oak partner's desk which gleamed in the light streaming in through the bowed window, between the heavy damask drapes. The desk was elaborately decorated with relief-carved female busts – often ascribed to Jenny Lind – together with paneled drawers with carved pulls. The top of the desk was bare of papers, its only decoration being a gold double-inkwell, the glass bottles devoid of any ink.

Gracing the white walls of the office were landscapes that Bertie thought were by John Constable, though he couldn't be sure without making a point of studying them. They looked to him to be original watercolors and oil sketches. Between them, and obtrusively to Bertie's mind, were photographs of Spiritualist mediums. From pictures he remembered seeing in *The Illustrated London News*, he thought he recognized Daniel Dunglas Home, the American Fox sisters, Miss Florence Cook, and the infamous Mrs. Samuel Guppy. There were others he did not recognize.

"Yes," Bertie replied. "Yes, Dr. Price. I am very interested in the subject and very much desire to be part of a group such as the one to which I understand you belong."

Price snorted. Bertie wasn't sure if it was a comment on what he had said or if the good doctor habitually breathed in noisily through his nose.

"Such groups do not spring up overnight, don't you know?"

"No. No, of course not."

"We have been studying and advancing together for some considerable time. It takes dedication, don't you know? Strict observance of the rules, and all that."

"The rules?" Bertie hadn't heard of any special rules.

"The Golden Rule, I suppose is the primary," said Dr. Price. He stood in front of a classically-inspired fireplace mantel in Aegean limestone with inset panel work; the upper frieze featuring Palladian style leaf and flower decoration.

There was no fire alight but the doctor stood as though warming the seat of his trousers, gently swaying very slightly from side to side.

"Of course," murmured Bertie.

"So what have you read, then?"

Bertie thought quickly. Truth to tell, he had not read a great deal on the subject of spiritualism but Taffy had primed him on some of the questions Dr. Price might ask.

"I found Viscount Adare's account of Mr. Home's experiences interesting," said Bertie. "Along with Home's own books, of course. Also Mr. Coggshall's history of spirit rappings in America and Count de Gasparin's *Treatise on Turning Tables*."

"Did you catch William Crookes' *Researches in the Phenomena of Spiritualism?*" asked Price.

Bertie tried to look serious. "I have not yet had the pleasure of reading that, though it is on my list," he said.

Price nodded. "Quite right. And you might also take in John Edmonds' and George Dexter's two volume tome on the subject. Just finished that myself."

Price continued his swaying in front of the fireplace, nodding his head slightly as though approving of all that had been said.

"Gurney, Myers and Podmore have just produced their book for The Society for Psychical Research," he said suddenly. "We've been waiting for that, don't you know? Just came out a couple of months ago so you may not have caught it yet." His head nodded more emphatically. "And of course we must not overlook those wonderful works of William Stainton Moses."

"Oh, no. Of course not," murmured Bertie, nodding in time with his host. After a discreet pause he added – prompted by Taffy's coaching – "It would seem that the majority of works are those published in America, would you not say, Dr. Price?"

Price stopped swaying and looked up with an expression somewhat akin to that of a startled rabbit. "What? Why yes. Yes, dammit! You're right, Hawkins. Very astute."

Bertie felt pleased. The interview seemed to be going well.

Price suddenly reached up to the mantelpiece and took down a gold cigarette box. He opened it and offered a cigarette to Bertie. Bertie declined but Price took one for himself. He struck a lucifer and was soon blowing blue smoke into the air. Bertie wished he had his old briar pipe with him, and some of his favorite Gallager's Rich Dark Honeydew tobacco to add to the smoke.

"Well then, Hawkins," continued Dr. Price. "You seem to be the right sort, don't you know? But it is dedication we're looking for. Lady Marlborough cannot abide dilettantes. No more can I. Dedication is what is called for."

"Yes, of course."

Bertie allowed a moment to pass then ventured: "This Captain Grimsby I will be replacing . . . what kind of a man was he, if I may ask?"

"What?" The startled rabbit again. "Oh, Grimsby! Bounder. Should never have been in the circle in the first place. Don't know who let him in. Well," he snorted again. "He's gone now, that's certain. Won't be missed, if you ask me."

"I see."

"So are you ready to sit in circle?"

"W-what? . . . er, yes. Yes, of course. Very much so."

"Good! Good man."

*Chapter Three*

Bertie led the way into the Reading Room at the British Museum. Arnold, close behind, looked inquisitively about him as they mounted the marble stairs. The Reading Room had been designed by Sydney Smirke, brother of Sir Robert Smirke who built the main museum building. The famous round room was made of cast iron, concrete and glass, and incorporated the latest heating and ventilation systems. It was a masterpiece of mid-nineteenth century technology. The room housed copies of all the many books ever published in England. The book-stacks around it were also made of iron to take the great weight of the books and protect them against fire. In all, they contained three miles of bookcases and twenty-five miles of shelves. The huge dome overhead had been built, forty years before, in what originally had been the central courtyard of the museum building.

"I'll take the Kelly city directories for London, Arnold, and you check through the White directories." Bertie had taken the precaution of writing down the names they were to look for and he now handed the list to his brother-in-law. "We don't know whether or not Miss Winifred Dobson or Miss Alice Bell is married. I doubt it and I certainly hope not. It might make finding them that much more difficult. The newspaper article did refer to each of them as 'Miss' but that may have been because the reporter didn't know any better."

"Hasn't Campbell got their addresses?" asked Arnold.

Bertie nodded. "Yes, but he's playing his Scotland Yard card and not sharing them. But we can find them without him, don't you worry, Arnold."

"So what am I looking for, Bertie?"

"The directories list everything, Arnold. It's extremely doubtful, I think, that either lady runs her own business but you never know. Might have a hat shop or do type-writing; who knows? But there are sections in the directories by streets – everyone who lives on a particular street – for private residents, tradesmen, professionals, banks, churches . . . you name it. We'll concentrate on private residents, I think. If we start with the area around Knightsbridge we can then expand from there."

"There are a lot of people there, Bertie."

Bertie sighed and tugged at his mustache. "I know, Arnold. It's a bit like looking for the proverbial needle in the haystack, but at least it's a start. If we can find where these ladies live, we can then try to discover their complete backgrounds."

To himself, Bertie thought that it was embarking on a quest that could take weeks, if not

months. Should he even start it? There were many
names contained in the eleven hundred fifteen pages
of the Kelly's. Since they were listed by streets and
not alphabetically by name, he'd have to look
through all of them to weed out any and all Dobsons
and Bells. And then there was no guarantee that the
directories included the names of lodgers in
rooming houses. Did the two ladies in question have
rooms, or did they perhaps still live with their
respective parents? It was a daunting task.

"Let's give it a try, Arnold. If we haven't
got anywhere by tea-time we may have to re-think
this whole thing."

But tea-time came and went with their
finding only three Dobsons and two Bells in the
immediate vicinity of Kingston House. One of the
Dobsons was listed as a fish and chip shop, another
a coal merchant. The latter was next door to the
stables belonging to the Cavalry Barracks so Bertie
crossed it off the list as unlikely. He felt the fish and
chip shop address equally unlikely. That left one
Dobson and two Bells. The Dobson was on Hill
Street and one of the Bells was just around the
corner from there on Montpelier Terrace. The other
Bell was farther away on Launcelot Place.

"We'll start our search with these," said
Bertie.

"Tea first though. Right, Bertie?"

Bertie was ready for a cup of tea himself. He
replaced the directories and picked up his bowler
hat and cane. "Right you are, Arnold. There's an
ABC just down Museum Street. Let's pay that a
visit."

"How did it go, Bertie?" Nellie gave a quick peck on the cheek to Bertie as he and Arnold came into the kitchen and sank down onto the chairs at the kitchen table. They both looked tired, she thought. She and Isobel were putting the finishing touches to the evening's dinner.

"Well, I think we've located the home of Miss Winifred Dobson. She resides on Hill Street in Knightsbridge. I had hoped that Miss Alice Bell might have been close by, but no. Neither on Montpelier Terrace nor at Launcelot Place."

"Can't you talk Campbell into sharing that information?" She finished placing the dishes on the trays and signaled to Isobel to take up one of them. "Come on up to the dining room. We can talk there, over a good meal."

The men needed no urging. Soon they were all four seated about the big dining table, Isobel being allowed to join them.

"I don't want to press Campbell on something like this," said Bertie, taking up the carving knife and fork and starting to dissect the roast duck. "I'd rather wait until there's something more important I need from him. Besides, if I'm to join the circle of sitters, then I will eventually get that information anyway."

"But we do have Miss Dobson's address," said Arnold, accepting his plate and adding peas and roast potatoes to it.

"Well then, that's a start," said Nellie.

"Yes." Having served all the others, Bertie took his own plate and sat down, urging Arnold to pass the potatoes. "There are a few more days before the first séance so that gives us time to do a little investigating. I'd like to go in there knowing as much as possible about the others."

"What about the men?" asked Nellie.

"It's much easier with them," said Bertie. "Their names, addresses, clubs, interests are all pretty much on public record. That's the advantage of dealing with the upper classes. They may have their deep, dark secrets but their everyday lives are open books."

"Cor! They got deep dark secrets?" asked Isobel.

"Eat your dinner, Isobel," said Nellie. "None of this concerns you."

"But in that last Penny Dreadful what Mr. Middleton got me . . ."

"Eat your dinner, Isobel!"

"Yes, Mrs. 'awkins."

"Do you think the two ladies are the main suspects, Bertie?" asked Arnold, his mouth full of meat and potatoes.

"I don't think we can jump to that conclusion, Arnold. It could have been any of them, including Lady Marlborough."

"A lady is a murderer? Cor!"

Isobel's exclamation of choice seemed, to Nellie, to have become "Cor!" She tried hard to educate the girl, though not formally, but certain expressions just seemed to come naturally or by way of the Penny Dreadfuls the maid absorbed.

"We're not saying that Lady Marlborough *is* the murderer, Isobel," Nellie said patiently. "Only that she could be, just as easily as anyone else. The fact of her being Lady Marlborough doesn't make her any different in that respect."

"Cor!" Muttered this time, as the girl cut-up her piece of duck and smothered it in mint sauce.

"So what do you expect to find out about these ladies, Bertie?" asked Arnold.

Bertie finished cleaning the meat off a drumstick and pushed the bone over to the side of his plate. "One thing will be whether or not either one of them is, or was, involved in any way with any of the gentlemen of the circle."

"Romantically, you mean?"

"Whether or not there's any romance in the relationship – if one exists – may play a part. I think Campbell has a notion that Captain Grimsby was killed by a woman scorned. It has certainly happened before – on many occasions – so it's something we can't overlook. Just part of the enquiry process."

"So what have you uncovered about this Miss Winifred Dobson?" asked Nellie.

"Unmarried," said Arnold.

"And living with her parents," said Bertie. "She's in her early thirties; volunteers time with a charity or two; plays the pianoforte. Her parents, although not top drawer, are well off enough. Her father is a Higher Executive Officer in the Ministry of Health. Although her parents are staunch Methodists, Miss Dobson is independently thinking enough to have become quite absorbed in the

Spiritualist movement. She has been a member of Lady Marlborough's group since its inception almost four years ago."

"No dallying with any of the menfolk?"

Bertie shook his head. "If she does, it's nothing obvious."

"And what about Miss Alice Bell?"

Bertie shrugged. "We know very little about her as yet. That's why Arnold and I are trying to track her down. She doesn't seem to live anywhere close to Lady Marlborough, but then she could live anywhere within a hansom cab ride I suppose."

"We could question the cab drivers who cover that area, Bertie," suggested Arnold, eyeing the apple pie dessert.

"Good idea, Arnold. It might come to that."

"Isobel, serve the dessert," said Nellie. The girl scrambled to her feet and started separating the cut slices of pie and putting them on to individual plates. She passed them out to the others and then started the cream jug on its way around the table.

"Thank you, Isobel," said Arnold, accepting his plate and then commandeering the cream. He ladled a generous amount onto his pie.

"Save some for the rest of us, Arnold," murmured Nellie.

"The trouble is," continued Bertie. "I can't imagine any one of the group murdering anybody. I know that's silly; anyone is capable, if driven to it."

"Cor!"

"Isobel!"

"So we really do have to dig a little deeper into their backgrounds."

"I wonder what Campbell has come up with," said Nellie.

"Yes," agreed Bertie. "I'd love to know that myself."

Police Detective Inspector Campbell Moss sat at his desk and frowned down at the open manila folder in front of him. It was, he felt, painfully thin. Beside the folder sat a mug of rapidly cooling tea.

Sergeant Tobias (Toby) Gilmore stood just inside the doorway, clutching his own mug of tea and shifting his weight from one foot to the other. He was a large man with a red face, bulbous nose, and friendly-mutton-chop sideboards . . . so-called because the sides were connected by way of a substantial mustache. Recently seconded to the inspector, Sergeant Gilmore had been hoping for a desk job for the remaining few years he had before retirement, but he had found that Inspector Moss was frequently going out of the office and walking the streets. Not a good thing for the sergeant's bunion-ridden feet.

"This all we got on those spirit people?" Moss asked.

"Yessir." Caught off-guard, the sergeant started and slopped some of his tea over the side of the cup. The inspector didn't seem to notice and Gilmore surreptitiously slid one foot out to smear the splash into the stained wooden floor. It had just missed the small piece of carpet that lay forlornly in front of the inspector's desk, but since that was old and multi-stained it might have been better if the tea had landed there.

"Just the names and addresses?"

"Yessir. And their statements, of course, inspector."

Moss turned to the next sheet and looked it over. Since the séance had taken place in darkness, nobody admitted to seeing anything. One sitter had remarked on the sound of the trumpet falling over on the table, but it seemed that was often accepted as a sign that the spirits were present. The trumpet was a tall aluminum cone that was used – purportedly, as Moss understood it – as a megaphone to amplify the voices of the deceased. Sometimes, it was claimed, the trumpet would lift right off the table of its own accord and float about the room, its movements observed by the rings of luminosity about each end of the instrument. Moss lifted his mug of tea and sipped it, making a face when he found it was no longer hot.

All of the statements were short. There was the one from Professor Harold Sedgeworth, President of the Society for Psychical Research and retired Professor of Philosophy at Trinity College, Oxford. He had attended a number of séances conducted by Prince Honoré and most other prominent mediums, and was well familiar with all aspects of spirit communication. He had heard and seen nothing untoward throughout the whole proceedings. He had no particular feelings regarding Captain Grimsby.

Dr. William Price, Harley Street specialist and ardent Spiritualist, claimed that the séance went

along normal lines, with nothing unusual for such a
sitting. He had attended a number of Prince
Honoré's demonstrations, all of which had been of a
high standard. He had heard nothing unusual. He
regarded Captain Grimsby as a neophyte but neither
liked nor disliked the man.

Mr. Maurice Austin, newspaper reporter and
columnist for the *Daily World News*, claimed that
he was there simply to research for a series of
articles he had planned. He was very much a skeptic
though professed to keep an open mind. He was
suspicious of Prince Honoré yet had so far seen and
heard nothing that would indicate the medium was a
fraud. He did believe that he had heard the trumpet
topple over onto the table but did not believe that to
be significant. He did not like Captain Grimsby but
then, he disliked most of the group.

Miss Winifred Dobson claimed to be a
"medium-in-training", though Moss was not
entirely sure what that entailed. She said that she
was "attuned" to Prince Honoré and knew him to be
pure. "His life force was on the vibrational level of
the spirits and she felt that the sudden passing of the
Captain must have put unusual stress upon his
trance" . . . so Sergeant Gilmore reported. She did
claim that at one point in the séance the spirits
tugged at her hair.

Miss Alice Bell had nothing to report,
having been absorbed by the séance and noticing
nothing unusual. She also commented that she
thought she felt a spirit touch her lightly on the
head. She originally had quite liked the Captain but
her opinion had changed when he attempted to press

his attention on to her. However, she claimed that she did not really know him well. No one, it seemed, had any reason to seriously wish ill to Captain Grimsby.

Prince Honoré himself had pointed out to the sergeant that he had been in a trance throughout the entire séance and so had no knowledge whatsoever of what took place on the physical level. Lady Marlborough had peered at the policeman over her lorgnette and passed no comment.

"No one heard or saw anything unusual then." The inspector sighed, and then tapped the list of names. "I'd like you to get out and check these. See if any of them are in debt – might have owed money to the victim and didn't want to repay it. Might have played the ponies a bit too much. You know the sort of thing."

Sergeant Gilmore sighed. *More walking*, he thought. "Yessir," he said.

"Get on it then."

"Yessir." The sergeant turned and left the office, bearing his mug of tea ahead of him as though carrying a trophy.

It was the inspector's turn to sigh. He enjoyed his job – couldn't think of anything else he'd rather do – but it did occasionally get bogged down in routine. That was why he enjoyed talking with Bertie Hawkins. Bertie always seemed able to point out the unusual factors in a case; to offer something he could get his teeth into. Bertie would make a darn fine policeman; not that Moss would ever tell him that, of course.

He sighed again, scratched the bald spot on top of his head, tugged on his mustache, and then ran his finger down the list of suspects.

There was a tap at the door.

"Yes?" he called, without looking up.

The door opened just enough to allow a uniformed sleeve to come through and wave a large envelope at him. "Just came for you, inspector," said a disembodied voice.

Without looking up, Moss reached out and took it. The sleeve disappeared and the door closed. The inspector tore across the top of the envelope and extracted the single sheet of pale blue paper it contained. The letterhead proclaimed it to have come from Her Majesty's Coroner's office. It gave details of the pathologist's post-mortem examination of Captain Cyril Harold Grimsby and the coroner's conclusions. Moss read it and then re-read it. He pursed his lips and wished that he could whistle.

*Chapter Four*

"It's Hattie's husband Herbert again, Bertie," said
Nellie, pausing in her dusting. Bertie was sitting in
the drawing room with Arnold at his side. The two
men were going over their list of the séance sitters,
making notes alongside each name.

"What's he up to this time?" asked Bertie,
his head down over the notebook.

Herbert Parker had a history of getting into
trouble; trouble from which Bertie invariably had to
extricate him. His wife Hattie was a close friend of
Nellie's. Happily Herbert had a good job at a bank
on Leadenhall Street and so Hattie was more than
happy to pay the Penny Court Enquirers' fees for
whatever work had to be done to bring home her
husband and save him from his own foolishness.

"It's something that just might tie-in with
your other work," continued Nellie, carefully
dusting the collection of bric-a-brac on the whatnot.
"It seems that Herbert has been bitten by the spirits-
and-ghosts bug."

Bertie looked up sharply. "Spiritualism?"

"I suppose so." She continued what she was doing. "Hattie says that he's become 'addicted' – that's her word – to the Belgravia Spirit Association in Belgrave Square. Originally it was just a brief visit or two out of curiosity, she says, but now he's there almost every evening."

"It is fascinating work," observed Arnold.

"Not when it takes you away from your wife and family," responded Nellie.

"No. You're right, Nell," agreed Bertie. "Hmm. Well, I'm up to my neck in this séance circle murder investigation." He looked at his brother-in-law. "I think this may have to be something for you to handle, Arnold."

"Really?" The big man looked up in surprise. In the past he had proven himself capable of dealing with real problems but still lacked the confidence that Bertie would have liked him to have.

"Not a big job, Arnold. Much like you've done before . . . with Herbert. Just go along and keep an eye on him. See exactly what it is he's got himself into – or is getting into. See if there's any real cause for alarm. You can do that."

"You think so, Bertie?"

"I know so, Arnold."

Arnold beamed. He admired Bertie and was always delighted when praised. Nellie, too, was pleased that her husband encouraged her brother.

"You've done good work for Bertie before, Arnold," she said. "You know you have. How difficult can this be?"

Arnold busied himself preparing his own notebook for 'his case', as he put it. He headed it with Herbert Parker's name and added the word "Spirituli . . ." crossed it out and then wrote "Spirits" in bold letters after it.

"Hattie says he'll be going there today, so you can start on it right away."

Arnold nodded, a worried look on his face.

A flush-faced Isobel burst into the room and then, remembering, turned back and knocked on the door.

"A bit late," commented Nellie. "What is it?"

"It's the hinspector," she announced. "Shall I bring 'im up?"

"Of course you should bring him up," said Bertie. "Inspector Moss is a regular enough visitor you should know that by now, Isobel. Go and bring him in."

The girl swung around, red curls bobbing, and rushed out of the room again.

"It's not her fault," said Nellie. "I told her she should always announce visitors first. I wasn't thinking of regulars like Campbell."

Inspector Moss greeted them as he always did; a dour Scotsman's expression on a face that was unfathomable. It always became quickly obvious that he enjoyed being there but he seemed incapable of showing any emotion about it. As usual his prominent eyebrows were knitted together as though he had the cares of the world on his shoulders.

"Sit down, Campbell," said Nellie. "Isobel, make a pot of tea."

"What brings you here, my friend?" asked Bertie, as the maid scurried away. "Not that you're not welcome at any time, but is this anything to do with the Spiritualists?"

"Aye! Aye, it is that," he said, dropping into an armchair just inside the door.

"Good news or bad?"

"That you'll have to judge for yourself." Moss looked about him as though to be sure no one else was in the room. "I have the coroner's report . . . not that I'm at liberty to reveal the contents to anyone not officially connected with Scotland Yard, of course," he said.

"Oh, no. Of course not." Bertie looked suitably impressed and winked at Nellie.

"For instance, I canna' tell you what the good doctor has to say about the murder weapon."

"A thin-bladed knife, you suggested, was it not?" asked Bertie.

"Aye! Aye, you could describe it as such."

"Oh come on, Campbell!" cried Nellie. "We're all friends here. Get on and tell Bertie what you came to tell him, for goodness sake!"

"Now Nell," said Bertie. "The good inspector has to go through the motions. I understand that." He looked back at Moss. "So what is it you've got, Campbell?"

A sly smile broke out on the inspector's face. A rare occurrence, Bertie thought.

"Our Captain Grimsby was stabbed with a hat pin," he said. "A long hat pin right into his heart!"

Promptly at two of the clock in the afternoon, Herbert Parker emerged from number 52 Warwick Lane and turned right towards Ludgate Street. Arnold, two or three houses away, put down the newspaper he had been pretending to read, folded it, and slipped it into his pocket. *Now the chase is on,* he thought. Not that it would be much of a chase with Herbert leading. He wasn't known for rapid movement, which suited Arnold very well. It was a brisk late-September day and he was happy to be out walking.

They plodded down to Ludgate Street, with Arnold thankful that Herbert never once looked behind him. From following Herbert on previous occasions, necessitated by his addiction to a variety of inappropriate pastimes, Arnold knew that the man could become obsessed to the point of looking neither to right nor left as he pressed on to his final destination. In this case that was Belgrave Square, home of the Belgravia Spiritualist Association. It would involve traveling on two different omnibuses, or summoning a hansom cab or growler. Arnold prayed that Herbert would not opt for a hackney carriage.

Omnibuses, of which there were approximately 150 lines, cross the Metropolis in every direction from eight o'clock in the morning until midnight. Herbert waved down a dark green omnibus and disappeared inside it. Arnold broke into a run and managed to climb aboard as it pulled away. At Piccadilly Circus, Herbert jumped off and made for the chocolate-colored bus going to Hyde Park Corner. Again, Arnold just managed to scramble aboard and plopped down in the only empty seat, kicking at the dirty straw on the floor. He paid his twopence fare and looked around to find himself gazing into Herbert's vacant face, his prey ensconced in the seat beside him.

"Arnold!" Herbert's reedy voice bleated. "What are you doing here? Where are you off to?"

Arnold was never good at thinking fast. He decided it would be better in the long run if he was honest. "I'm on my way to Belgrave Square, Herbert. And you?"

"By Jove! So am I. What a small world."

Herbert was a nervous little man – much shorter than Arnold – whose eyes, behind his bottle-lens, black-rimmed spectacles, seemed to be darting in all directions at the same time. It was as though he was afraid that someone, or some*thing*, might creep up on him and surprise him. His eyebrows looked to be perpetually raised, as in surprise. His hair and small, square-cut mustache, were dark brown; almost black. His eyes were the same dark brown. He had no beard but had a habit of stroking his chin as though regretting the lack of this facial adornment. His hair, although by no means full, was adequate to cover his head but showed signs of strain at the apex. With his top hat resting on his knees, Herbert's balding spot became a fascination to Arnold.

"What takes you to Belgrave Square, if I may make so bold as to ask?"

Again, Arnold could not concoct a story on the spot. "I – er – I'm going to that spirit place," he said, mumbling a little since he did not wish to share the details with any of the other passengers.

Herbert almost squealed in delight. "The Belgravia Spiritualist Association? The famous B.S.A.?" He looked as though he couldn't believe his ears. "But – but that's where *I* am going! Can it be that you too, Arnold, are a devotee of the Summerland?"

"The what land?"

"The Summerland. That mysterious place where all must reside when their earthly existence has drawn to a close."

"Hyde Park Corner!" called the omnibus conductor.

"Ooh! That's us, Arnold." Herbert pried himself loose from the seat and followed close behind two middle-aged ladies who were disembarking.

Arnold followed them, thinking that it was a good thing that he had made contact with Herbert since now he could stay close to him and observe what he was doing. The two men started walking along Grosvenor Place.

"The B.S.A. is truly amazing, don't you think, Arnold? Which of the mediums have you sat with?"

Arnold scratched the top of his bald head. "Mediums? Oh, no. No, Herbert. This will be my first time there."

Herbert looked smug. "Then you are in for a rare treat, you can take it from me. I have an appointment this afternoon at three o'clock with Madam Lillian Stanhope. She is one of the best, you know? There is always a waiting list for her."

"Oh!" Arnold was a little disappointed. "So I wouldn't be able to go to that same sitting with you then, Herbert?"

Herbert stretched his neck and rotated his head as though his collar was too tight. He ran a finger around it before replying. "Well, I suppose you might be able to get in there. It's not the evening sitting, of course, so it may not be too crowded. But she is normally very difficult to get into," he finished, as though that proved his own regular acquaintance with the medium.

In fact there was no problem at all. It seemed to Arnold that anybody willing to pay the requested two shillings and sixpence "donation" could be a part of Lilly Stanhope's séance. He counted just six people besides himself and Herbert; five of them ladies. The other male was a brusque man in a dark green, rumpled, sacque suit. He had a habit of sucking on his teeth, which Arnold found annoying. He introduced himself as Maurice Austin and said that he was a journalist writing a series of articles on the London Spiritualist scene.

"You must go to a lot of these things then," said Arnold. They were gathered in the hallway

outside the séance room, waiting for Madam
Stanhope to arrive and usher them all inside.

Austin grunted. He nodded to Herbert.
"Seen you here before, haven't I?" he asked.

Herbert preened, delighted to have been
recognized. "Indeed you have, sir. I am a regular at
these gatherings."

Austin grunted again and turned away. At
that moment Madam Stanhope arrived. She was a
tall, angular lady with a prominent lantern jaw.
Despite her height, she wore a single long peacock
feather in her turban-like hat. It waved and bobbed
as she nodded and smiled at the little group of
devotees.

"Come along then, my darlings. You've all
paid your half-crown fee – your donation – I take it?
Yes? Good. Must keep the Society running, you
know. This way now. Some of you have been here
before, I know."

She swept into the small room, its center
filled by a large circular table with heavy chairs set
about it. From glancing in at open doors, Arnold
had seen that there were several such rooms off the
center corridor of the Belgrave Square Spiritualist
Headquarters.

Madam Stanhope sat down in one of the
seats and the others scurried around seating
themselves. Arnold found himself between two
corpulent ladies, both of whom wore more than
sufficient amounts of lavender-scented perfume.
Nobody introduced the sitters to one another and
Arnold deduced that they liked to preserve an air of
anonymity in order for the spirit – or the medium –

to prove him or herself. But it transpired that the sitters were nearly all regulars and well known to the medium anyway, so Arnold didn't really see the point.

Madam Stanhope stood and turned down the gasolier. She reseated herself and they all took hands around the table.

"I can give you only a quick look, Bertram," said Inspector Moss, leading the way up the stairs off Long Acre.

It was an older shop building with rooms for rent above it. Captain Grimsby had rented a third floor flat and Bertie was puffing by the time he got up to the rooms. Moss was in no better shape and Bertie felt that the climb was one of the reasons for the inspector's reluctance to allow Bertie to visit.

"A bachelor's rooms," said Moss, moving over to stand by the window and look out at the passing traffic on Long Acre.

Bertie looked about him. "Strange that there are no photographs," he said.

"What?" Moss swung back to look about the room. "You're right, Bertram. I never noticed that."

"These days people love photographs. There are always photographs in homes," said Bertie. "Relatives, friends, acquaintances, places visited. Everyone has them."

"Everyone except our Captain Grimsby, it would seem. Well, I don't suppose it's important."

"No," agreed Bertie. "No, it may not be."

The room, and the adjoining bedroom and kitchen, possessed little to reflect the Captain's life and interests. A set of Indian clubs stood on the floor beside the wardrobe, in the bedroom, attesting to Grimsby's physical fitness.

*He could probably manage those stairs all right*, thought Bertie.

There was little food in the kitchen cupboards but a number of half-filled liquor bottles stood on the top of the sideboard.

"He obviously had his priorities," said Moss.

"Had he been living here long?"

"No. Apparently he was living at his club for a short while . . . the Army and Navy. But he was asked to resign when his tab got too high and he couldn't pay it. They're not cheap, those gentlemen's clubs." Moss rubbed the top of his head ruefully as though he had himself considered taking out membership. "Twenty or thirty guineas just to join and then ten guineas a year. But it's the bar fees and dinners that add up . . . so they tell me. It seems that Grimsby had originally applied to join the United Service club but they don't accept anyone with a commission less than Major, so he was out of luck there."

"Then how could he afford to pay a guinea a week for Lady Marlborough's séances?"

Moss tugged at his mustache. "There's a rum do, Bertram. I would guess that he had some scheme in mind. He couldn't have kept that up for more than a couple more weeks, judging from his bank account."

"Perhaps he was hoping to gather information he could use to blackmail someone?"

"Aye! It's possible. Anything seems possible with our Captain Grimsby. Now we may never know."

"What of his books?" murmured Bertie, moving across to a small bookshelf next to the window. He perused the volumes. "A couple of military biographies, some books on India, a price guide to Chinese porcelain – but no pieces in sight – two or three cheap novels and a Baedekers for London and its environs."

"Hrmph." The inspector moved back to continue his appraisal of the Long Acre traffic.

"I'm still amazed that he was murdered with a hat pin," said Bertie, as he looked about the flat. "Is that not unusual?"

"Aye. But not unknown. There was a woman stabbed her young man on an omnibus in Hammersmith a year or so ago. She claimed she hadna' meant to kill him but it went right into his heart . . . just like with our Captain Grimsby."

"You think whoever it was, meant to kill the captain?"

Moss shrugged.

Bertie returned to the bookshelf. "Any personal papers that told you anything, Campbell?"

"No." Moss stuffed his hands into his trouser pockets and rocked slightly on his feet as he gazed out of the window. "Just his bank account – showing he was extremely low in funds, with a hefty overdraft – and a large number of unpaid bills."

"Letters?" persisted Bertie.

"Nothing recent. Nothing personal."

"Doesn't that seem strange?"

"In what way?"

"I don't know." Bertie shrugged and walked over to join his friend looking out at the busy road outside. "Wouldn't you think that a man of some social standing – presumably he wouldn't be in Lady Marlborough's circle unless he had some sort of recognition – wouldn't you think that he'd receive a letter or two once in a while? An invitation to something, somewhere? A request for a meeting or comments as the result of a meeting?"

"Some people are like that," said the inspector. "I don't get much in the way of letters myself, as a matter of fact."

"Hmm. Perhaps you're right." Bertie found himself rocking in time with the policeman and made a point of turning away. "Perhaps he just destroyed them as soon as he'd read them. He wasn't married, I take it?"

"What?" Moss also turned away from the charms of Long Acre and looked at Bertie. "Married? What made you ask that? These have all the signs of being bachelor quarters."

"I know. I know." Bertie looked about him. "But things are not always what they seem. Just because a man is living alone doesn't mean that he isn't married . . . or hasn't been at some time."

Moss looked worried, then pulled out his blue-covered notebook, stub of pencil, and started jotting down some notes.

"It may be worth checking," murmured Bertie. He moved back to the shelf of books and studied them again, running his finger along the spines. He stopped at one and pulled it out.

"What have you got there?" asked Moss, glancing up from his note-taking.

"Something rather interesting," said Bertie. "A book by a Charles Devereaux titled *Venus in India.*"

"Ah!" Moss nodded and returned to his notebook. "Yes. I saw there were books on India. Apparently he spent some time there."

"This isn't exactly a 'book on India'," said Bertie, turning the pages.

"What do you mean?"

"I thought the title sounded familiar," Bertie continued. "I think I heard mention of it when I was in Germany earlier this year. Something scandalous about it, as I recall."

The inspector's head came up and he moved over to stand beside Bertie. "Scandalous?"

Bertie nodded, read a brief passage and shook his head sadly. "Scurrilous might be a better description," he said. "I don't know what Lady Marlborough would make of this!"

"Here! Let me see." Moss took the book from Bertie and – a little too eagerly, Bertie thought – turned pages and read passages. His face became redder and redder. He finally dragged his eyes away and snapped the book closed. As he did so, a piece of paper fell out and fluttered to the floor.

"What's that?"

Moss bent down and retrieved it. To Bertie it looked like an official form of some sort. He read it over the inspector's shoulder. They both looked at one another.

"Well, I'm blowed!" said Moss. "You were right, Bertram."

Alice Bell was a young woman with a mind of her own. She had left home at the age of seventeen after a violent argument with her father on the subject of women's rights. Her mother had pleaded with her to stay but would not join with her daughter in standing up to the head of the household. After a lean year, Alice had been lucky to find work as a seamstress for Cy Berman, a tailor on Warwick Street in Pimlico. She had eventually taken rooms at number eleven Denbigh Street, living there for the past two years, and was now firmly ensconced as the supervisor of four junior seamstresses at Berman's. Her employer was a tailor who made suits for some of London's professional gentlemen and, although very careful with his money, he showed proper appreciation for the work that Alice did.

Ten months ago Alice had received word that her mother had passed away and Alice had felt a strong urge to try to connect with her mother through the rapidly developing religion of Spiritualism. Through the agencies of Dr. William Price, one of Cy Berman's customers, she had made the acquaintance of Lady Marlborough and her

Spiritualist group and had become one of the regular sitters at that lady's séances.

Alice had felt no sorrow for the passing of Captain Grimsby. The man had proven himself to be a chauvinist who had absolutely no respect for women. He had been charming to Alice on their first acquaintance at Lady Marlborough's but that had changed very quickly when she agreed to meet with him outside of the séance circle. He had taken liberties and expected responses from her which she had not been prepared to give. However, he had not been content to allow her a gracious exit from their extremely brief and chaste liaison. Captain Grimsby had threatened to have her expelled from Lady Marlborough's circles unless she acquiesced to his demands. She was outraged, especially since she had been a part of the group for far longer than he. But Alice had by no means concluded her business with her late mother so she refused to be bullied by the likes of Grimsby, just as she had refused to be bullied by her father. And now Grimsby was dead. She was glad. She was not happy to think of anyone's life being taken but in this instance felt quite unmoved by his death. Indeed, Alice looked forward to the next few séances when it might be possible to contact the recently deceased Captain and see if he might have already learned the error of his ways. Death, she believed, was the great revealer; the door that opened on the greater truths of life . . . or of life after death.

Bertie sat filling his pipe with his favorite tobacco, his big brown eyes on his brother-in-law as he listened to Arnold's report on his Belgrave Square experience.

"It was nothing!" said the big man, stretching out his long legs under the kitchen table. "No ghosts. No white sheets. No cold hands reaching out for you! Just a whole lot of talk. I don't know what Herbert sees in it. It certainly wasn't worth the half-crown, I can tell you that!"

"Don't forget to mark that down in your expense book," said Nellie, without looking up from where she sat at the other end of the table, writing out the week's menus.

"She told Herbert some mumbo-jumbo about his dead grandmother and he was as happy as a puppy with two tails."

"Tell me about this journalist who was there," asked Bertie, then put the pipe in his mouth and struck a lucifer.

Arnold nodded. "Maurice something."

"Maurice Austin?"

"Yes! That was it. You know him, Bertie?"

"He is one of the regular sitters at Lady Marlborough's séances. I'll be meeting him." Bertie puffed smoke, which Nellie tried to wave away. A blonde ringlet had made its escape from her mop cap and she poked it back with a finger.

"He said he was writing some articles."

"Hmm." Bertie removed the pipe for a brief moment, studied the glowing tobacco, and tugged at his mustache. "I suppose he would have to go to a number of different séances to get an overall picture."

"He was there when that man got stabbed with the hatpin?" asked Nellie, still not looking up but frowning at the amount of smoke Bertie was generating.

"Yes. Or so Campbell said. I think I'd like to talk with him."

"Why not do it before your first sitting with Lady Marlborough?" Nellie laid down her pencil and looked at her husband. "That's on Friday, isn't it? You could probably find out from Taffy what newspaper he works for and go along and see him."

"Good idea." Bertie looked around. "Where's that girl? I wouldn't mind a cup of tea."

"Isobel is out doing some shopping for me," said Nellie. "But I wouldn't mind a cup of tea myself. Arnold, would you put on the kettle?"

At talk of tea Arnold was only too happy to get to his feet and start the process. "You wouldn't happen to have some biscuits as well, would you Nell?" he murmured.

"I did do some digging around after Campbell took me to Captain Grimsby's flat," volunteered Bertie, fussing with the tobacco in his pipe and tamping it down. "And what I found was interesting."

"Oh?" Nellie was curious.

"It seems that the murder victim was indeed a married man," said Bertie. "The marriage certificate fell out of a . . . a book that he had. He was married to one Jessica Elisabeth Grimsby, née Drury. They were married in India; in Lucknow.

They separated a little less than a year ago and divorced last July, hence his living as a bachelor. I haven't yet been able to find out what became of her."

"Perhaps he killed her," said Arnold darkly, gazing into the teapot as he poured the boiling water onto the tea leaves.

"Arnold!"

"Sorry Nell."

"Anything is possible," said Bertie. "You could be quite right there, Arnold. But I think it's just as likely that she's left the country and perhaps gone across the Channel to the Continent."

"Why leave the country?" asked Nellie.

"True." Bertie nodded, puffing clouds of smoke all around himself. "She could just as well have moved out *to* the country, here in dear old England . . . anywhere out of town."

"Why wouldn't she have stayed in London?" asked Arnold.

Bertie waved his hand in the smoke in a feeble attempt to disperse it. "Again, why not?" he said. "Yes, Arnold, she could just as well have stayed in the area. Until we can find out for sure, all we can do is guess."

"So," said Nellie, summing up. "This mysterious Jessica Grimsby either moved to France, bought a house in Cornwall, stayed in London, or got herself killed by her ex-husband. Is that the sum of it, Bertram?"

Bertie would not be drawn and simply shrugged. "Close enough, Nell. Close enough."

# *Chapter Five*

"Now do hold still, Bertie. I can't tie your tie if you keep wriggling around."

"I'm not wriggling." He tried to remain still and watched, in the bedroom mirror, as Nellie expertly manipulated the white, impliable, neckwear so that it ended with both ends projecting equally from the center knot; something Bertie had struggled to do for the previous half hour. "How do you do that?" he asked.

Nellie gave a last brush to his dark brown, wavy hair. "Now get into your waistcoat and jacket and run along, or you'll be late. You don't want to create a bad impression at your first séance."

Although in the past, on the rare occasions when Bertie needed to wear evening dress, he had borrowed Herbert Parker's suit, Nellie had proclaimed that it was time he had one of his own. Herbert owned such sartorial elegance because of his involvement in the rites and rituals of the Freemasons. Nellie reminded Bertie of the times when, due to the involvement of the Penny Court Enquirers, he had needed to fit-in with what she termed the 'Upper Class' (Arnold said 'the Swells' and Isobel called them 'the Nobs'). Bertie had agreed, although he doubted that the time would come when Arnold, too, would need to be so outfitted.

Bertie had to walk to the end of Penny Court to hail a hansom cab but then quickly found one and directed it to take him to Knightsbridge and Lady Marlborough's residence. He had not yet had occasion to meet the lady, his acceptance into her circle being affected through Dr. William Price. It seemed she was still distraught enough over the loss of Captain Grimsby that she was willing to accept an immediate replacement when endorsed by someone of the good doctor's caliber.

"'ere you are, guv," said the cabby, opening the trapdoor in the hansom's roof and peering down at Bertie. "That'll be three bob."

Bertie descended, paid the driver – giving him a sixpence tip – and looked through the wrought iron gates at Kingston House; the elegant residence beyond. There were lights burning in two of the ground floor windows, plus a gaslight outside over the imposing twin entrance doors. Bertie advanced and knocked on the left hand door with the knob of his cane, too late noticing the heavy brass knocker in the center of the right hand door.

Almost immediately the door was opened by an elderly parlor-maid, whose eyes remained downcast as she put out her hands to take his hat, gloves and cane. It was still mild enough autumn weather that he had not troubled himself with a top coat. She led him in through a portrait-hung vestibule papered in blue velvet flocking, to an open

double-doorway. From inside came the murmur of
quiet conversation.

"Ah! It is our new sitter, I do believe. Mr.
Bertram Hawkins, is it not?"

A tall lady dressed in the aesthetic style, in
an un-corseted Liberty gown of pale lilac velvet,
with a white central panel of smocking, approached
Bertie and peered at him through a gold-rimmed
lorgnette. He noticed that her hair had been given
the red tinge so often favored by the followers of
the aesthetic movement. However, a startlingly
brilliant diamond necklace destroyed the bohemian
theme. She had a thin, black, lace shawl about her
shoulders, which she shrugged off. A maid –
probably her lady's maid, thought Bertie – moved
forward, took the shawl, and left the room.

"Lady Marlborough," he murmured, giving
a slight bow. "I must thank you for accepting me
into your exclusive circle."

"William speaks well of you," she said,
glancing around to nod in the direction of Dr. Price,
whom Bertie spied in deep conversation with one of
the other ladies in the room. "Do please make
yourself at home. We will be sitting shortly. Please
help yourself to some light refreshment."

She waved her fan in the direction of the
sideboard, resplendent with a variety of fruit,
several plates of pastries and petit beurre biscuits,
and even small servings of  green salad. Lady
Marlborough then moved off to speak to the two
ladies. As Bertie approached the offerings a liveried
footman proffered a silver salver bearing glasses of
grenadine sucré. Bertie took one but decided to

pass-up the confections. He looked about him at the other participants.

"You must be Hawkins."

Bertie recognized Professor Sedgeworth, from pictures he had seen of him in *The Illustrated London News*. He inclined his head to the older man. "Indeed," he acquiesced. "I'm afraid I'm stepping into the dead man's shoes, so to speak."

Sedgeworth took a thoughtful sip of his wine and then nodded. "Somebody had to, I believe. Welcome aboard. You been to these 'does' before, I take it?"

Bertie didn't want to confess to being a complete neophyte. "This is certainly my first time with this Prince Honoré," he said. He looked about him. "Is he here?"

"Oh, he pops in at the last moment," said the professor. "Likes to build up an entrance, it seems. But he is certainly an amazing medium. We are blessed that Lady Marlborough managed to acquire his services."

William Price joined them, nodding briefly to Bertie. "What do you think, Harry," he said to the professor. "Will our late lamented Captain Grimsby put in an appearance tonight, or is it too soon?"

"Too soon for me, thank you very much." Sedgeworth put down his empty glass on the end of the sideboard and pulled out a gold cigarette case.

"We are just about to start, professor." Lady Marlborough's unraised voice was quite audible. Sedgeworth muttered darkly and put the cigarette case back in his pocket, unopened.

"Shall we take our seats?" her ladyship continued. She led the way through to the library, the others following her like a line of school-children trailing their teacher.

Bertie found that the gaseliers and wall sconces were turned low in the bookshelf-lined room. The chairs, which he had fully expected to be set out around a central table, were arranged in a curved row facing one end of the room. At that end stood what looked to Bertie to be a large wooden wardrobe with double doors. It was of plain polished wood, with no adornment.

"A cabinet," murmured the professor, who was closest to Bertie.

"By George!" exclaimed Doctor Price.

"Something new!" added Maurice Austin.

Bertie had tried, unsuccessfully, to meet and speak with the journalist prior to the séance evening, but the man never seemed to be in his office. Bertie now looked at the newspaperman, who was dressed in a somewhat rumpled evening dress suit that had certainly seen better days. Bertie silently thanked Nellie for insisting he purchase a new one.

"May I present my cabinet."

The high, refined voice issued from a figure Bertie had not noticed, standing half in shadow at the end of the library's fireplace, close to the wardrobe item. It was a young man wearing a white turban, floppy black jacket and baggy black trousers. A green stone in the front of the turban caught the light and twinkled at the attendees.

"Good evening, Prince Honoré."

Everyone mumbled a greeting to the personage. Bertie noticed that the ladies – with the exception of Lady Marlborough – gave a slight curtsey as they greeted him. Bertie himself kept his eyes on the slight figure and watched as the prince moved gracefully across to stand before the wooden piece of furniture.

"I would like to invite you all to examine my cabinet. Until now we have sat in circle and enjoyed the visitations of the spirits as they conversed with us, through my humble self. But the spirits have told me that tonight we are about to take a step forward. Tonight, we are to experience more of what the Spirit World is all about. First, however, so that none may doubt the power of our ethereal friends, I request – nay, I ask – that you come forward and ensure that this temporary fixture is all that it appears to be. No more, and certainly no less." With a flourish, he stepped back once again into the shadows beside the fireplace.

There was the briefest of hesitations and then the group, led by Professor Sedgeworth and Lady Marlborough, advanced upon the addition to the library furniture.


"I want you to go over that flat with a fine-tooth comb," said Inspector Moss, addressing Sergeant Gilmore. "Empty all of the cupboards, look under the carpet, pull out all of the books on that book-shelf and then flip through the pages of every single one of them. I want you prying into every possible nook and cranny."

"What exactly am I looking for, sir?" Gilmore had out his notebook and was recording the instructions on a fresh page.

The inspector paused and pursed his lips. "Aye! That's a good question, sergeant. What are we looking for?" He paused a moment longer, then sighed. "If I knew, I'd tell you. Now just cut along smartish, my lad, and see what you can find. Anything that is out of the ordinary – any tucked-away pieces of paper, for instance – you just bring them right back here to me." He tapped the top of his desk, even though it was hidden beneath an untidy mass of loose papers, folders, flyers, and dog-eared memos. "My good friend Mister Hawkins wasn't in there five minutes and he found something of immense value. Why hadn't *we* found it, you might ask?"

The sergeant looked hopeful.

"Well, *don't* ask?" concluded the inspector. "Now just get out of here and start looking."

"Yessir." Sergeant Gilmore hurried from the room.

The cabinet seemed innocuous enough, thought Bertie. It was not large, though it held a chair and small table inside of it. The side and back panels of the cabinet seemed smooth and without any cracks that might indicate possible hidden doors or similar. He noticed that the professor spent some time studying the walls for such clues. Stepping outside again, Bertie ensured that the compactum was tight against the rear wall of the room, with no space for anyone to secrete themselves behind it. The top of the structure was close enough to the room's ceiling that no one could lie up there. Satisfied, Bertie resumed his seat. Soon everyone had satisfied their curiosity and returned to sit down and await events.

Prince Honoré came forward once more and, after a small bow to Lady Marlborough, spread his arms in welcome and smiled at the sitters.

"On the sideboard to my left you may see some musical instruments – a tambourine, small bell, rattle, and concertina. I would ask two of you to take these instruments and place them on the small table within the cabinet. There is also a table-cloth there. Please place this over the instruments as they lie on the table, and secure the corners of the cloth to the table legs with the cord you see, so that it is not possible to easily access the instruments. Would you do this?"

Dr. Price and Alice Bell rose and did as the prince requested. They then returned to their seats.

"Excellent. Thank you." With another slight bow the medium then turned, stepped inside the cabinet, and sat in the chair. He rested his arms along the arms of the chair. "Perhaps you, Professor Sedgeworth, and you, Mr. Austin, would be kind enough to tie my arms to the arms of this chair. There is plenty of solid cord on the sideboard there."

The two gentlemen did as requested. Bertie leaned forward to make sure that the medium's arms were well secured to the chair's arms.

"Very good," continued the prince. "Now if anyone is in any doubt, please feel free to come forward and examine the cords and the knots."

Maurice Austin half rose but then, seeing that he was alone, sat down again, nodding as though acknowledging that all was well.

"Lady Marlborough? Would you be kind enough to finalize the proceedings?"

Her ladyship rose and went to the seated medium. She was carrying a short scarf which she used to blindfold the prince. Then she turned away, closed the two doors of the cabinet, and returned to her seat.

"Dr. Price? The lights, if you would be so kind?" she said.

Price rose and turned down all the gas jets until Bertie could only just make out the outline of the cabinet. He leaned forward again, straining his eyes to see if anything became visible about the cabinet. Dr. Price returned to his seat.

"Prince Honoré suggested that we start the sitting with a song, to create harmony and to draw the spirits to join us. I would suggest our old favorite, *Abide Not In the Realm of Dreams*, by Mr. William Henry Burleigh."

There were murmurs of assent and Bertie, not knowing the words, contented himself with humming along as the others sang. They were into the second verse when suddenly the sound of the tambourine came from the closed cabinet. Bertie was surprised. There was the slightest faltering in the singing but then it renewed with extra vigor. As the song came to an end the concertina in the cabinet took up the tune. It was shortly followed by the rattle and the bell sounding in unison.

"The spirits are with us," murmured her ladyship.

Bertie's straining ears thought that there was the faintest sound of a footstep from behind the closed doors but no one else seemed to be aware of it.

"Greetings!"

A muffled voice escaped the confines of the cabinet.

"The Earl of Beaconsfield," cried Lady Marlborough. "Our beloved Benjamin Disraeli! We are honored."

"I don't know about that," muttered Austin.

"Ssh!" hissed her ladyship.

"Greetings, my dear Lady Marlborough and friends," came the voice.

*If this is Disraeli,* thought Bertie, *he's lost that 'Jewishness' everyone always noticed in his voice. Still,* he conceded, *perhaps that's what death does for you.*

"Lord Beaconsfield," cooed her ladyship. "So very good of you to call."

"He's not an afternoon caller," complained Austin, obviously no great follower of Disraeli's politics.

"Ssh!" It was Winifred Dobson. "Let's hear what he has to say."

"Indeed," added the professor.

"My devotions to you all on this remarkable occasion," said the Disraeli voice coming from the cabinet-enshrouded medium. "It has been but a short time since my transition to the spirit realm but I feel that I have learned much. All is mystery but he is a slave who will not struggle to penetrate the dark veil."

"Amen," said Lady Marlborough, echoed by the others.

"All power is trust. We are accountable for its exercise; that from the people and for the people, all springs and all must exist. It is knowledge that influences and equalizes the social condition of man; that gives to all, however different their political position, passions which are in common and enjoyments which are universal."

Bertie thought to himself that what the purported spirit was saying sounded very much like Disraeli had sounded when making a speech in life. In fact, he was not certain but that the medium was not simply repeating part of an old speech by the late Prime Minister.

"The greatest good you can do for another is not just share your riches, but to reveal to him your own," continued the sermon.

Maurice Austin fidgeted and Alice Bell suppressed a cough. The Disraeli voice droned on.

"The more extensive a man's knowledge of what has been done, the greater will be his power of knowing what to do."

After a half hour of these platitudes, the voice seemed to hesitate and fade a little. Lady Marlborough resumed command.

"We do not wish to tire you, Prime Minister. We thank you for attending on our humble circle and hope that you will grace us with your presence again in the future."

"Hear, hear!" murmured Professor Sedgeworth, obviously a Disraeli supporter.

Suddenly the tambourine sounded again, and then the bell. Then all was quiet. Lady Marlborough gave thanks to the spirit world and concluded the proceedings with a short prayer. Dr. Price got to his feet and turned up the gas lamps. "Will you open the cabinet?" he asked her ladyship.

Lady Marlborough opened the doors to reveal Prince Honoré still secured to his chair, his arms still securely tied there. The table-cloth seemed to be undisturbed in its attachment to the small table; the musical instruments inaccessible. Bertie was surprised by this. He caught the glance of the newspaperman, Maurice Austin, squinting one eye and lifting an eyebrow as though questioning what he was seeing. He did not, however, say anything.

It was not long afterwards that the sitters prepared to take their leave. Prince Honoré had excused himself shortly after the circle closed. Refreshments had again been served and Lady Marlborough's lady's maid returned, bringing her mistress the shawl and remaining in the background while they all commented on the success of the evening's séance. Bertie tried to be unobtrusive as he circled around the ladies. He studied their hatpins as he did so, seeing them protruded sharp and gleaming in the gaslight.

Bertie made a point of walking out alongside Maurice Austin and got into conversation with him as they left Kingston House and strolled in the direction of Knightsbridge, looking for a hansom cab.

"Your thoughts, Hawkins?"

Bertie shrugged. "I am relatively new to this," he said. "I must take it at face value for now. Was that really the spirit of Benjamin Disraeli, do you think?"

Austin snorted derisively. "I never cared for the man's politics when he was alive and I have heard nothing to seduce me to his way of thinking tonight. As to whether or not it was him . . . well, I suppose we will have to wait and see what transpires at future sessions."

"Are you impressed with the prince?"

There was a pause before the newspaperman answered. "I think it remarkable that the various instruments were played within the cabinet, yet they seemed to remain fully covered and the medium was most definitely secured in his chair."

"You *were* impressed then?" Bertie persisted.

Another pause before a reluctant "Ye-es. Yes, I suppose I was – after a fashion. Again, I think I must reserve final judgement until future sessions. This is the first time Honoré has worked inside his cabinet. It's a rare gift, they say. But familiarity may bring revelations." He stopped in mid-stride, as an idea came to him. "You know, I've just thought of someone who may be able to add to our information; who knows something of these Spiritualist cabinets." He started walking again.

"Really?" Bertie was interested. "Someone you can talk to about all of this?"

The newspaperman nodded. "I think I just might pay him a call on Monday."

At that moment a hansom turned the corner ahead of them and came in their direction. Austin stepped to the curb and hailed it.

"Any chance I might accompany you to see this person?"

Austin looked at him. "Why not?" He climbed into the cab ahead of Bertie. "What is your destination, Hawkins? I'm going to stop off in Fleet Street myself."

"That's perfect," said Bertie, closing the flaps over their legs. "I'm not far from there myself. I can continue on after you get out."

*Chapter Six*

Isobel Wilson, the Hawkins's red-haired, freckle-faced, maid-of-all-work, peered out of the basement kitchen window up to the street level. She could just make out the figure that had descended from a four-wheeler, which still stood outside number 27 Penny Court. The cab driver lifted down a large trunk and two carpet-bags. The man looked up at the ground floor windows of the house, to Isobel obviously hoping that someone would come out and take charge of his luggage.

He was a thin, tight-lipped man with departing grey hair, which Isobel was able to see when he took off his bowler hat to mop his forehead. His face was lined and sallow; his eyes rheumy and glistening with moisture. The scraggly hair made its way down his cheeks to bunch on his jaw-line, though his chin was bare of beard and no mustache caped his upper lip. He fumbled in a purse and extracted a few coppers to tip the cab driver. The cabby continued to hold out his hand for some little time, apparently surprised that there were no more copper coins forthcoming. Finally, with a muttering, he climbed up back into his seat and snapped the reins to start the horse away from the curb.

Still the man stood there, uncertainly.

"What are you gazing at, Missy? Don't forget you've got potatoes to peel."

Nellie's voice interrupted Isobel's thoughts and brought her back to the kitchen. She turned from the window and told her mistress what she had seen.

"'e's just sorta standin' there, Mrs. 'awkins. Is 'e hexpected, then?"

Nellie moved across and peered out of the window herself, being careful not to disturb the curtains and alert whoever it was on the pavement outside.

"Oh, no!" she exclaimed.

"What is it, Mrs. 'awkins? 'Oo is 'e?"

"It's Bertie's cousin George. The proverbial bad pen . . . Get out there, Isobel, and help him with his things. I'm sure I don't know what he's doing here. It looks as though he thinks he's coming for a long stay, too!"

Isobel started for the basement door.

"No! Wait! First let Mr. Hawkins know he's here. And see if Arnold – Mr. Middleton – is anywhere about. You're going to need him to move that trunk."

"What'll I do first then, Mrs. H?" Isobel looked perplexed.

Nellie started removing her apron. "Oh, go and tell Bertie. I'll go out and talk to George." She made her way up the stairs, following behind the scampering maid.

There was a distinct odor of fish that seemed to follow Cousin George, Bertie had to admit. Since the man was a fishmonger by trade it was perhaps hardly surprising, yet Bertie found it offensive. He had feigned pleasure at seeing his cousin but he knew that it did not bode well. The last time he had encountered George – again turning up unexpectedly at Penny Court – it had led to a misunderstanding between George and the daughter of the local newsagent, which had almost resulted in George's arrest. Luckily Bertie was on friendly terms with Officer Boggs and was able to explain Cousin George's fascination with phrenology and that he was only trying to feel the "bumps" on the young lady's head.

Bertie sighed and looked at his cousin across the dinner table. "How's Penelope?" he asked, picturing the mouse-like wife of his cousin who must surely, he thought, be glad to be rid of George for a few days.

"What? Oh, Penny's fine. Same as usual. Now, as I was saying, of course I thought of you and Our Nell," George studied his dinner plate. "I'm going to be running for public office. The Municipal Corporations Act of 1883 provided for the abolition of unreformed borough corporations unless they obtained a new charter. Well, that charter for Bridlington has to be got by the end of this year. If I can get the votes, I will help get that charter and be 'someone' in East Yorkshire!"

"I thought you already were 'someone,' George," said Nellie, winking at Bertie. "You have the largest fishmonger's shop in the town, or so you've always told us."

Bertie sliced the roast beef and passed a plate to Arnold, who sat listening to the conversation with a look of puzzlement on his face.

"Why did that make you think of Nell?" he suddenly asked.

George looked at him as though noticing the big man for the first time. "Why, because I've got to be in London, haven't I?"

"You have?"

"Well, of course."

"Arnold's right," said Bertie. "You haven't yet told us why you are here, George. We are delighted to see you, of course. And you are welcome to stay as long as . . . for a few days." He caught the look in his wife's eyes. "Though we can now gather that your *unexpected* visit has something to do with your local politics."

George heaped peas onto his plate, rivaling even Arnold in the size of his helping. "If I'm to be recognized as anyone, then I need something special to make 'em notice me. Am I right?"

Bertie slowly nodded his head.

"All right then," George continued. "What better, I says to myself, than to link my business with the famous Worshipful Company of Fishmongers? And the Fishmongers' Company Hall is right here in the nation's capitol. Am I right? They have this big building at London Bridge and I was thinking that if I visited there, then going home with some sort of connection to them would really give me some status."

Bertie and Nellie exchanged looks of puzzlement.

"You mean you can get 'status' just from going there?" asked Arnold.

"No! No, of course not." George stabbed at the Yorkshire pudding. "But there has to be some connection I can make; something that I can display in my shop to show that I'm one of them."

"You mean, like with a royal endorsement?" asked Nellie. "Like when they put *By Appointment to Her Majesty* on things?"

"Yes!" cried George excitedly. "That's it!" Then, more soberly, "Only not quite up to that standard, of course. No, it just shows that it's . . . well, *special*. 'The Worshipful Company of Fishmongers'. Has a real ring to it, doesn't it?"

Bertie shook his head. He accepted the bowl of potatoes Arnold passed him and set it down on the dinner table.

"So you'll just be here until you've visited this Fishmongers' Hall?" asked Nellie.

Two peas rolled off George's knife and bounced across the table cloth. He didn't seem to notice them. "Unless there's anything I can do to repay you for your kindness in having me." He smiled around at everyone. "What are you up to these days, Bertram? Anything I can lend a hand with?"

Before Bertie could stop him, Arnold announced "Oh, didn't Bertie tell you? He investigates murders and things. And I help him.

The Penny Court Enquirers is what we are." He
beamed at George. Bertie tried desperately to kick
his brother-in-law under the table but couldn't reach
him.

George's knife and fork clattered onto his
plate. He looked at Bertie with his eyes wide. "You
investigate murders? What? With the police and
all?"

Arnold caught sight of Nellie's accusing
stare and dropped his head, mouthing the word
"Sorry!"

"Nothing fanciful," said Bertie. "Just our
own little form of . . . of amusement, if you like."
He looked hard at Arnold, who kept his head down.

"Amusement? With murders?" George
picked up his cutlery again and sliced into the beef.
"Now, I know you Bertram. Always modest. Am I
right?" He unconsciously spat a half-eaten pea onto
the tablecloth. Nellie's eyes locked onto it. "Don't
try to fool me." He chewed thoughtfully for a
moment.

Bertie opened his mouth to say something
but George continued. "So what case are you
working on now, cousin? Some gruesome murder in
the East End, perhaps?"

Arnold looked up, determined to rectify his
faux-pas. "Bertie is very good at it," he said,
looking George in the eye. "He solves things that
Scotland Yard can't. Right now he's mixing with
high society and going to Spirit mediums . . . and so
am I!" He thrust out his jaw as though daring
George to deny the worth of the Penny Court
Enquirers.

For the second time George's knife and fork clattered to the plate, this time bouncing off and scattering peas, gravy, and bits of mashed potato about his place at the table.

"Spirit mediums? Is that true, Bertie? Yes, I can see it is. Well now, I can help you there." He beamed and returned to his plate of food. "Yes. Very familiar with mediums, I am. We've got all the best ones up in Yorkshire, you know." He nodded his head and smiled a broad smile.

"Is that right?" It was Nellie, intrigued despite herself.

"Oh, yes." George shoveled a pile of mashed potatoes and peas into his mouth, not letting it stop him from talking. "Take Mildred Pratt for instance. What a medium! Amazing! Goes into a trance and speaks with a man's voice. And then there's Gladys Lofting. She's a physical medium. Started with table tipping and then went on to move trumpets and levitate pianos."

"What's that?" asked Arnold. "A physical medium?"

"It means she can produce physical phenomena. Spirits actually materialize . . . you can see one standing right there beside the medium. And like I said, lift up heavy furniture without touching it."

Arnold's eyes grew large. His knife and fork became still; an uncommon occurrence for Arnold at the dinner table. "What's a trumpet got to do with it?" he asked.

"Spirit trumpet," said George, matter-of-factly. "It's a long aluminium cone that sits on the table until it's needed. Then it floats in the air – held up by the spirits – and they speak through it."

"Why?"

"Well . . . so that everyone can hear them, I suppose."

"How do you know it floats through the air?" asked Nellie. "Aren't these séances taking place in darkness?"

"It has these bands of luminous stuff on the ends so you can see when it moves."

"You've seen all of this?" asked Bertie, suddenly seeing his cousin as a person who just might be of use after all.

George did not answer right away. He finished his meal, leaving a completely clean plate, and pushed back a little from the table. He stifled a belch, mumbled an apology, and then looked about him. "We got dessert then, Nell?" he asked.

Nellie was not to be used. "Bertie was asking if you'd actually seen these things," she said, her mouth a tight line.

George leaned forward, ran the tip of his finger around his clean plate, and then sucked the finger. "They are always in the newspapers. Can't keep 'em out, it seems. Am I right? One amazing thing after another."

"Have you actually seen them?"

He looked hard at the few remaining peas and small amount of mashed potatoes in the serving dishes, as though reconsidering whether or not he had really finished his meal. Then, with a sniff, he looked up at Bertie. "Not in so many words. No.

No, if you mean have I actually been *at* one of them Spiritual things, then no. No, I haven't."

Bertie sighed and relaxed. He smiled at Nellie, who shook her head and then got up from the table. "Dessert?" she said. "Anyone for dessert? I know you will, Arnold."


Maurice Austin was a veteran newspaperman and had originally joined Lady Marlborough's circle as a skeptic. He was inclined to doubt the validity of mediumistic phenomena, being a believer in Isaac Watts's 1725 work on *Logick,* in which the author stated: *The Dogmatist is in haste to believe something . . . The Sceptick will not take Pains to search Things to the Bottom, but when he sees Difficulties on both Sides resolves to believe neither of them.*

Austin was a short man with a rotund figure, speaking for many years of dining injudiciously. His carmine-purple nose attested to his love of brandy before, during, and after his meals. Sandy hair heavily laced with grey was brushed forward in a sad attempt to hide the receding hairline. Slightly old-fashioned, bushy mutton-chop sideboards framed his beardless face, with ruddy over-large ears protruding on either side as though alert for gossip, scandal, or whispered secrets. Despite his appearance, Maurice Austin had a sharp mind and an accurate memory. He seldom resorted to using a note book yet could write lengthy commentaries giving names, details of dress, mannerisms, and accurate quotations. Over the years he had acquired a number of enemies.

In a worn sacque suit, with an incongruously large gold watch chain spread across the waistcoat, and sporting an obviously new, brown bowler hat, Maurice Austin stepped off the omnibus and turned east along Fleet Street. He did not, however, enter any of the various newspaper offices for which the street was known.

Bertie was waiting for him at the corner of Whitefriars Street and together the two men turned down that thoroughfare and entered a small shop with the name *MASKELYNE* in small gilded letters over the door. The shop was a studio, with a large Turkish-influenced couch, upholstered in maroon tufted velvet, in pride of place in the center. There were two matching chairs and a variety of small tables and mahogany stands scattered about. Bertie paused at one such stand, noticing a wooden, flesh-colored object shaped like a human hand resting on it. Along one wall stood a pair of flatwall whatnots holding a variety of small devices on their shelves. A tall aluminium cone – a spirit trumpet – stood between them. An impressive walnut pump organ, with windpipes, took up much of another wall.

As they closed the shop door, a smartly dressed, middle-aged man emerged from a curtained doorway in a back corner and greeted them. He wore a brown velvet jacket, with black velvet collar and cuffs, over dark-brown striped trousers. His waistcoat was of ivory over a white shirt. The green cravat he sported made a bright splash of color. His black hair was brushed straight back and he wore a walrus-type mustache. Brown twinkling eyes appraised Austin and Bertie as they entered.

"I wish you a very good morning, gentlemen. I am John Nevil Maskelyne. How may I be of service to you?"

Austin did not remove his bowler hat. He stood looking about him for a moment before responding.

"I heard that you are familiar with the cabinet workings of the famous – or should I say 'infamous' – American Davenport Brothers."

Maskelyne inclined his head. "I did have the honor of bringing certain anomalies in the Brothers' performances to the attention of their audiences. Yes." He gave the barest hint of a smile.

"As I heard it, you exposed them."

Maskelyne indicated the chairs. "Won't you please be seated. And you are?"

Austin plumped down in one of the upholstered chairs and finally removed his hat, placing it, along with his gloves and cane, on the couch. He fumbled in his pocket and produced a business card which he gave to the other man. Bertie, in turn, offered his own Penny Court Enquirers card, and took another chair.

"A journalist and an enquirer." Maskelyne looked up from the cards. "And you are enquiring about spirit cabinets?"

"In a sense, yes," said Austin.

"We recently attended a séance where the medium employed a cabinet," explained Bertie.

"Ah! I see." Maskelyne walked over to a walnut and burl Davenport desk standing next to the whatnots. He opened one of the brass-handled side drawers and drew out some papers, which he carried across to his two visitors.

"You might like to peruse these. They are the plans for the construction of such a cabinet as you describe. With the help of my good friend and cabinet maker, George Alfred Cooke, we designed and built a spirit cabinet after studying the Davenport Brothers' performance. You will see that although outwardly it seems solid, in fact there are certain hidden cupboards and doors that can be extremely useful to a fraudulent medium."

It was nearly an hour later that Bertie and Austin left Maskelyne's shop. John Nevil Maskelyne had made a name for himself as a stage magician – one of Britain's finest – and his emporium on Whitefriars Street catered to others of that profession. There he designed and constructed stage illusions, sold large and small items of that ilk, and taught legerdemain to aspiring entertainers. Although he was not especially connected with the exposing of fraudulent Spiritualist mediums, he did have occasion to unmask some of the worst of that type. He had not heard of Prince Honoré, he claimed, and certainly had nothing negative to say about him.

Bertie now felt much better informed about the construction of spirit cabinets. He did note, however, that John Maskelyne had made the point that just because some mediums were fraudulent, it did not mean that *all* mediums were so. Only by examining individual mediums and their cabinets would it be possible to tell. Bertie couldn't wait to again examine the prince's cabinet.

## *Chapter Seven*

The four-wheeled carriage slowed as it entered the Victoria Station yard.  Dr. William Price leaned out of the window and, catching the eye of a young lady strolling slowly along the pavement, raised his hat. The young lady was Alice Bell. She was wearing a navy blue, homespun dress trimmed with silk and lace, with satin bands and gilt buttons. She had a fashionable grey, brocaded satin cape about her shoulders and a matching grey, taffeta silk hat trimmed with a large bunch of violets, on her head. Her dark brown hair showed in ringlets on either side of the hat. She smiled and approached the growler.

"Miss Bell."

"Dr. Price."

He opened the door and stepped down, then handed her into the vehicle. He followed her in and the driver started off again. They turned onto Grosvenor Place and continued in the direction of Hyde Park. As the growler entered the park, the blinds on the windows were discreetly pulled down.

"Insofar as I am able to ascertain, sir," said Sergeant Gilmore, "all of the suspects is clean insofar as their private lives is concerned."

"You're sure about that?"

Gilmore hesitated. *You can't really be sure about anything these days. I thought the inspector knew that. Well, I'll assume he knows and is speaking in general terms*, he decided.

"Yessir."

"Hmm. Well, we'll see."

The sergeant thought it might help to enumerate. He had his notebook open and referred to it. "Dr. William Price seems to have no debts of any sorts; no indebtedness, you might say, sir. No vices apparent. Mister Austin is a journalist so – er – of course I expected some sort of 'outside activity,' if I can put it that way, sir?"

"Go on." The inspector scratched the top of his head and then yawned. He stretched his feet out under his desk and bumped his knees on the bottom of the desk drawer – something he'd been doing for some years and had still not learned to avoid. He muttered to himself and waved the sergeant on.

"It seems as how our Mr. Austin is a not uncommon figure at the races, sir. The horse races, that is. A bit of a flutter that is not often successful, it seems. But he don't overdo it, apparently. Not our Mr. Austin."

Moss nodded and waved him on again.

"Miss Winifred Dobson was not easy to pin down, sir, in a manner of speaking."

"Go on."

"It would seem that Miss Dobson's main interest lies in this Spirit business and she is bound and determined to become a medium herself."

"Meaning what, sergeant?" The inspector straightened up again, and once more banged his knees. He muttered a curse.

"She lives with her parents, who are middle class, sir. Viz; her father works for the Ministry of Health in a upper position, so Miss Dobson receives a plentiful allowance."

"Which she spends on what?"

"On this spirits business, sir, it would appear. Miss Dobson takes classes at the . . ." He referred to his notebook. ". . . Belgravia Spiritualist Association in Belgrave Square. She purchases books and magazines on the subject and also goes to other séances besides them of Lady Marlborough."

"What about the other lady; Alice Whatshername?"

"Miss Alice Bell, sir. Yes. She is a quiet one."

"Aren't all women," the inspector observed. "So what can you tell me?"

"Steady job, inspector. Lives alone. Employed by a Pimlico tailor. No special interests . . . none that is apparent, at any rate. I suspect that she has a gentleman friend but I have, as yet, been unable to ascertain who that might be, sir."

Moss sniffed, shrugged, and said nothing.

"Professor Sedgeworth, as you know sir, is . . ."

"Aye, aye. We know who he is. Get to the facts, Sergeant. Anything suspicious?"

Gilmore grunted at having his flow interrupted but continued. "The gentleman in question would appear to spend a great deal of his money on books and a certain amount on paintings – considers himself something of a coin . . . conn . . . an expert on the arts, sir."

"Does he now? And who does that leave?"

"Just Lady Marlborough and her medium, inspector."

Moss got to his feet and stretched. Gilmore's eyes followed him as he walked over to the small window that let in so little light that the overhead gas mantle always had to be lit when the office was occupied. The window looked out onto a small, cobbled courtyard where broken wooden boxes and forgotten sacks of rubbish had been growing into an untidy heap for as long as Moss could remember. He stared, unseeing, out of the window, eventually noticing that it had started to rain. He turned back to his sergeant, who now stood contemplating the framed print on the wall, clipped from *The Illustrated London News*, showing the proposed new Tower Bridge.

"I don't think we need trouble Lady Marlborough, but her medium is another story. What's his name again?"

Another quick look at the notebook. "Calls himself Prince Honoré, inspector. I have not, as yet, managed to track down exactly who he is or where he comes from."

Inspector Moss thought for a moment, alternately tugging at his mustache and scratching the top of his head. "All right, Gilmore. You get back to your list and dig a bit deeper on the professor's art interest and on the two misses. I'll have to take a look at our medium friend myself, as soon as I can."

"Yessir."

"Ouch!"

"What is it?"

"Devil take it! Your deuced hatpin stabbed me!" Dr. Price sucked the back of his hand where a red spot of blood appeared.

"Oh, I am so sorry, William." Alice's head came up and she reached up to her hat, to gingerly feel for the offending pin. "I should have taken this off anyway." She did so and threw the hat onto the seat opposite.

William Price tried to recapture the bliss he had been enjoying, as the carriage made its leisurely way through the park.

George Hudson stood on London Bridge and looked down at Fishmongers' Hall; known locally as "Fish Hall". The earliest recorded building had been constructed in 1310. A newer hall was built in 1434 but was destroyed in the Great Fire of London in 1666. This was replaced in 1671 and then again replaced – with the construction of London Bridge – in 1827. This present hall, which George so much admired, held many treasures including the dagger used by Lord Mayor Sir William Walworth when he killed Wat Tyler in 1381, thus ending the Peasants' Revolt. Contained in the hall was also a famous collection of seventeenth and eighteenth century silver, an embroidered fifteenth century funeral pall, two portraits by George Romney and river scenes by Samuel Scott. None of these treasures seemed to George Hudson's mind to have anything at all to do with fishmongers. He was, however, willing to learn if it would allow him entry into the distinguished company.

"Do you have an appointment?" The uniformed commissionaire looked down his thin pointed nose at George and sniffed disapprovingly.

"Appointment? No, I don't have no appointment. Why would I need one?"

"Everybody needs one," he was informed. "Do you think the Wardens have nothing better to do than open their doors to the riff-raff?"

George pulled himself up to his full five feet seven inches – still some few inches shorter than the man he faced – and spluttered, "Riff-raff? *Riff-raff?* How dare you, sir? Do you know who I am?"

The commissionaire stepped back a pace the better to look George up and down, which he did slowly. He did not seem assured by the appraisal.

"And your name . . . sir?"

George swallowed and reminded himself that it wouldn't do to get off on the wrong foot with the Worshipful Company of Fishmongers and that the man facing him was their representative; albeit an employee. He tried to put on a friendly face.

"My name is George Hudson. I am the major purveyor of fish in the whole of East Yorkshire. I have traveled down here to London for the express purpose of speaking with someone here at Fishmongers' Hall."

"And do you have an appointment, sir?" The face was unsmiling.

George breathed deeply and mentally counted to ten. He smiled his broadest smile.

"Forgive me," he said. "No, I do not have an appointment. Being a humble fishmonger from the North of our fair country, I was unaware of the necessity for such. Now, I would very much like, if you would be so very kind, to speak to someone as knows something of the art and science of fish selling. Someone, if I may make so bold, as is higher up on the fish scale, as it were, here at the Fish Hall. Would that be possible, do you think?"

The commissionaire regarded him silently for a long moment. Finally he turned on his heel.

"Follow me," he said.

With George close behind him he walked, with what George considered something of a swagger, across the gleaming marble floor back to a distant corner where a messenger boy sat biting his fingernails.

"Samuel, conduct this – gentleman – up to the third floor and introduce him to Mr. Wickersby."

"What for?" questioned the boy, not getting to his feet.

"Just do as you're told," hissed the commissionaire.

"All right, all right." The messenger boy got to his feet, tugged his uniform more or less straight, and then, with a grin at George and beckoning to follow, led the way towards the curving marble staircase that ascended to the upper floors. "Come on, mate. Never mind 'is nibs. I'll steer you right."


"So where did you end up?" asked Bertie. He had packed his pipe with his favorite Gallaher's Rich Dark Honeydew tobacco and now, applying a light, contentedly puffed smoke out at his cousin.

George drew on an Ogden's Guinea-Gold cigarette, the better to blow smoke back. Nellie, ignoring their smoke, smiled contentedly as she sat darning Bertie's socks and listening to their conversation.

"With some gent named Alexander or Alexandria or something. It seems the Worshipful Company is more interested in organizing boat races and regattas and in managing charities and trusts than in selling fish these days. Am I right?" He sadly shook his head at the very idea. "What is this country coming to?" he asked of no one in particular.

"So you didn't get your endorsement?" Bertie asked.

"Oh yes. Yes, they agreed to me mentioning them in my business." He paused before continuing.

"Mind you, I had to make a contribution to their 'dowment fund?"

"*En*dowment fund, I suspect," said Nellie without looking up.

"Something like that," George agreed. "I just know it cost me more than I thought it would. Any chance of a cup of tea, Our Nell?"


It was the purest chance that Sergeant Toby Gilmore was approaching Denbigh Street from one end when a four-wheeler turned into the street from the other end and came to a halt outside number eleven. Thinking quickly, the sergeant moved across to the other side of the street, hopping lithely over piles of horse manure missed by the crossing sweeper, and tried to give the impression that he was more interested in the houses on that side of the street than on the occupants of the growler. He was far enough along that his angle of sight allowed him to see what was taking place.

"Miss Alice Bell, if I am not mistaken," he murmured to himself. "And who might we have with her, I wonder?"

As if in answer, a gentleman stuck out his head and looked up and down the street, not noticing the policeman on the other side. He then descended and assisted a young lady out of the carriage.

"As I thought," murmured Gilmore.

There was a brief touching of hands – nothing too intimate – and then the gentleman returned to the carriage and it drove away. Miss Alice Bell went into the house.

Sergeant Gilmore took out his notebook and pencil and made an entry. After many years on the beat, he had learned to mark the more pertinent points of both a person and a scene. He now wrote down: *Tall gentleman with oiled dark hair touched with grey. Beard and mustache. Flushed or ruddy face. Gold-rimmed pince-nez. Spats.* He couldn't be totally sure but he suspected that it was Dr. William Price, so he appended *Dr. William Price?* and tucked the notebook back in his pocket.

Scotland Yard is situated at 4 Whitehall Place. The back entrance, used by visitors to the Commissioners, is in Great Scotland Yard. The building in the center of Scotland Yard is partly occupied by the Chief Superintendent and his subordinates and partly by the functionaries who look after the cab-drivers of the metropolis. This is where those drivers get their licenses and, more importantly, is where they must deposit any property inadvertently left in their vehicles by their fares. When lost articles are claimed, a percentage of the value is demanded and this is passed on to the finder as a reward for his honesty.

On the right, as one enters, are the offices of the Commissioners. It was there that longtime Commissioner of Police of the Metropolis Sir Edmund Henderson held reign, until his forced resignation following the "Black Monday" riots in Trafalgar Square and Hyde Park at the beginning of the year. He had been succeeded by Sir Charles Warren. Also on the right is the telegraph office of London's police system; the center of a mighty spider's web extending to the limits of the district. Lower down, on the opposite side of the Yard, is the printing office and alongside it is the Central Prisoners' Property Store, where released prisoners apply for the return of their personal property. The library, upstairs from there, contains over twenty thousand photographic portraits and details of felons from all over the United Kingdom.

Bertie and Inspector Moss entered Scotland Yard and made their way to the area of the library, but passed on from there to what had become known as the "Black Museum" – that collection of artifacts used by past and present criminals; many of them notorious. There were axes and spades used in murders, smashed gambling tables, articles of clothing, blood-rusted blades of razors, skeleton keys, leaden hammers, knives, daggers, walking-stick swords, pistols, jemmies, and much more. There was the paraphernalia of Professor Zendavesta, Charles Peace's expanding ladder, the irons in which Jerry Abershaw was hanged, the tanned hide of John Belligham who was the only successful assassin of a British Prime Minister.

Among the multitude of burglars' tools on display was an admirable set of skeleton keys.

"These are made of both iron and steel," said Moss, pointing them out to his friend. His voice was hushed as though in a library or a church. "Mostly of scrap iron though."

"Oh? Why is that?"

The inspector rubbed his chin. "It has nay grain to it and they say it's tougher. Burglars and housebreakers usually make their own skeleton keys, though some of them are pretty rough."

Bertie looked down at the selection, laid out on a piece of old canvas.

"There are two kinds," continued Moss. "The pick-locks made of stout wire and, for larger locks, the stronger keys."

"What on earth is this?" asked Bertie. He pointed to a battered top hat with a crude black mask attached to it. The mask was made out of American cloth with two eye holes cut out. There was a piece of cord tied to the bottom of the mask to tie around the neck.

Inspector Moss looked at it and laughed. "That was a most unfortunate gentleman of the road. He tucked himself away out of sight in a room at a lodging house on the New North Road, planning to come out after closing time. The landlord found him under a bed and chased him. The gent dashed to a window to get out but, because of his mask, he didna' really see that there were bars on the window. He lunged forward and got his head stuck between two of them. The landlord then proceeded to prod him with a sword-stick. The poor man screamed and screamed until the police arrived!"

They both laughed.

"And what's this display?" asked Bertie.

"Ah! Now that's Charlie Peace's things. Remember him? Back about ten years ago?"

Bertie nodded. "Oh, yes. *The Daily Chronicle* ran a number of front page stories about him."

"Aye! Well, these are some of his clever tools."

"What's this? It looks like a dummy arm!"

"That's exactly what it is, Bertram. Charlie had a finger missing and that piece of information was on the description that went out and was posted to every police station in the country. So what did he do? He wore a fake false arm so while we were looking for a man missing a finger, he was parading around like a man missing a whole hand!" Bertie laughed. "Oh, aye! Very funny. But he was a very successful man, doing everything by himself; working alone. He stole; he had nay receiver so he melted down metals himself and then sold them. He built that ingenious ladder you see there. When we finally caught up with him at Blackheath, he was wearing those blue-lens spectacles and had his face stained with walnut juice to look like a Mulatto." He sighed. "Ah, they dinna' make them like him any more . . . thank the good Lord." He looked around. "Tell me again what we're looking for Bertram."

"Anything like a hatpin," replied Bertie. "I just thought it might be that our murderer was inspired in his choice of weapon by some confounder from the past."

"Well, there is certainly a vast selection of gruesome weapons here," said Moss, studying the items on display.

They moved slowly along the displays, pausing occasionally and then moving on again. They found murder weapons that were thin, beveled-edged stiletto daggers, sharpened metal rods, screwdrivers, even a knitting needle, but no hatpins. After almost an hour of study, and with a queasy stomach, Bertie was ready to give up.

"I think this may not have been one of my better ideas, Campbell," he said. "The closest I've found is a knitting needle. No hatpins that I can see."

Moss grunted in agreement. "Still, it was an idea, Bertram, and one I hadna' thought about."

With a final sweep of the display cases, they made their way out of the area and headed for the fresh air.

"So what is our next move?" asked Moss.

"How about a cup of tea?"

"Sounds about right to me."

Together they made their way to the closest Aerated Bread Company teashop.

With a cup of hot tea and a digestive biscuit in front of him, Bertie felt a little more relaxed. "How is your own investigation going, Campbell?" he asked.

The inspector stirred three sugar lumps into his tea and grunted. "Very slowly, Bertram. Very slowly. Sergeant Gilmore has been doing some background checking for me but that hasna' brought any great revelations. It does seem, though, that our late lamented Captain Grimsby was a bit of a ladies' man and also had been abusive to his wife . . . the reason she finally left him, I imagine. Oh, and it would seem that our Miss Alice Bell and Dr. Price are rather more closely associated than had previously been thought, but that's nay a crime."

Bertie raised his eyebrows, and then reached for a second biscuit. "Is it significant, do you think? Any possible rivalry between Price and the deceased, perhaps?"

Inspector Moss paused with his own biscuit halfway to his mouth. He looked hard at Bertie. "You mean, jealousy might have caused Dr. Price to kill the Major? Hmm. I hadna' really thought of that. I wouldna' have thought it of Dr. Price but you never can tell." He set down both his biscuit and his cup and pulled out of his pocket his dog-eared blue notebook. Searching his waistcoat finally produced a pencil stub and he made a notation. "I'll get the sergeant on to that when I get back," he muttered.

"Both of our ladies sport sizeable hatpins, I've noticed," said Bertie. "Hardly surprising, of course. All ladies do. But it would have been a simple matter for the murderer – whoever he, or she, may be – to pull a pin out of a hat belonging to one of the ladies, stab the victim, and then return the hatpin to where it would not be noticed . . . back in the hat. Though returning it may not have been too easy to do in the dark, of course."

"Aye! Aye!" The inspector had returned to his tea and biscuits. He chewed thoughtfully for a few moments. "So it wouldna' necessarily have been the woman wearing the hat herself, I suppose. It could have been whoever sat close to her. Do you think it was really meant to kill the man?" he asked suddenly. "I mean, to stab a man in the dark with a hatpin . . . I could see it being done just to hurt him, for whatever reason, but it would be a tricky job to stick it into his heart, would it not?"

Bertie nodded his head. "I agree. No, I doubt that it was meant to kill, but it was certainly meant to hurt and to do some sort of damage. From what you told me – what you were kind enough to share, Campbell – the pin entered his chest far enough to strike his heart, so it was thrust in with some force and certainly not to just prick the man."

"Very interesting choice of weapon," said Moss. "Thin enough to nay cause a lot of blood yet stiff enough to go in under pressure."

"When I was at Lady Marlborough's séance," said Bertie, "I managed to get a look at the ladies' hatpins. Both ladies retained their hats throughout the evening, which is normal for such a sitting I understand."

"And what did you see?"

"I couldn't really tell without asking either lady to remove her headgear and allowing me close inspection," said Bertie. "But there is no doubt that any one of the larger pins these ladies use would have done the job."

The inspector pursed his lips and his brow furrowed. "Nay sign of any blood on the pins, I suppose?"

Bertie shook his head. "If the murderer had pulled the pin from Miss Dobson's hat, say, stabbed the Captain, withdrawn the hatpin and then stuck it back in her hat, it's just possible it might have retained a little of his blood on the end, but I saw no evidence of it."

"Could someone, other than Miss Dobson or Miss Bell, have done all of that in the dark, do you think?"

Bertie nodded. "All of their heads were bent over the table, I would imagine. I'm sure that even in the extremely dim light, it could have been done. And don't forget that both Miss Dobson and Miss Bell mentioned that they thought a spirit had touched them. That was in all probability the murderer pushing the hatpin back into place."

"Aye. Aye. It is nay an impossibility, I suppose."

They both drank their tea and chewed on their biscuits as they thought about the case.

# Chapter Eight

"You must be anxious to get home again, George," said Nellie, pulling the carpet-beaters out of the pantry. "Get back to Penny and the children."

"Oh, no! No, I don't think so."

Nellie made a face. George sat at the kitchen table nursing a cup of tea. Bertie sat beside him, trying to go over the notes he had made in his Penny Court Enquirers notebook.

"Much as I'd love to go running off back up North, Our Nell, I feel I can't possibly leave here till I've repaid cousin Bertram's and your kindness in having me here. Am I right?" He turned to face Bertie.

Bertie looked up, startled. "What? Oh, no, George. You feel free to go home any time you like. You don't owe us anything."

"Not a thing," added Nellie.

George chuckled. "Ah, you're such good family! But I know you two. And don't worry about Penny. She's got plenty to occupy herself, especially with the children. Yes! But you two are always giving and never taking back. Well, that won't do, you know?"

"It won't?" Bertie looked and felt worried. "W-what did you have in mind, then?"

"Why to help you and Arnold in this spirit thing you've got yourselves into, of course. Am I right?"

Bertie closed the book. "No, George." He tried to sound as firm as he felt. "No, this is something we are doing along with Scotland Yard. It's not anything that you . . ."

"But it's my speciality, Bertie. I told you that. I know all about these spirit gatherings."

"Séances," said Nellie.

"That's them." George nodded.

"But you said you hadn't actually been to a séance," said Bertie.

"Well, that's easily remedied, isn't it? Am I right? I'll just go along to the next one that you or Arnold's going to. I bet they'd be pleased to have someone of my expertise there. Am I right again?"

Bertie looked desperately at Nellie. She held up a carpet beater. "Why don't you come outside and help me do the carpets, George?" she asked.

The Yorkshireman quickly gulped down the rest of his tea, pushed back his chair, and got to his feet. "No, I think I'd best be finding Arnold and see what's what for this work. See when he's next going to a gathering. Right?" Without waiting for a response, George scuttled out of the room and up the stairs.

The Army and Navy Club, at 36 Pall Mall, had 2,400 members and a lengthy waiting list of would-be members. It was situated on the corner of Pall Mall and St. James's Square and was of unremarkable appearance. It was a square, two-storey edifice with simply dressed windows in a rustic face on the ground floor, and the entrance marked by a Doric portico of three bays. The upper floor was slightly more interesting, with the windows set in arched recesses between Corinthian columns. There were statues in niches and an ornamented balustrade stretched across the entrance.

Bertie took the white No. 5 horse-drawn omnibus from Ludgate Circus to Whitehall and then walked to Pall Mall. He had been wondering about Cyril Grimsby's flat and its lack of clues regarding the Captain's life. Then he had remembered Inspector Moss's comment that Grimsby had been ejected from the Army and Navy Club for non-payment of bills.

"I wonder," Bertie had said to Nellie, "if any trace of Grimsby remains at his old club? Such institutions are notoriously slow in updating all manner of things. I wonder if, by any chance, there are still some of the late Captain's possessions there?"

"You really think there might be?"

Bertie tapped the side of his nose in a way he had seen Taffy Owens do when thinking through an idea. "There's only one way to find out," he said.

The commissionaire at the Army and Navy Club was trying to answer questions from an impatient red-faced gentleman in the uniform of an army colonel; was receiving three or four brown-paper-wrapped boxes from a delivery boy; was repeatedly banging on a bell for a messenger-boy's attention; and was trying to oversee a sign-in book, when Bertie appeared before him. He half-listened to Bertie's query while trying to field the colonel's complaints at the same time.

"You'd best talk with Snooky Thompson," the commissionaire told Bertie. "Batman to Colonel Sir Winston Caruthers. Snooky often did double-duty for Captain Grimsby. Quite unofficial, of course. He may be through in the squash court at this time. Now, colonel . . ." he turned away from Bertie to the red-faced, uniformed gentleman.

Bertie hurried away into the farther reaches of the building. He found Snooky Thompson lounging outside the squash court smoking a cigarette. The batman was in uniform but hatless. He had sandy-colored hair and bushy sideboards. He seemed to be developing a mustache but without a lot of success. The result was an upper lip bearing straggly hair that was unkempt and stringy. He had a habit of sucking on it.

"An enquiry agent?" Snooky raised his eyebrows and looked up from the card Bertie had given him. "What's this then?" He threw down his cigarette and ground it into the floor with his heel. He pulled himself upright and straightened his jacket. "And 'oo's been talkin' then, might I ask? 'Cos whatever they said, I deny it!"

"No, no." Bertie spread his hands in what he hoped was a calming gesture. "I am here just to ask a few questions about Captain Cyril Grimsby."

"Grimsby? What's Cyril been up to, then?"

"Well, right now, he's dead."

"Dead?" Snooky Thompson's puzzled face cleared and he dug in his pocket for another cigarette. "So old Cyril's kicked the bucket, 'as 'e? Shot by a jealous 'usband, was 'e?" He chuckled as he struck a lucifer and inhaled deeply.

Bertie patiently explained what had happened to the Captain and why he was there. "I was wondering – hoping, actually – that the late Captain might have left some of his belongings here? Perhaps letters, or a notebook, or . . . anything?"

Snooky studied the end of his cigarette, his brow furrowed again, and sucked on his mustache. "First off, Mister 'awkins, Cyril weren't no captain. That's what got 'im thrown out of this pangless billet."

"But – but I thought he had exceeded his club bar bill and was in arrears . . ."

"Ho, yes! Yes, indeed. Cyril 'ad spent one 'ell of a lot more – if you'll pardon my French – than 'e could pay, no question about that. But it was for impersonating an officer that 'e got the boot. 'e weren't no more'n a Second Lieutenant. Captain? Hah! Mind you, I told 'im 'e'd never get away with it. But that's Cyril for you . . . *was* Cyril, I suppose I should say. I knew 'e'd come to a sticky end."

"Quite. About any letters or anything? . . ."

Snooky took a long drag on his cigarette and then flung it away. He turned on his heel and beckoned Bertie to follow him. "You just might be in luck, my old son. Foller me."

Snooky's room was next to that of Colonel Sir Winston Caruthers. Snooky saw to it that the colonel's quarters were immaculate, but the same could not be said of his own. Bertie thought that it was an odd mixture of neat and untidy . . . clothes were precisely pressed and hanging in a wardrobe and the bed was tight and Spartan. Brightly shined boots were arrayed along the end of the bed. Yet books and papers were dropped in casual heaps about the room, partly covered by outdated newspapers and discarded underwear. There was little light entering the room, which had only a single narrow window heavily draped with plain, mud-colored curtains. Snooky led the way in and turned up the gas light on the wall sconce.

"Welcome to my abode, Mr. 'awkins. It ain't the Savoy 'ere, but the service is good and the eating's the best. 'Ere! Take a pew." He swept some clothes from a straight-backed wooden chair onto the floor and gestured for Bertie to sit down. "Now, let's see. We 'ave something of old Cyril's, I know. Now where did I put it?" He stood thoughtfully rubbing his chin.

A scob, or small trunk, was pushed against the wall alongside the wardrobe. Snooky Thompson got down on his knees and flipped open the lid. He rifled through a number of papers before pulling out a well-worn envelope. He passed it to Bertie.

It was marked *Cyril Harold Grimsby*, in pencil, and bound by an old rubber band that snapped as soon as Bertie tried to stretch it to remove it.

"Cyril left this stuff with me 'cos 'e left in something of a 'urry, you might say. I was supposed to send it on to 'im when 'e found somewhere else to stay but I suppose I never did get around to it." Snooky didn't seem too contrite, thought Bertie.

Inside the envelope were a number of bar chits, every one of them stamped *OVERDUE* in red ink. There were four letters. One, without return address, was from a William Macklesthwaite, threatening to severely injure Grimsby if he did not repay the fifty pounds that was owed. Two of the others were made out on a type-writer and sent from a lawyer named Mortimer in Chancery Lane. The letters from the lawyer were both the same; one a duplicate of the other but they were dated a month apart. They stated that Grimsby was to "cease and desist" his abuse of his wife Jessica. The fourth letter was a single small sheet, handwritten and signed *Jessica*. This said simply: *I cannot allow you to so abuse me and thus I am leaving.*

"Jessica was Cyril's wife," said Snooky, peering over Bertie's shoulder. "'e was not an easy man to deal with, especially when 'e 'ad a drink or two in 'im. She – poor thing – put up with 'im longer than I would 'ave done. But then she just couldn't take it any more."

"She took him to court?" asked Bertie, indicating the lawyer's two letters.

"No. She couldn't do that very easily. That Mortimer was a friend of a friend of 'ers, as it were, 'oo wrote those letters more to frighten Cyril than anything. But they didn't have no bite to 'em, so she finally just up and left."

"Do you know where she went?"

Snooky shook his head. "Cyril never said but I don't think 'e knew. 'e didn't seem to care anyway. Said as 'ow 'e'd get 'isself a nice little bachelor flat, when they threw 'im out of 'ere."

"Who was this Macklesthwaite, threatening bodily harm?"

Snooky shrugged. "Could 'ave been any of a number of blokes. Cyril owed money all over the place."

Bertie looked over the letters again. He noticed an address penciled on the bottom of the handwritten note: *Kingston House*. It sounded familiar but he couldn't place it.

"Do you think I might keep these for a while?"

Again Snooky shrugged. "Don't make no never-mind to me, now do it? If 'e's dead, 'e's dead. 'e won't be looking for 'em. You can burn 'em as far as I'm concerned, and good riddance."

"No, I won't burn them," said Bertie, getting up to go. "I think Scotland Yard might find them of some interest. I thank you, Mister Thompson."


"What-ho, Arnold! This must be George?" Herbert's high-pitched, slightly nasal voice stabbed the fog and reached the big man as he and cousin George alighted from the omnibus at Hyde Park Corner.

"Been waiting long, Herbert?"

"Just stepped off an omnibus myself, Arnold."

"Bit murky, isn't it?" said George, straining to see through the gloom. "Have we got far to go? Do you think it's really worth it, in this fog?"

"I thought you wanted to sit at a séance," said Arnold.

"Oh, yes. Yes, I do. No question, Arnold. Is it far from here?"

"Follow me!" Herbert set off hesitantly, his arms stretched out in front of him. "Madam Stanhope says that this is a good time to contact the spirits, when the fog is thick."

"Why would that be?" asked Arnold, cautiously following the other two men.

Herbert did not answer. He sidestepped around a lamp-post, its dim light reflecting back off the fog. It was more than a half hour later that the three of them were able to make out the Belgravia Spiritualist Association's dim lights burning bravely through the fog.

They found that a surprising number of people had been drawn out into the murky weather by the lure of spirit communication. As Arnold dropped his half-crown into the box he looked about him to see nearly a dozen people gathered in the séance room. He recognized one or two from his last visit but there were many new faces.

"Lend me a florin, Arnold," said George, counting pennies and coming up short of his admittance money. Arnold sighed and gave him the money, making a mental note to write it into his accounts.

"Please take your seats, ladies and gentlemen," cried Madam Stanhope, her smiling face and lantern jaw swinging from side to side as she beamed at all of the sitters. Arnold thought that she possessed an extremely prominent set of teeth. "This is going to be an exciting séance I know. The spirits are with us, drawn here through the fog like moths to a flame. One must send out one's love to those near and dear to one, and let the spirits know that one is open to communication."

There was a scraping of chairs as everyone hurried to take a seat. In the center of the otherwise bare table sat a trumpet. Arnold found himself sitting between two ladies; one extraordinarily fat and the other painfully thin. Both seemed to be seasoned séance-goers, immediately placing their hands on the big oak table and spreading their fingers to touch those of their immediate neighbors. Arnold looked down at his large hands between their more petite ones. As the gas light was turned low, he glanced up just in time to see George, across the table from him, smiling brightly at the young lady sitting beside him. Herbert was on the other side of the young lady.

Madam Stanhope took her seat and directed her fellowship to sing a song . . . apparently, thought Arnold, a Spiritualist hymn well known to most of them. As they sang, their medium sat back in her chair, her prominent chin slowly descending to rest upon her chest and her breathing deepening and slowing. A white-haired gentleman seated next to her acted as master of ceremonies, obviously having led such séances many times in the past. Arnold recalled noticing, before the lights were dimmed, that he was dressed in a well-worn suit with a soup-stained waistcoat. As the singing faded away he turned down the light completely and spoke.

"Now let us all join our thoughts with those of our beloved medium Madam Stanhope and send her all of our energy as she opens the door to the Summerland, welcoming those who have passed across that threshold."

Nothing happened for a very long while and then the medium gave what Arnold thought to be a snore. *She's fallen asleep!* But apparently not. She gave another snort and then spoke loudly and forcibly in a high-pitched, sing-song voice as though trying to sound like a very young girl.

"Hello, everybody."

"It's little Ellie!" cried one of the sitters.

"Yes. Yes . . . Ellie," said another.

"Hello, Ellie!"

"Hello, everyone," responded the child-like voice, brightly. "I'm come to see you all again."

Arnold was not impressed. To him, it just sounded like the medium trying to impersonate a young child. But many of the other sitters seemed to be familiar with this particular spirit, if spirit it was.

"We are going to play that game again," said the voice. "You know the one. Where I hide something and you have to find it."

"Oh!" the thin lady on Arnold's left exclaimed. "Ellie. Don't forget that you already have something of mine. You said that you would return it this time."

The master of ceremonies, who had given his name simply as "Mr. Smith", spoke softly to the group. "Ellie has been showing us how apports and asports work. She asported a necklace belonging to Miss Fotherington at our last session and promised to return it – as an apport – at this one."

Ellie giggled. "Was I naughty, Miss Fotherington? I'm not really, you know. I said I'd return it and so I will . . . before the sitting is done."

Arnold wasn't sure what all of that meant but he listened carefully, trying to commit it all to memory so that he could write it in his notebook after the meeting. Bertie would be interested in this, he was certain.

After some further banter, the child spirit faded away and others took her place – relatives of various of the sitters, acknowledged by them as the spirits came through. Herbert's grandmother put in another brief appearance, telling her grandson that she watched over him at all times and still loved him. Herbert seemed delighted to hear that, although it seemed to Arnold that was what she had said the previous time.

Towards the end of the séance the luminous rings around the ends of the spirit trumpet were seen to rise above the surface of the table, pointed out by Mr. Smith in case anyone had not noticed. It apparently floated the length of the table and then dipped down. Something was heard to fall and hit the table's surface, and then the trumpet floated around again before alighting gently in the center. When the séance ended and the lights were once again turned up, the sitters saw that something sparkling lay beside the trumpet.

"My necklace!" cried the thin lady, Miss Fotherington. "Ellie has returned my necklace, just as she said she would!"

"For those of you unfamiliar with the words," said Madam Stanhope, now fully conscious again, her teeth flashing in the bright gas light, "an asport is something which seems to disappear from a sitter. One knows full well that one has placed an item firmly in one's reticule, or in a pocket, and yet when one checks, after the séance, it is no longer present. The spirits have taken it . . . as proof that they are present." Her smile spread even broader, to Arnold's amazement. "Invariably that which was taken – or 'borrowed' – is returned at a later date. An apport, on the other hand, is a gift from spirit. It is something which suddenly appears – often tumbling out of the trumpet – and might be a totally new item or might be that which had disappeared at a previous time." She indicated the necklace. "On this occasion – as promised by the spirits – Miss Fotherington's temporarily missing necklace is returned, safe and sound."

Miss Fotherington snatched it up and, snapping open her lorgnette, examined the jewels in the necklace very closely.

"Have no fear, my dear," said the medium. "It is as good as when it first was taken away."

"I would hope so," said the young lady, through tight lips. "It was my late mother's diamond necklace. As I intimated when it was asported, I was not happy to see it gone."

A gentleman sporting a broad, checkered waistcoat and wearing a monocle leaned forward as far as his ample stomach would allow.

"Have no fear, my good lady. I understand your hesitancy but perhaps I can set your mind at rest. I am a jeweler by profession. Mr. Reinhart Kaster, at your service. Perhaps I might inspect the piece and ascertain its authenticity?"

Arnold realized that Miss Fotherington, without spelling it out, was concerned that the necklace returned to her might not be the same one that had disappeared. She allowed the jeweler to take it from her. He screwed his monocle more firmly into his eye and stood up under the gas mantle, turning the necklace slowly through his hands. No one said a word; all was quiet around the circle. Finally he looked up, smiled, and allowed his eyeglass to fall.

"I compliment you on the beauty of these diamonds," he said. "They are all of excellent quality."

There was a collective sigh of relief around the table.

"All – all of them?" asked Miss Fotherington, in a quiet voice.

"Every last one," smiled Mr. Kaster. He resumed his seat.

"The spirits are such a joy to us all," cried Madam Stanhope. "Now, we all have need to find our way home through the fog beyond these walls. I urge you now to take your leave, and to exercise all caution as you traverse this city to your respective abodes. I hope to see you all about this table once again. Good night to you, one and all."

*Chapter Nine*

"We have to follow up on this medium character, Prince Honoré," said Inspector Moss, as he stepped up into the hansom cab he had hailed. Sergeant Toby Gilmore stood on the pavement close behind him. "I see you didna' note his place of residence in the report. I think you had better track him down and remedy that short-fall, Sergeant."

"Yessir." The sergeant prepared to climb up after his superior. "Where will you drop me off then, sir?"

"Drop you off? Drop you off? Oh, I dinna' think so, sergeant. Nay, you can walk like any good policeman. I did my fair share when I was in the ranks. Drive on, driver!" He snapped the doors closed over his legs and rapped on the roof of the conveyance. Sergeant Gilmore jumped back as the hansom lurched forward and then made off at a brisk pace along Whitehall Place, its metal-rimmed wheels clattering over the cobblestones.

"Yessir. Thank you, sir!" muttered Gilmore sarcastically. "Now where do I start with this bloody prince?"

After thinking for a moment, he turned along Whitehall and started north towards Charing Cross. Trudging along in the direction of the Strand, he turned down Craven Street and, picking his way through offal, detritus, and dung, sought out a small hole-in-the-wall tavern which bore no name but had only a weather-worn, once-gilded figure of a fighting cock painted on a board above the doorway. After first glancing up and down the street, Sergeant Gilmore opened the blackened oak door and slipped inside.

It took a while for Toby Gilmore's eyes to adjust to the dim lighting in the tiny tavern. It was little more than a medium-sized room, with a low, beamed ceiling and a pair of long wooden tables and backless benches filling the restricted floor space. Its once-white walls and plaster ceiling were blackened with coal-fire and tobacco smoke. Dirty straw was scattered across the floor, long past time of refreshing. At the back of the room was a makeshift counter at which stood a bald-headed man in a dirty canvas apron, in the midst of pouring water from a copper jug down a funnel into a bottle of rum. He glanced up briefly and then went on with what he was doing.

"Bit early for you, Jug, in'it?" he said.

Tobias "Toby" Gilmore – known by some of the locals as "Toby Jug" – took off his bowler hat and hoisted himself up onto a three-legged stool alongside the counter. "Still doctoring the good stuff, I see," he said.

The landlord laughed, which turned into a coughing fit. When he recovered himself, he put down the water and banged a cork into the rum bottle. "What 'good stuff' would that be, Jug? Ain't 'ad no good Jamaica in 'ere in a dog's age. What'll it be, then?"

"Give me a shilling pale ale, and no funny business."

Gilmore sipped his beer and looked around at the empty room. "Not much in the way of customers, Jacob."

The landlord leaned on the counter on his elbows and shook his head. "'Tis a bit early for the reg'lars. They'll be sleepin' off larst night's corning, wouldn't wonder." He paused a moment to pull out a stub of a cigarette he had tucked behind one ear. He studied the end of it and finally decided to smoke it, striking a match on the rough edge of the counter. "So what you lookin' for, Jug? Information, I'll be bound." He blew smoke in Gilmore's direction.

The sergeant ignored the gesture, took a drink of his beer, and then stared down into the glass. "You know anything about these here Spirit professors? Mediums, they call themselves. They are all the rage with the society swells these days."

The landlord laughed, and again broke out in a fit of coughing. He looked accusingly at the cigarette, but then took another long drag on it anyway, blowing out smoke across the counter. "There's a few of 'em as I knows of, as it 'appens. Mostly they works around Piccadilly. Often pops in 'ere to wet their whistles after they done their stint, sometimes afore they do it. 'oo in particular you lookin' for then, Jug?"

"Ever hear of one calling himself Prince Honoré?"

"Prince, eh? Lordy! Some of 'em do get carried away, don't they?"

"Have you heard of him? This is worth half a bull to you if you can help me out."

The landlord whistled through his teeth. "'alf a tusheroon, eh? Hmm! Then let me fink."

He screwed up his face and looked up at the ceiling, as though expecting information to come fluttering down.

"'alf a tusheroon, you say? Hmm. 'ow soon you need to know this then, Jug?"

"I'd like to find out today, Jacob. The Inspector's down on me on this one. That's why I'm offering a half crown of my own money."

The landlord dropped the cigarette butt on the floor and stepped on it. "You leave it with me then. Look back in 'ere this afternoon. I may 'ave somefing for you then."

Sergeant Gilmore drained his glass and put it down on the counter. "Thanks, Jacob. I'll do that." He slipped out of the door and back into the street.


"It's just more of the same," said Arnold. "These spirits don't seem to have much more to say than they had when they were alive, it seems to me. Just 'We love you,' is about all it amounts to."

"Well," said Bertie, "for some that may be enough. How is Herbert behaving himself?" Bertie and his brother-in-law were sitting in the drawing room, going over their respective notebooks on Penny Court Enquirer activities. Bertie looked about him. He would dearly have loved to have a library that he could retire to, as his office. It seemed that all the better class of people had such a book-lined room, but it was not meant to be for him. He sighed. He really could not complain. He and Nellie had chosen this little house together and together had turned it into a warm and comfortable home. Not just comfortable, but comfor*ting*, he thought. That was evidenced by the continuing visitations of not only Arnold but also Inspector Campbell Moss. Both men seemed to look for opportunities to visit number 27 Penny Court. Of course, Bertie realized that Nellie's cooking had much to do with it, but still . . . He sighed again, but this time a sigh of satisfaction.

"Herbert seemed to be doing no more than sitting in the circle," said Arnold. "At first, anyway."

Bertie raised an enquiring eyebrow.

"But now he seems to have formed some sort of attachment – or at least an attraction – to one of the regular young ladies. The trouble is, it's the same young lady that cousin George has taken a shine to."

"Oh, no! Who is she, Arnold? Does she show any interest in either of them? Doesn't cousin George remember that he has a wife waiting for him back in Yorkshire?"

"I don't know about that," said Arnold. "This young lady certainly doesn't encourage either one of them."

"Well that's a relief."

"She's just very polite. Seems much more interested in the séance than in them. I think I heard that she attends a number of different groups in the area."

"So how was this last séance?"

"A bit different, Bertie. They had that trumpet thing George told us about, and what they called 'apports' – things that the spirits took away and brought back later."

"Yes, I've heard of that."

"But this Miss Fotherington . . ." Arnold referred to his notebook to be sure of the name. "She was not happy. She spoke to me afterwards. I think she overheard George saying something about the Enquirers. She thought I – we – might be able to help her."

"What did she want?"

"It seems that the spirits took away her diamond necklace at the last séance and then brought it back again at this one."

Bertie looked up. "Took it and then returned it a week later? That doesn't sound good."

"I think that's what she thought," said Arnold. "But it was all right . . . or so it seemed. There was a man there who said he was a jeweler. He examined the necklace for her and said that all the stones were good. She had nothing to worry about."

"So what did worry her?"

"The fact that, as she told it to me, two of the diamonds had been lost some years ago and had been replaced with artificial ones. So the jeweler couldn't have been right when he said they were *all* genuine."

Bertie pursed his lips but didn't actually whistle. "I see! Yes. So someone had replaced the original necklace with a fake one and this man claiming to be a jeweler vouched for its authenticity just to satisfy this Miss . . . ?"

"Fotherington, Bertie."

"Had other people let their jewels be taken and returned by the spirits?"

Arnold nodded. "Miss Fotherington said that quite often some lady's ring or earrings were app . . . asport . . . taken away and then brought back later."

"Were they always looked at by this same jeweler."

"I think so, though she didn't say if it was the same man each time."

"Hmm. I think this is something you can follow up on, Arnold."

"Really?" Arnold's face lit up.

"This is your case, Arnold. For the Penny Court Enquirers, of course. Yes. See if you can check on this jeweler. Do you have his name?"

Arnold again referred to his notebook. "Mr. Reinhart Kaster."

"If that is indeed his name. All right, Arnold. See what you can find. Meanwhile, I've got to track down our Prince Honoré. No one seems to have determined where he lives nor where he actually originated."

"Sorry, Jug. No one's got the book on this cove. There ain't that many princes running about, not even in London, outside o' Bucking'am Palace, o' course."

Sergeant Gilmore gazed in dismay across the dirty counter of the dingy tavern. He had been counting on Jacob, the landlord, who had never previously failed to dig up needed information.

"No one has heard of him?" he asked. "Not even by reputation?"

"Seems like a closed shop, if you asks me. You say as 'ow 'e works for this Lady Something?"

"Lady Marlborough, yes, in Kensington."

Jacob rubbed his grizzled chin and closed one eye as he concentrated. "I'd still like to get that 'alf a bull you talked about, Jug. Can't tell you nothin' right now, but you give me a couple o' days and I'll get someone as can peach on 'im. Guaranteed!"

Sergeant Gilmore had no choice. The inspector was breathing down his neck. He needed to produce something. "Get it to me quickly and I'll double the money; make that a cartwheel," he said. He turned and left.


Arnold had no idea how he was going to check on this Mr. Reinhart Kaster. If the man really was a jeweler then there was a good chance he did business in Regent Street or Bond Street. Nellie had also suggested that her brother might check with the

Goldsmiths' Company, at the back of the General Post Office in St. Martin's le Grand, which was not far from Penny Court. Arnold went there first.

The home of the Goldsmiths' Company was an immense mansion. The staircase within was made entirely of marble and was famous. But Arnold had little time to admire this structure. An officious commissionaire, in Goldsmiths' Company livery, barely listened to his request to identify one Reinhart Kaster as a member of the worthy company before escorting the big man out of the building again, with the admonition that the Goldsmiths' Company no longer dealt with individuals but only with charities and institutions. Arnold had heard the stories of how, in days gone by, the Company had fought with the Merchant Taylors and with the Fishmongers on a question of precedence, and that there had been much cudgeling on the streets at night. Those days were reportedly behind them, but Arnold did not feel comfortable lingering where he was not wanted. He determined to focus his search in the Regent Street area. Tired from his walk to the Goldsmiths' Company building, Arnold opted to take an omnibus to his new destination, even though it meant two changes of vehicle.

The shops found on Bond Street and the more fashionable Regent Street were stylish and expensive. Arnold felt extremely self-conscious when he entered one of the several jewelers he found there. A dark-haired, mustachioed jeweler or, possibly, diamond-merchant, Arnold thought – one could hardly simply call him a salesman – dressed in an impeccable swallow-tail frock coat with pin-stripe trousers and a silver satin waistcoat, fixed a wary eye on Arnold as he approached.

"Sir?" he asked, in a tone that indicated he did not actually consider Arnold worthy of that mode of address.

"Er, yes." Arnold could feel himself blush – a rare occurrence in the big man. Suddenly realizing that he was a good three or four inches taller than the other man, Arnold drew himself up and attempted to look down on the salesman. However, when the man brought out a pair of pince-nez spectacles, clipped them on his nose, and took a step back the better to appraise him from head to toe, Arnold felt that he had lost his advantage. *Better to get this over and done with!*

"Do you have in your employ a gentleman by the name of Mr. Reinhart Kaster?" he asked, speaking much too quickly.

"Mr. Reinhart Kaster." The man repeated it, sounding each syllable as though tasting the words. "The name is not one familiar to me, I am afraid. But I must advise you that I am not at liberty to discuss personnel matters with . . . just anybody."

Arnold swallowed. "I see. And is there anyone here who can . . . with whom I can . . . I *may* discuss this, er, matter?"

"No one at all . . . sir! Good day to you." So saying the man turned his back on Arnold, moved around behind the counter, and began to straighten displays of jewelry. Arnold stood a moment digesting this before turning and, red-faced, leaving the shop.

Of the several jewelers on Bond Street, and along Regent Street, none seemed interested in discussing their employees and the majority displayed much the same reaction as the first. At the end of the day Arnold turned for home feeling frustrated and unhappy. He knew that Bertie would not fault him but he was disappointed in himself. He would have liked to return to Penny Court with definite news regarding the jeweler.

"You did well, Arnold," said Bertie, over a cup of tea before dinner. "If, as I suspect, this Mr. Kaster is *not* a jeweler, then of course you'll find no record of him anywhere. It was a long shot, no question about it."

"And even if he is a jeweler," added Nellie, as she tipped a saucepan of boiled potatoes into a serving dish, "there's no guarantee that he works in that area. He could be in any one of the hundreds of jewelers about the city. Or he could even work by himself."

"Wish I'd thought of that before I started," said Arnold. "So how do I find him, Bertie?"

"We may have to follow him home from one of the séances, Arnold. But before we do that, there's one place you might check. Remember when we were looking for the two ladies from Lady Marlborough's group? Go to the British Museum and go through the White directory. Look under *Jewelers*, and probably *Goldsmiths* and *Diamond Merchants* as well. There's a better chance of finding him there than going shop to shop in Regent Street."

"I'll do that tomorrow, Bertie."

# *Chapter Ten*

To Inspector Campbell Moss's eyes, Detective Chief Inspector Malcolm Villiers's perpetual red face would seem to be the result of the tight, three-inch high, starched collar that he wore. Despite being a winged collar – which allowed his Adam's apple to bob up and down at a sometimes alarming rate – the overall height and tightness must surely somehow constrict the blood's flow, reasoned the inspector. Such flow must also, he further reasoned, be obstructed in its continuing route to the Chief Inspector's brain. Such were the thoughts that passed, unhindered, through Moss's mind as he stood in front of his superior's desk.

Chief Inspector Malcolm Villiers was a hirsute man, with large, bushy, salt-and-pepper, mutton-chop sideboards almost meeting on his otherwise smooth chins. The whole was topped by a small, bald apex to his head. In his right eye he gripped a monocle that looked as though it had been screwed in there at birth. He was always dressed as though he had just come from his tailor, with his pumps polished to a high gloss and with the ever-present wing collar cutting into his flabby red neck.

"*Tempus fugit*, Moss. *Tempus fugit*. Where are we with the death of this . . ." he looked down at the single sheet of paper on his otherwise virgin desk. "This Captain Cyril Grimsby? Should we not have the miscreant under lock and key by now? It is the Yard's reputation that is at stake, don't you know?"

"Yes, sir. I'm well aware . . ."

"The murder took place at the home of her ladyship Lady Constance Marlborough, in Knightsbridge. Knightsbridge, dammit Moss! That's my backyard."

"Yes sir. I . . ."

"Lady Marlborough is the daughter of the late ninth Earl of Marlborough, don't you know?"

*What has that to do with Grimsby's murder?* thought Moss, but he remained silent. *Let the old man blow off steam,* he thought.

"Six suspects," added Villiers, picking up the sheet of paper, the better to focus his monocle. "Just six. All in the one room together."

"Actually eight, sir," ventured Moss. "With her ladyship and Prince Honoré, the medium."

"Pshar!" Villiers waved a dismissive hand. "I'm talking *suspects*, Moss. You can't consider her ladyship and a prince, for the good Lord's sake! Now then, what is going on? Where are you in what should be an open and shut case?"

Inspector Moss took a deep breath. He had been here before, he knew. Whatever he said would not be acceptable, so why not just plunge ahead and explain the intricacies of the case to Villiers? *Because the old fool will refuse to accept it!* He nodded his head as though to confirm his feelings.

"Yes? I see you nodding. Speak up, man! Do you have the miscreant or don't you?"

"We . . . we have narrowed down the suspects, sir, and you can expect an arrest . . . very shortly."

"Hrmph!" The Chief Inspector placed the sheet of paper in the previously empty basket on the corner of his pristine desk. He waved a hand at Moss and looked about him as though he had urgent business elsewhere. Moss knew when he was being dismissed and hurried from the room.

"It's the hinspector," announced Isobel, standing back to allow Campbell Moss access to the kitchen.

"Thank you, Isobel," said Nellie. "Now get on about your business. You have beds to make, I believe?"

The diminutive maid sniffed and, with a toss of her red curls and many a backward glance, went off up the back stairs leaving Nellie, Bertie and Inspector Moss about the kitchen table.

"It's good to see you, Campbell," said Bertie, moving his Penny Court Enquirers' account book to one side as the policeman took a seat. "To what do we owe the pleasure of this visit?"

"Not that it isn't always good to see you," added Nellie. "Cup of tea?" she got up to see to the refreshment.

"Thank you, Nell. Bertram." He nodded to his friend and then let out a sigh as he relaxed onto the now familiar kitchen chair. "I must say it's good to see friendly faces for a change."

"Oh?"

"The Chief Inspector," Moss said, as though the mere mention of his name would explain everything.

"Ah, yes." Bertie nodded understandingly.

"I was wondering if we might, as it were, compare notes, Bertram?" Moss looked at his friend from under lowered eyebrows. "See what you've picked up at those séances." He tugged at his straggly mustache.

Bertie didn't answer right away but waited while Nellie set out three cups of steaming tea and a plate of ginger biscuits, which she knew to be the inspector's favorites. Bertie further kept Moss hanging by taking his time adding milk and two lumps of sugar to his cup. He stirred the tea thoughtfully, sipped it, nodded in satisfaction, and then looked at his friend.

"What have you got so far, Campbell?" he asked.

"I'm hung up on this medium. Prince Honoré. *Is* he a prince? If so, where's he come from? His first séance with Lady Marlborough was at the beginning of August; 6 August to be precise. But more to the point, where is he living now? I canna' find him registered at any of the big hotels. None of Sergeant Gilmore's usual informants know of him. Where's he hiding himself, that's what I want to know? Have you found out anything;

anything to suggest he might be a faker, for example?"

Bertie shook his head slowly. "No, Campbell. I'm afraid I don't have much there. I did speak at length with Maurice Austin, who seems to have pried into most people's background at one time or another. He says that the prince – if he is indeed such – comes from Luxembourg. That's according to Lady Marlborough herself, apparently. He hasn't been in this country for too long and Austin's guess – and I'm inclined to agree with him – is that the man is staying at Kingston House as a guest of Lady Marlborough."

"Well, nay wonder we couldna' find him anywhere."

"I think there may be some truth in it," said Bertie, selecting a ginger biscuit. "It would certainly make sense. If her ladyship had been instrumental in bringing him here from the Continent, then she would certainly entertain him as a guest. And it seems she is keen on keeping his mediumship exclusively to her circles. Oh, and there's one more thing you may find of interest."

The inspector raised his eyebrows questioningly.

"It seems that the prince is available for private consultation with the sitters . . . at a rather high fee. I don't know what he tells them but it would seem to me that it is an opportunity for him to learn more about his sitters' backgrounds; to do some prying."

"Aye! You're right, Bertram. I think I must visit Lady Marlborough and insist on having a word with our prince. All right then." Moss nodded and transferred his own attention onto the biscuits. "So without him it still keeps our main suspects down to the five: Austin himself, Professor Sedgeworth, Dr. Price and the two young ladies."

"I'm inclined to discount the professor," mused Bertie. "Though I know that history has shown all sorts of people, from all walks of life, have been guilty of murder."

"Aye." Moss nodded his head as he nibbled on a biscuit. "But I agree. The professor is at the bottom of my list."

"And what about Dr. Price?"

The inspector unthinkingly dipped his ginger biscuit into his tea before eating it. "I have to reserve judgement on that gentleman I think, Bertram. Sergeant Gilmore reports a possible liaison between the good doctor and one of our other suspects – Miss Alice Bell."

"Oh?" Bertie looked up, as did Nellie.

"Aye. They have been taking carriage rides together around Hyde Park . . . with the blinds down, if you please!"

"Not enjoying the view then," Bertie murmured.

"How does that fit in with your suspicions then, Campbell?" asked Nellie.

"It brings in the ugly possibility of jealousy," Moss replied. "We know, from various reports, that Grimsby was a womanizer. Miss Bell herself complained of his unwanted attentions. If Dr. Price was aware of those – and if the couple is at all, er, *close* then surely he must be – then there is

cause to suspect him of taking matters into his own
hands to get rid of the man."

"I think I did suggest that some time ago,"
murmured Bertie. Moss did not acknowledge it.

"It seems a bit extreme to me," said Nellie.

"Aye, well . . . murder *is* extreme."

"I had wondered how Miss Bell managed to
afford the circle," said Bertie. "Perhaps her
paramour was footing the bill."

"I think that is quite probable."

"What of Miss Dobson?"

The inspector gazed silently into his tea cup
as though it might be a crystal ball. Nellie wondered
whether she should offer him another ginger biscuit
but he finally looked up.

"Now there's another strange one. She's a
spinster and still lives with her parents. Her father is
a minor government employee. She seems to be
interested only in the spirit business."

"Yes," agreed Bertie. "I heard that she wants
to become a medium herself. At Lady
Marlborough's she keeps very much to herself.
There is general chit-chat before the sitting, when
refreshments are served, and sometimes a little
afterwards, though many times people just want to
get home. But she seldom gets into any
conversations other than with Miss Bell."

"Have you spoken with Miss Dobson?"
Moss asked.

"Very briefly. Once again I have to rely on
hearsay from Maurice Austin. He infers that if she
has any romantic interests anywhere then it is . . ."

he glanced at Nellie before continuing. "Well, it is with Miss Bell."

Nellie stopped what she was doing, looked thoughtful for a moment, and then turned and started sorting a pile of laundry lying on the back table.

Inspector Moss paused with a dunked biscuit halfway to his mouth. The soggy half dropped off and fell into his tea. "Aye! Well, then. Hmm! Well, I suppose that would give her the same incentive that Dr. Price might have, would you not think?"

"*If* there is any truth in the allegation," said Bertie, refilling his teacup. "Personally I think Austin has an overactive imagination. Perhaps part of being the type of newspaperman he is. He wouldn't have found a job in the old *Chronicle*, I can tell you that."

"Well, keep your ears open at these spirit things, Bertram. The answer has to lie there."

"Oh, have no fear, Campbell. I will."


George stood uncertainly on the corner of the street, watching the progress of Miss Winifred Dobson as she crossed behind a crossing sweeper who was clearing freshly-deposited horse manure from the cobblestones in the center of the road. The young lady had emerged from the public library, where she had spent the past hour writing in her notebook as she perused a number of volumes taken from the shelves housing books on spiritualism. George had spent some time in the library himself, peering at her from behind the stacks. He had artfully, so he thought, rearranged a few books so that he could look through the shelf to where she sat without being seen by her, even if she should look up. But she never did look up. She was engrossed in what she was doing.

George had been seated next to Miss Dobson at the séance he had attended with Arnold and Herbert. She had not revealed a great deal about herself but, under his questioning, she had mentioned that she spent time at the Lambeth Free Library on Brixton Road. Something about Miss Dobson fascinated George, though he would be hard pressed to put a finger on it. Perhaps it was simply the air of mystery, since she was so reticent about herself.

He allowed her to cross the street and set off along the main road. For the last day of September, it was very mild weather and Miss Dobson had only a shawl across the shoulders of her organdie dress. She carried a striped parasol, though the sun was not really bright enough to warrant it, and a fine Milan straw hat decorated with a ribbon band to match her dress. George admired her walk and saw himself, in his mind, as he was some twenty years ago. An observer might have noticed an unusual spring in his step that was normally missing. However, after walking some distance, his gait returned to its more normal near-shuffle.

George spent time summoning up his courage to catch up with the young lady and to pretend to be surprised to encounter her there. *My goodness me,* he could hear himself exclaiming. *Is it not Miss Dobson? What a delight to encounter you here on . . .* Where exactly were they? He looked around for a road sign. When he turned back, it was to see his quarry climbing into a hackney carriage, which whisked her away into the stream of horse-drawn traffic that made up Brixton Road. George felt in his pocket and pulled out a few pence. Not enough for a cab. He cursed.

## *Chapter Eleven*

Bertie made a point of arriving early at Kingston House for the next séance. When he got there only Professor Sedgeworth and Dr. Price were in the drawing room. There was no sign of Lady Marlborough nor of Prince Honoré, though Bertie knew that the medium never did put in an appearance until the sitting was about to begin. Light refreshments had been laid out as usual, with the stoic footman in attendance. The two other men were nibbling on cucumber sandwiches and sipping white wine when Bertie entered the room.

"Ah, Hawkins!" acknowledged the doctor. "We were just discussing Mrs. Guppy-Volckman. Have you ever been to one of her séances?"

"Er, no. No, Dr. Price, I haven't."

"Neither has either of us," acceded the professor. "It's a treat I keep promising myself."

"Mrs. Guppy is best known for her apports, is she not?" asked Bertie, who remembered stories that Taffy had told him.

"Exactly," agreed Price. "We were just saying that she recently had a sitting with the Duchess d'Arpino and that that good lady requested the apporting of some sand from the sea."

"And did she get it?" Bertie asked. Both men laughed.

"Oh, yes!" cried the professor. "Not just sand, either. What fell out of Mrs. Guppy's trumpet was sand, sea water, and even a starfish! Incredible!"

"I remember hearing of an earlier séance – can't remember who was there – but someone wanted a sunflower. It arrived all right . . . over five feet tall and with a big clump of earth still clinging to the roots, as though it had just been pulled up out of the ground. Amazing!" Dr. Price shook his head in bewilderment as he sipped his wine.

"Frank Podmore couldn't find anything to criticize in her," added the professor. "He's on the council of the Society for Psychical Research and tends to be very skeptical, don't you know."

"Will we be seeing anything like that here?" asked Bertie, beginning to feel excited.

"Who knows?" Price had the footman refill his wine glass from the decanter. "One can never tell what the spirits have in store for us. Personally I was surprised with the cabinet work we saw here last time."

Bertie helped himself to a fish paste sandwich and tried to sound casual as he asked, "If I might ask, does Miss Dobson exhibit any of these abilities?"

"*Our* Miss Dobson?" asked the professor. Bertie nodded. "I have not heard of any physical manifestations by her. Have you, William?"

Dr. Price shook his head. "No. I know that she is awfully keen to learn and wants to progress, but I have not heard that she has even led a séance to date, though I may be wrong."

Bertie looked around. "Does the prince not even join us for pre-séance snacks?" he asked.

Dr. Price shook his head. "I believe he likes to partake of a small salad to settle his stomach – or so her ladyship once mentioned – but he does that privately, before we join him."

At that moment the door opened and Lady Marlborough entered the room accompanied by her maid and closely followed by Miss Bell and Miss Dobson.

"Ah! Gentlemen!" exclaimed her ladyship. "Our two ladies have arrived, as you see. Now we just await Mr. Austin and we may begin."

"You need wait no longer, m'lady." Close on their heels, Maurice Austin was shown in by the footman. "I hope I am not too tardy. Traffic about Hyde Park seems to get heavier by the day."

"We are in good time, I think," responded Lady Marlborough. "Do, please, partake of some light refreshment, Mr. Austin . . . you know I do like my sitters to find something lickerous here before we sit." She glanced briefly at her maid. "You may leave us, Lisbeth." The girl quietly left the room, closing the door behind her.

"Are we to witness anything new this evening, my lady?" asked Alice Bell, selecting a petit beurre.

"The B.S.A. seems to be abuzz with talk of the latest exploits in High Holborn, concerning Mrs. Guppy," said Winifred Dobson.

There had been reports of a séance held by Messrs. Herne and Williams when it was claimed that they had actually apported the large figure of Mrs. Guppy herself from her townhouse to land on the table in the Herne and Willliams' circle.

"The professor, Mr. Hawkins, and I were just talking of her," said Dr. Price. "Apports are certainly fascinating, though I find this latest report hard to swallow."

"Perhaps the prince will favor us with something like that this evening," said Alice.

"Let us proceed and see for ourselves. Ladies? Gentlemen?" Lady Marlborough led the way to the library, the others dutifully following behind her.

This time the cabinet was not in evidence. Chairs had been placed around the large walnut library table and Prince Honoré was already seated at one of them. A tall trumpet sat in the center of the table. Lady Marlborough seated herself beside the medium.

"No cabinet tonight, Prince?" asked the professor, taking the chair beside his hostess. "You only introduced it last week; I do hope you are not already tired of it."

"Not at all, professor." The medium smiled at his questioner. "We shall utilize it next time, I assure you. However, I understand that there is still a large interest in the phenomena of apports and asports. Our good Spiritualist friends Frank Herne and Charles Williams, not to mention the ebullient Mrs. Guppy, have been making quite a name for themselves in this field. It would never do for our dear Lady Marlborough's select circle to be left behind."

There were murmurs of agreement and her ladyship gracefully inclined her head towards the medium.

"Shall we then begin?"

Professor Sedgeworth reached up and turned down the gasolier. To Bertie the room immediately became as black as pitch, but gradually his eyes did adjust until he thought that he was able to distinguish vague shapes.

The proceedings started with a short prayer, an entreaty from her ladyship for the spirits to attend, and the singing of melodic songs. At the conclusion of the second song – *I dreamt that I dwelt in marble halls* – Bertie became aware of the deep breathing issuing from the direction of the medium. Apparently Prince Honoré had entered his trance.

There followed a repetition of the first séance that Bertie had attended, though without the presence of Benjamin Disraeli. The voices which first came through the Prince's lips claimed to be connected with various of the sitters. Later, however, Professor Sedgeworth got into a dispute with a spirit claiming to be Allan Kardec, the famous French Spiritist. The professor stated that he had recently written an article about the man and so was very familiar with everything about him. More so, it seemed, than the medium. Kardec's birth name had been Léon-Dénizard-Hippolyte Rivail. Apparently Prince Honoré – or the supposed spirit, Bertie assumed – was not aware of that complete birth name. When the professor began asking probing questions, Prince Honoré suddenly allowed a completely different spirit to come through – one claiming to be the grandmother of Alice Bell – and permitting the French spirit to depart in all haste. Professor Sedgeworth was most put out and continued to murmur his aggrievance for the rest of the evening.

The voice of Miss Bell's purported grandmother faded away. There followed a long silence, during which Bertie could still sense the professor tut-tutting. Then a strong female voice said "I bring you gifts, from the Summerland." Something rattled onto the table top.

"Apports, I do believe," breathed Lady Marlborough.

"Wonderful!" said Winifred Dobson.

"I had hoped as much," added Miss Bell.

Bertie said nothing but inwardly he thought that the séance had fallen far short of the previous one. To his mind, the display of music issuing from inside the cabinet, when the medium was bound into a chair, was far stronger evidence of the working of spirits than the production of any assorted apports.

The rattle of arriving spirit gifts seemed to go on for a very long time, before finally tapering off. Shortly after the percussive sound had stopped, the medium could be heard settling back into his chair and his breathing slowed and softened. There then followed a lengthy sigh from the prince. After a brief pause, Lady Marlborough led a prayer and the séance came to a close.

"Lights, if you would be so kind Professor?"

The turning-up of the gas returned everyone to the mundane world and Bertie blinked his eyes and looked around. In the center of the table lay a pile of what turned out to be semi-precious stones; smooth, shining pebbles of different shapes and hues. The number of them was surprising. *How could the medium hide that many stones about his person and then tip them out when needed?* Bertie asked himself. Meanwhile, Prince Honoré pleaded tiredness and excused himself, leaving the library before he could be drawn into any sort of discussion with the professor about Allan Kardec.

Lady Marlborough and the two ladies enthused about the séance, delighting in the apports that were there. The professor and the doctor remained unusually quiet, thought Bertie. Suddenly all eyes were drawn to their hostess.

"Oh!" a sharp exclamation came from Lady Marlborough. She raised her right hand in the air, fingers wide-spread and extended. "Oh! My ring! My ring! It has gone."

"Are you sure?" asked Doctor Price

"Well or course I'm sure!" snapped her ladyship. "I know when I am wearing my rings and when I am not. I tell you it has gone! My diamond and ruby ring that belonged to my late mother; it is gone from my finger!"

"The spirits!" exclaimed Miss Bell, in awe.

"Of course," agreed Miss Dobson. "It was asported."

"Asported my . . . !" Her ladyship seemed to Bertie to be monetarily out of words. She did not seem to him, at that moment, to be one entranced by the marvels of mediumship.

Lady Marlborough moved quickly to the mantelpiece and pulled on the bell cord to summon a servant. After a few moments her lady's maid, Lisbeth, appeared at the door.

"I need . . . I must see Prince Honoré," she said. "It is important. My ring has disappeared."

The maid seemed to hesitate a moment before turning and leaving the room.

"But we were expecting such apport and asport activity, were we not?" asked the professor.

"We had certainly hoped for it," agreed Dr. Price. "Remember? We were talking about Mrs. Guppy . . ."

The door opened and Lisbeth reappeared. She stood just inside the doorway.

"Well?" demanded her ladyship. "I asked to see the prince. Where is he?"

"He offers his apologies, your ladyship," said the girl, in a quiet voice, her eyes cast down. "He says that he is overcome with fatigue, but assures you that anything that was asported will be returned by the spirits at the next séance." She bobbed a quick curtsey and then turned and left the room. Bertie was surprised that she did not wait for Lady Marlborough's dismissal but then, realizing her ladyship's obvious annoyance, he could hardly blame her.

"I – er – think that we should adjourn the evening, perhaps?" said the professor. "Until next time?"

"Yes. Yes, let us do that." Lady Marlborough nodded in agreement, but her mouth was set in a tight, thin line and her brow furrowed.

"I am sure that the spirits will return your ring next time," said Dr. Price. "Just as Prince Honoré suggests. It is just yet another of their demonstrations . . ."

"Yes. Thank you, Doctor. You will excuse me, I'm sure. Parker will see you all out." So saying, Lady Marlborough swept from the room, leaving the door open. The butler almost immediately appeared, followed by the elderly footman bearing hats, canes, and the other personal items of the attendees.

# *Chapter Twelve*

The *Daily World News* was a newspaper with a rapidly growing circulation. At fourpence a copy it was the cheapest newspaper in London, catering to the newly literate working classes and featuring purportedly true reports of bizarre criminal acts, complete coverage of vice prosecutions, transcripts of police descriptions of brothels, and various other forms of titillation. Its back page was the only page in the whole newspaper that bore the more mundane news reports and, to his credit, Maurice Austin's column was usually featured on that page.

Bertie was well aware of the newspaper's reputation and had been surprised when he had discovered that this fellow member of Lady Marlborough's séance room was an employee of such a journal.

"I don't care for the rest of the rag," Austin had commented when he and Bertie had been visiting Maskelyne's. "My column is legitimate and the publisher keeps me on because I set the tone for the whole newspaper." Bertie had doubts that this one column could raise the standards of such as the *Daily World News*, feeling that the "tone" had been set long before the reader got to the last page.

"Fleet Street" is used as a metonym for the British national press since most newspapers had made their home on this thoroughfare, named after the subterranean River Fleet. The first newspaper, *The Daily Courant*, had started there in March of 1702, though printers and publishers had operated in the area from two hundred years before that. The office of the *Daily World News* was, perhaps symbolically, just off of Fleet Street.

Bertie made his way along the famous street, with St. Paul's behind him and Temple Bar ahead of him. At Shoe Lane he turned the corner and entered a narrow red-brick building that seemed to be squeezed between two taller edifices. An over-weight, red-faced commissionaire directed him to the third floor editorial offices.

"Mr. Austin?" A harried-looking office boy Bertie met on reaching the head of the stairs, answered his query. "'E's in there . . . somewhere." He gestured over his shoulder with his thumb and hurried off, several bunches of papers clutched in his arms.

"In there" was a large open area filled with desks at assorted angles, the majority manned by men in shirt sleeves. Many of these men were pounding away on type-writers – the click-clacking filling the otherwise quiet room – while others scribbled in notebooks or sorted through piles of papers, newsprint, memos, brochures, and books. A visible layer of grey-black cigar smoke hovered over all.

Some few desks were empty of their owners yet still liberally covered with the detritus of the

industry. Bertie, familiar with the layout and
running of a newspaper, made his way towards the
far end of the room where glass-enclosed offices
housed the editors and senior editor. He paused at
one desk where a thin-faced man wearing a bowler
hat, despite being in the office and in his shirt
sleeves, was sitting back with his feet up on his
desk, reading a long sheet of column proofs.

"Excuse me," said Bertie. "Mr. Maurice
Austin? Is he available?"

Echoing the earlier office boy, without
letting his eyes leave the paper he held, the man
jerked his thumb in the general direction of the far
wall. "Out!" was all he said.

Seeing an empty desk against the wall, close
to the only window on that side of the room, Bertie
gathered that Austin was not in the office. He
sighed and continued on to the empty desk. There
was a vacant chair beside the desk and Bertie sank
down onto it, to give himself time to think and
decide what to do next.

"Hawkins? Is that you? What are you doing
here?"

Bertie looked up to see Maurice Austin's
round figure marching down the aisle between the
desks, slipping out of his jacket as he came. He
arrived at his desk and threw the coat over the back
of his chair. "Didn't expect to see you here," he
said, as he dropped into his seat and dumped a large
notebook together with several unopened letters
onto the desk top beside the type-writer. "What can
I do for you?" he asked "Not got a lot of time, you
know. Deadlines, and all that." He pulled his watch

out of his waistcoat pocket, studied it, held it up to his ear briefly as though to check that it was still ticking, then gave it a wind and replaced it in his pocket.

"Of course," said Bertie. "I just hoped that perhaps you could spare me a few minutes to tell me a little of what you know, or knew, of Captain Grimsby?"

Austin peered at Bertie from under the fringe of the brushed-forward hair he sported. "Grimsby? Why d'you want to know about him? He's dead and good riddance, I say."

"Why would you say that," persisted Bertie. "Did you and he not get along?"

Austin snorted; a sound that Bertie was coming to recognize as the newspaperman's way of indicating disapproval. "Look. I knew the man before ever he turned up at Lady M's. He was no good, all right? Let's leave it at that. Why do you want to know, anyway?"

"Let's just say that, since the police claim he was murdered, I find the whole subject fascinating and would like to learn more about the man."

Another snort. "You're not with the police in any way, are you?" Austin sounded accusatory.

"I am in no way officially connected with the police," said Bertie truthfully. "How did you come to know him?"

Maurice Austin seemed to relax a little and settled back in his chair. As he spoke he shuffled through the unopened envelopes he had brought in with him before dropping them back on his desk, still unopened.

"I like to have a little flutter at the track once in a while. Same as anyone. No harm in that." Bertie nodded understandingly. "Well, I bumped into Grimsby there a couple of times. He was just a Second Lieutenant then, as I recall, not a Captain. We'd give each other tips, if we had them. One day Grimsby gave me what he claimed to be a major tip – 'straight from the horse's mouth', as he put it. He claimed he'd got friendly with the horse's jockey. Anyway, at his insistence I dropped a load on the nag's nose. Then I wandered around to the stables behind the grandstand and what do you think I saw? Our friend Grimsby, and he was giving something to this horse. Just a bucket of water he claimed, and then he walked away. To make a long story into a jaw-snapper, the horse dropped dead in the final stretch! I lost my shirt. Could have killed that damned Grimsby . . . Oh! Just a figure of speech, of course."

"Of course," said Bertie, making a mental note of it. "Anything else you can tell me?"

"The man was a blackguard. A knark who beat his wife."

"You know this for a fact?"

Austin nodded. "Oh, yes. He boasted of it; of 'knocking some sense into her', he put it. I never met the woman but I wasn't at all surprised when he told me she'd run off. I didn't blame her."

"Do you know where she went?" asked Bertie.

The other man shook his head. "As far from him as she could get, is my guess." He had another quick look at his watch. "What do you think of

Lady M's reaction to the disappearance of her ring at the last circle? Bit over the top, wouldn't you say?"

Bertie nodded. "I was a little surprised, considering that we had been looking at apports and asports and expecting them. Perhaps it hit a little too close to home for her."

"Hmm. Perhaps."

"Well thank you. I won't keep you any longer," said Bertie, getting to his feet. "Thank you for the information."

"I really think we should wait and tell Bertie where we're going," said Arnold, as he and George hurried along the Strand and then crossed it and went up St. Martin's Lane.

"I thought you were half of your Penny Court thing," George responded, pushing his way through a group of begging children and avoiding a chimney-sweep with his sooty brushes slung over his shoulder. "Aren't you equal partners with cousin Bertram? Don't you decide where you need to go to investigate?"

Arnold felt uncomfortable at being put on the spot. "The thing is, George, Bertie needs to know where I am – where we are – in case he needs me . . . us," he said. "Where *are* we going anyway?"

"I told you, I was talking to Miss Dobson at the last sitting and she said that she wanted to conduct a séance herself. Your friend Herbert said that he'd go to it and so I said the same."

"So she's holding a séance? And we're going?"

"Well, not exactly." George ducked around an organ-grinder as he turned into Cecil Court. Arnold hurried after him. The monkey on top of the barrel organ snatched at Arnold's coat but missed. "Miss Dobson has consented to have a preliminary working with George and myself . . . as practice, you might say."

"I see. And where exactly is this to take place?"

"Right . . . here!" George came to a stop, looking up at the numbers on the shop fronts in the small courtyard between St. Martin's Lane and the new Charing Cross Road. "I think this is the place." Arnold thought he didn't seem too sure of himself.

They entered a book shop and stood looking about. A harried-looking little man with untidy hair and clutching an armful of books glanced up as they came in. There was no one else in the shop.

"Yes?" was all he said.

"Mr. Hudson, *and* Mr. Middleton! How delightful." Miss Dobson suddenly appeared at the back of the shop, coming through a door leading to a rear room. "Do come in, gentlemen. It's all right, Clarence," she said to the book man. "My cousin," she said, by way of explanation. "Come on back. Mr. Parker is already here."

They followed her into the rear room, Arnold closing the door behind them. Herbert was sitting in a straight-backed chair but came to his feet when they entered.

"Hello, Arnold. George."

It was a small room, obviously used for inventorying, accounting, and other necessary activities. An accounting desk sat in the center of the room and two or three small tables, laden with books, were scattered around the walls. Book shelves covered two of the walls.

"I only just got here myself," said Herbert. "As did Miss Dobson. We met at the door."

"This is my cousin's book shop," said Miss Dobson. "He very kindly let's me use this back room on occasion, so that I might study in private . . . and without my parents' knowledge, I'm afraid." She shook her head. "I regret that they are not entirely in approval of my metaphysical leanings."

"We understand," volunteered George. "Bit of a secret, eh?"

"I don't like to go behind their backs, but I am resolute in my endeavors to become a Spiritualist medium."

"And for that, practice most certainly does make perfect," said Herbert. "So what do you have in store for us today, Miss Dobson? Apports? Materializations? Transfigurations?"

"Goodness, nothing so advanced!" She moved across to take up a small wooden board that was leaning against the wall, beside a tea-chest filled with old, worn books and bearing the inscription *Lot Number 17*. "Perhaps you gentlemen would be so kind as to move any books and papers off those chairs – you can set them down on the floor – and place the chairs close together so that we may sit in circle."

When they were all seated, she took up the board and laid it across her lap. Its top surface was marked off with letters of the alphabet and numbers.

"This is what is known as a spirit board," she said. "It can be used for communicating with the deceased."

"I've never seen anything like that before," said Herbert.

"No." Miss Dobson seemed pleased with herself, thought Arnold. "It was invented by an American gentleman, Mr. Elijah Bond. He visited here last year and spoke at the B.S.A. He told us how he had based this board on an old Chinese idea. He has plans to patent it. He said he may call it 'Nirvana' and will sell it through his company The Swastika Novelty Company."

"And how did you come by it, if I may enquire, Miss Dobson?" asked George.

"Mr. Bond distributed a half dozen of them on the understanding that we use them and write to tell him how effective, or otherwise, they may be." She produced a small piece of polished wood and set it down in the center of the board. "So we are all here as part of an experiment in spirit communication."

"Oh! I am honored," said Herbert, looking well pleased with himself. Arnold and George murmured in agreement. "What is that object?" Herbert continued, pointing.

"It is termed a 'planchette', from the French meaning a platform, I'm given to understand."

"And how does it work?" asked George, leaning forward.

"You will see. Now then, let us all move our chairs in sufficiently that the board can be settled on our knees. Oh! Not too close, Mr. Hudson, if you don't mind."

George beamed and edged back very slightly. Arnold thought that his knees were still extremely close to those of Miss Dobson.

"Now, the planchette, as you can see, is heart shaped and has been well varnished so that it will slide over the surface of the Spirit Board, which is similarly varnished." She placed her fingertips on the small platform and slid it around the larger board. "When it stops, as you can see, the point of the heart is pointing at a letter or a number. In this way it will spell out a message."

"You mean, it just moves by itself all around the board?" asked Arnold.

"Alas, no." Miss Dobson shook her head. "Would that it did. And perhaps with a more experienced medium it would." She sounded wistful, thought Arnold. "But for us, spirit uses our muscles to make it move. We each rest a fingertip on the edge of the planchette and then I as medium ask a question and, calling upon our energy, spirit moves it around to answer the question; spelling out a message. You will see, as we progress."


"It moved around and spelled out messages?" Nellie was incredulous. "All by itself?"

"No," said Arnold. "It was like Miss Dobson said, it depended upon our muscle power to actually move it, but then it was spirit – so she said – that actually directed it to give the message."

"Cor!" murmured Isobel.

Arnold had returned to 27 Penny Court to bring Bertie up-to-date with the proceedings. George had insisted upon escorting Miss Dobson home, despite her protests that it was unnecessary. Bertie, Arnold and Nellie sat around the kitchen table, with Isobel at the vegetable table chopping onions for Nellie's popular curried mutton. Isobel alternately sniffed and blinked back tears from her watering eyes.

"So what messages did the spirit produce?" asked Bertie, helping Nellie fold napkins.

Arnold shook his head in despair. "It started out well but then suddenly took a turn."

"Took a turn?"

Arnold continued shaking his head. "Yes. It seemed to depend on the people using it. But then cousin George took it into his head to push the little platform thing to make it spell out messages to Miss Dobson."

"What?" Bertie and Nellie spoke together. Isobel added another quiet "Cor!"

"Of course, Miss Dobson was most upset and said that the whole experiment was ruined. Herbert said a few sharp words to George and the meeting broke up."

"And yet George is accompanying Miss Dobson to her home?" asked Nellie.

"He said he wanted to explain things to her."

"What else can he possibly do?" Bertie raised his eyes to the heavens. "The man is a disaster."

"Not directly connected with that," said Arnold. "But in the course of conversation, before George got carried away, Miss Dobson mentioned that she does not trust most men so she is always on her guard."

"Well, George has certainly proven that she has good cause," said Nellie. "Poor young woman. Just wait till George comes back. I'll give him a piece of my mind!"

"As will I," said Bertie darkly. "Though I suppose we should be grateful he is not still into his phrenology. Remember the newsagent's daughter, Nell? What was her name?"

"The spirit board did start to say something about feeling her bumps," muttered Arnold.

"Good Lord!" said Bertie. "I think it's well past time for cousin George to return home. I think he has outlived his welcome here."

They were interrupted by a loud knocking at the front door. Isobel waved her hands in the air, one clutching a raw onion and the other wielding the kitchen knife. Nellie got to her feet with a sigh and went up the stairs to the front door. She soon returned.

"What is it, Nell?"

"I think you had better come, Bertram. It's a policeman. He says they've arrested cousin George."

George sat on the edge of the cot in the cell looking very angry. He came to his feet and started shouting as soon as he saw Bertie approaching.

"See what she did, Bertie! And I'm the one locked up! How can that be justice, I'd like to know?" He held up a hand that was wrapped in a soiled handkerchief stained with blood.

The constable leading the way stopped outside the cell and turned to Bertie.

"I ain't a-goin' to be lettin' you in there wif 'im, sir. Not in 'is present state of mind, if you get my meanin'? You can talk to 'im from 'ere and I'll come back and get you in a few minutes." So saying, the policeman turned away and quickly moved off back the way they had come.

Bertie took hold of two of the iron bars of the cell and stood studying his cousin. "Calm yourself George. And do stop shouting. That will get you nowhere. Now then, start at the beginning and tell me exactly what happened."

George came to the bars and gripped two of them himself. He glared at Bertie.

"Miss Dobson!" he spat out the name. "How could I have been . . . ? Well, never mind that bit. Look what she did to me!" He waved the bandaged hand in the air.

"And what did she do to you?"

"She stabbed me with her hatpin, that's what she did! Right through my hand . . . well, the fleshy bit between my thumb and finger. It really seems to bleed an awful lot from there."

Bertie raised his eyebrows. "And why did she do that, George? What led up to this . . . stabbing?"

George dropped his hands and turned away, to look up at the tiny barred window in the back wall of the cell. "I was demonstrating from *Dr. Fowler's Compendium of Phrenological Attributes*," he mumbled. "Miss Dobson possessed – possesses – the most extraordinary example of cranial *Sensus Communis* I have ever seen." He swung around again to face his cousin. "This was confirmed in Professor Combe's *Lectures and Moral Philosophy of Phrenology*."

"You have these books with you?" asked Bertie incredulously.

George tapped the side of his head with his bandaged hand. "In here, Bertie. In here. I have committed these books to my memory . . . well, more or less. Enough to be able to tell at a glance when someone is exceptional . . . as I thought Miss Dobson to be." He gave a long sigh.

"You no longer think she is?"

"It's the bumps, Bertie. The bumps. They don't lie, you know."

He looked serious, Bertie thought. "No. No, I'm sure they don't George. However, there is a proper time and place to examine the, er, bumps of a person . . . especially of a young lady. I thought we had dealt with all of this the last time you visited?"

"Oh, that was different!" George waved his hands in the air to dismiss the very idea. "Miss Dobson, I don't mind telling you Bertie, since you are, after all, my cousin . . . blood is thicker than water, you know?"

"What are you rambling on about George? Now listen. If you assaulted Miss Dobson you could be in very serious trouble. Do you understand me?"

"Yes. Yes, I do." George seemed very contrite, Bertie thought.

"All right. Well, I'll see what I can do to get you out of here. And I'll have to go and have a word with Miss Dobson, I suppose."

"Thank you, Bertie. Thicker than water, you know?"

"I've arrested Miss Winifred Dobson for the murder of Captain Cyril Grimsby – or Second Lieutenant Grimsby, or whatever rank he really was." Inspector Moss eased himself down into the chair closest to the fire in the Hawkins's drawing room. The weather had turned colder, as a reminder that October was well under way, and the coal-skuttle was full and ready to fuel the fire.

"You're certain that she committed the murder?" asked Bertie, tamping down the tobacco in his favorite pipe.

Moss pulled out a cigarette case, opened it, studied the contents for a moment and then closed it again and put it back in his pocket without taking a cigarette.

"Her action in stabbing your cousin prompted me to it. How is his hand, by the way?"

"Nellie smothered it with iodine before he left. He didn't seem to have any trouble carrying his carpet bag so I won't lose any sleep over it," said Bertie, leaning forward and lighting a taper from the fire. He settled back again in his chair and lit his pipe, blowing smoke like a railway engine getting up steam.

"He's off back to the North, then?"

Bertie nodded. "Overstayed his welcome, as usual. I'm sure his wife will be glad to see him again." He puffed and blew some more smoke. "Actually, I'm not sure she'll be glad, but that's neither here nor there. You're certain about Miss Dobson though?"

The inspector sank deeper into the chair and gazed into the fire as though hypnotized. He didn't respond for a long moment. "The Chief Inspector was really breathing down my neck, Bertram. I have to say that I wasna' happy about it; not as certain as I would have liked to be. But I feel that the truth will come out now that we've got the enquiry moving forward again."

"Meanwhile it's possible that an innocent young lady's reputation is being tarnished!" put in Nellie.

"Aye! Well . . ." Moss left the sentence unfinished. There followed a long silence.

"Have you found the murder weapon?"

"Miss Dobson claims that when she returned home after the séance on the seventeenth of September, when Captain Grimsby met his maker, she discovered that one of her hatpins had disappeared; was nay longer in her hat."

"And have you found it?"

Moss shook his head. "She described it as an expensive pearl-ended one, with filigree silver and a gold-plated pin." There followed another silence before he asked, "You'll nay be stopping your own investigation, I take it, Bertram?"

"I don't think I can, Campbell. At least as long as Taffy and the Yard pay my way at Lady Marlborough's. It seems to me that there's no real evidence – though you are Scotland Yard, of course, so you should know. However . . ." he took several long puffs at his pipe. "I don't see a motive."

"Aye! Aye!" was all that the inspector said. He sat gazing morosely into the fire before adding, "I'll see you attend at least one or two more séances, Bertram – I'll tell the Chief Inspector we have to tie-up loose ends – but then you'll either have to get your friend Taffy to pick up the full amount or we'll have to consider the case closed."

"Do you think Miss Dobson will be given bail, Campbell?" asked Nellie, looking up from darning some of Arnold's socks.

"I hope so," murmured Bertie.

"That'll be up to the magistrate," said Moss. "I dinna' think she poses any risk of running away, so there's a good chance. But it all depends on his lordship's mood and the way the wind blows! You know how that goes."

"I understand Lady Marlborough is encouraging her cousin Sir Mortimer Long to take her case," said Bertie. "That's what Taffy said, anyway."

"Aye! Well, we'll see."

*Chapter Thirteen*

Bertie and Arnold, with Herbert in tow, entered the Belgravia Spiritualist Association premises and headed for room number seven, where Madam Stanhope was scheduled to once again hold one of her séances. This was Bertie's first visit to the famed B.S.A. but Arnold had briefed him on what to expect. Depositing their half-crowns in the slot on top of the polished mahogany box outside the room, they hurried inside at the end of the short line of sitters following the medium. As they took available seats about the table, Arnold nudged his brother-in-law and nodded in the direction of a monocled man in a brown suit with a dark green checkered waistcoat.

"Kaster," Arnold mouthed. Bertie nodded his head and then took hands with his neighbors.

The séance proceeded along the lines that Arnold had outlined to Bertie. The spirit calling itself Little Ellie was again in attendance, apparently a favorite among the older ladies of the circle. Bertie found it hard to credit people of any intelligence with believing the voice to belong to anyone other than the medium herself but, he decided, if they felt that they were getting their money's-worth in entertainment then far be it for him to upset them. He sat through the departure of Little Ellie and then the arrival of a blustery old gentleman who claimed to have been a medium at the B.S.A. many years before and to be joyfully watching the development of Madam Stanhope. Again, to Bertie, it sounded like Madam Stanhope herself trying to deepen her voice to sound like a man. As the séance continued, messages were given for several individuals, apparently regular members of the circle. Once again Herbert received love and good wishes from his departed grandmother, though nothing that Bertie would have considered evidential.

Just as Bertie was getting restless and wanting to stretch his legs, the spirit trumpet rose up, its luminous bands marking its progress, and glided back and forth across the table. Suddenly it seemed to dip and something was heard to fall onto the surface of the table with a clatter. This was followed by the sounds of other smaller items landing. Bertie strained his eyes to see in the darkness. He thought that he could make out a tiny glimmer of some stray light reflecting off the glass dome enclosing an elaborate and ostentatious clock on the fireplace mantel. He could have sworn that something moved across, in the darkness, momentarily eclipsing the glint of the clock glass, but he couldn't be absolutely certain.

The séance came to a close and someone stood and turned up the gaslight. There on the surface of the séance table lay a man's meerschaum pipe, a bracelet and a ring. Mr. Reinhart Kaster, with a grunt of satisfaction, swooped up the pipe and cradled it in his hands.

"I knew that spirit would return this treasure," he cried, looking around at everyone. "It was borrowed by them over a week ago, but I knew they would return it." He beamed. "You see, you need never worry about the spirits. No matter how long they retain an object, they will always eventually return it in good condition."

A large-bosomed matron seated opposite Bertie pointed to the bracelet. "Then be so kind as to pass my diamond bracelet to me, so that I can be sure that it, also, is in good condition."

Someone slid it across to her. She snatched it up and peered closely at it. "I shall take it to my jeweler at my earliest con . . ."

"My dear lady," cried Kaster. "Pardon my interruption but please allow me to save you the trouble. I am a certified jeweler and diamond merchant. Mr. Reinhart Kaster, at your service. Pray permit me to examine your bracelet and set your mind at rest."

It was, Bertie saw, a re-enactment of the séance Arnold had attended. The self-professed jeweler gave the owner every assurance that the diamond bracelet was authentic. She seemed satisfied and gave him grudging thanks. Another lady laid claim to the emerald ring that had also dropped from the trumpet. Mr. Kaster was equally effusive in examining that.

"What are you going to do, Bertie?" asked Arnold, as people started to leave.

Herbert hovered behind him, looking slightly worried. "You are not going to be accusing Madam Stanhope of any improprieties I trust, Bertie?" he said, a slight quaver in his voice.

"Not at all, Herbert. Don't worry. Arnold, you and Herbert wait outside for me. I just want a brief word with our jeweler friend there."

Lady Marlborough studied Inspector Moss through her lorgnettes. She was a long time in coming to any sort of conclusion about him, which made the inspector nervous. In his job he had to speak to, and frequently question, people from all walks of life, but he had never quite got used to addressing the so-called nobility. The "upper classes" – those who obviously were and those who only believed themselves to be – were no problem. Campbell Moss felt that he was as good as any man alive . . . or woman. But this unique group of people who sported titles of one sort or another, many of them trailing back through their ancestors to by-gone ages, was always difficult to approach. "Just look at them and picture them in their undergarments," had been Chief Inspector Villiers's advice. "That'll bring 'em all down to size!" Maybe it would, thought Moss, but he had the greatest difficulty looking back at the matronly Lady Marlborough and imagining her in her . . . well, he just couldn't do it!

"Inspector Moss, is it?" she finally intoned.

"Yes, your ladyship. Of Scotland Yard."

"And you say that this is to do with the late lamented Captain Grimsby, who was one of my select circle of spiritualist followers?"

"The gentleman who was *murdered*, ma'am." He thought it might help to emphasize the obvious. "Yes. I find it necessary to ask certain questions of the – er – medium . . . of this Prince Honoré. It is my understanding that he resides here at Kingston House with your ladyship."

Another long perusal through the spectacles.

"Indeed, I do have the prince in my home as my house-guest, Inspector. But I fail to see how disturbing him at this hour of the day will in any particular aid you in the investigations into your murder."

Lady Marlborough sat at her desk in the middle of her library, her accounts book open in front of her. She had obviously been going over the household accounts when he called. With a final disdainful look at him, she reached out and rang a small bell which sat on the corner of the desk. Almost immediately – as though he might have been standing outside the study door awaiting such a call – the door opened and the butler entered.

"Madam?"

"Parker, inform the prince that a *person* wishes to speak with him here in my study."

"Very good, my lady." The butler went out.

"I am afraid I must ask to speak to him in private, Lady Marlborough." The inspector spoke quickly and then allowed his gaze to be drawn into studying a large tapestry covering the wall next to the window. It was ancient and in places a little threadbare, he noticed, but other than that he had no idea what it was depicting. There followed a long silence.

After what seemed to Inspector Moss to be a very long time, during which her ladyship sat silently gazing out of the window, the door opened again and a young man entered whom Moss assumed to be Prince Honoré. He barely paused to take in the inspector and then strolled over to stand beside the fireplace. A well-banked fire burned in the grate.

"This Scotland Yard gentleman wishes words with you," said Lady Marlborough, rising and moving to the open door. "I have told him that your time is valuable." She went out, closing the door behind her.

*She did not tell me that his time was valuable*, thought Moss as he scrutinized the prince's slight figure. *I suppose that is her way of telling me to hurry things along.* He took out his notebook and pencil and moved to stand with his back to the window. The young man stood as though posing, with one arm resting on the mantelpiece. He wore a somewhat baggy costume of long black velvet jacket over black velvet trousers. Moss's eyes were drawn to the white turban on his head and the glittering green stone in the front of it. The prince had a pencil-thin mustache and wore a pair of gold-rimmed spectacles with dark lenses, so that Moss could not see his eyes in any detail. The dark glass was a surprise to the policeman since there was not a lot of light in the room, despite being mid-afternoon. The day outside was dull and overcast.

"Am I to presume that your visit is as a result of the demise of Captain Grimsby?"

The voice was high and for a brief moment Moss wondered if there was anything homo-sexual about the prince. His manner seemed slightly effeminate yet Moss had no real knowledge of foreign princes and their manners and customs.

"Yes, sir, that is what brings me here," said the inspector.

"I already made a statement to your sergeant, did I not?"

"Yes, sir, you did. For which I thank you. However, I would like to ask you to repeat your story to me, if you would be so kind?"

"My story?" the prince smiled, as though he found the whole situation slightly humorous. "I have no 'story' inspector. As I have already stated, throughout the séance I was in trance. That is the whole purpose, the *raisin d'être*, of a medium, you know? Or perhaps you don't know."

"Oh, aye sir. We at Scotland Yard are not entirely disconnected from what goes on in these Spiritualist groups. I am aware of mediums." He made an entry in his notebook.

"Then you must know that when in trance we are, as it were, disconnected from the physical world. We have no knowledge of what goes on at the sitting until such time as we emerge from the trance. I do not, therefore, know anything of your murder nor who may or may not have perpetrated it."

Moss scribbled in his book, without comment. It seemed to him that the prince's voice had become slightly more shrill as he disclaimed any knowledge of events, but it could simply have been frustration at having to repeat what seemed needless. Moss could understand that. If he had a sixpence for every time he had to ask someone to retell a tale already told, he would be a rich man.

"And you have nothing to add to that, sir? No little detail that may have, shall we say, filtered through to you while in this entranced condition?"

"That is not the way it works, inspector."

"Nay. Of course not." He paused. "Just one more question, if I may? Where are you from, sir? I have heard various names in Europe suggested. Luxembourg, for example, I have heard?"

"What does my country of origin have to do with your murder investigation, inspector?"

"Ah! Aye, sir, you are right. Just filling-in background information, as it were."

"Unnecessary, I think you must agree." The prince stood quite still, studying the inspector.

Moss was annoyed that he couldn't see the medium's eyes. He closed up his notebook and tucked it back in his pocket. "Then I will bid you good day, sir. Sorry to have interrupted your . . . activities. Meditation, or some such, was it?"

Prince Honoré smiled slightly and said nothing.

"Then I will see myself out," said the inspector. "Thank you for your time, and please convey my thanks to her ladyship."

"You stay here, Arnold, until I've finished my business with him, and then you do as we said."

"Don't worry, Bertie. You can count on me."

Arnold sat in a seat next to the window in an Aerated Bread Company tea shop on New Bond Street. He watched his brother-in-law leave, cross the street, and approach a jeweler's shop next door to the prestigious Fine Art Society. As Bertie got there Mr. Reinhart Kaster came out of the shop, almost bumping into Bertie.

"Ah! Mr. Hawkins, is it not? I had almost forgotten that you were to call. Please forgive me."

"Yes," replied Bertie, withdrawing a small package from his pocket. "When I spoke to you at Madam Stanhope's séance you said that you would be willing to appraise my sister's diamond necklace."

"Indeed. Indeed." Kaster patted his pockets and looked about him as though uncertain as to what to do. "The trouble is that I had forgotten you were coming and I have an urgent appointment. However . . . are you able to leave the necklace with me? You recall I said that I would need to have it for a few days to thoroughly examine it?"

"Of course." Bertie looked up at the sign above the shop's entrance. "You had said to meet you here at Mathesons. An eminent jeweler. This is where you are employed?"

"A most prestigious jeweler, as I'm sure you are aware." Kaster nodded and drew his overcoat about him. "I would invite you inside to my office but, as you see, I am on my way out. A frightful nuisance! Do forgive me. You have the necklace there? I can simply take it, to save you having to return another time."

"Of course," replied Bertie. And then, as though an afterthought: "Oh! I suppose I should ask for a receipt. My sister would insist, you understand?"

"Of course." Kaster stepped out onto the pavement, away from the shop. "Why don't we duck into that tea shop across the way? It will save going back into my office – I don't want to get delayed any further; you would not believe how they rely on me. I can give you a receipt and be on my way and you can relax with a nice cup of tea. Come!" Without waiting for a response he marched across the road, ducking around a growler and springing over the sweepings in the gutter. Bertie followed him.

Inside the tea shop they took the table that happened to be next to Arnold. Bertie was pleased to see that the big man gave no sign of recognition.

Kaster again patted his pockets. "Bother! Of course I don't have my headed notepaper with me, but a simple hand-written receipt on a page out of my notebook will suffice, I'm sure." Without waiting for a response, Kaster drew a somewhat dog-eared notebook from his pocket, tore out a blank page, and scribbled on it. He ended with a signature done with a great flourish.

"Here you are, Hawkins. Good as gold. Now I must be off. See you in about a week, what?" He took up the packet Bertie had laid on the table and hurried out of the tea shop. As he went, Arnold stood up as though he had finished his tea, and also left the shop.

Arnold had learned enough from the many times he had had to follow Herbert that he took care not to get too close to Reinhart Kaster. The man walked at a brisk pace, considering his well-fed frame, along to where the southern section of New Bond Street became Old Bond Street. Partway towards Piccadilly, he then turned right onto Grafton Street and entered what Arnold took to be a building of flats.

Arnold waited a few moments before himself entering the building. All was quiet inside, with only a low murmur of voices coming indistinctly from some of the closed and numbered doors. There was no way to tell which flat Kaster had entered. Suddenly a door on the first floor, almost immediately above the entranceway, opened and Arnold heard Kaster's voice.

"I will be by again in four days to pick it up, Mr. Singh. Make sure it's ready."

Kaster had been in there for no more than five minutes. As he descended the stairs, Arnold stepped back into the shadows and watched him go out. The man left and hailed a cab. Arnold let him go.

Climbing to the first floor, Arnold tried to tread quietly as he moved along to the end door. As with all of the flats, a twist mechanical doorbell was set into the wall with a name-plate beside it. Penciled on the insert it said

## Chandra Singh

Arnold wrote the name in his notebook.

Sergeant Tobias Gilmore stood at the corner of Ennismore Gardens and Princes Gardens, not far from Kensington Road, stamping his feet to keep warm. The day had turned cold and the temperature had dropped considerably. Sergeant Gilmore's chilblains threatened to give him trouble. He didn't want a repeat of what had happened the previous winter so, better to spend twenty minutes stamping his feet than to have to pass his evenings with his feet soaking in a basin of Epsom Salts.

"You keep your eyes on Kingston House," Inspector Moss had said. "Watch out for a little man in a turban. If you see him come out, follow him. Dinna' let him see you and dinna' interfere with him. Just report back to me as to where he goes."

"Yes, sir."

A little man in a turban, indeed! What was London coming to? Foreigners even in the depths of Kensington!

But no such figure emerged. On separate occasions two different domestic servants came up the area steps and hurried away. *Probably off to the market*, thought the sergeant. A knife-grinder stopped by and spent almost an hour sharpening knives and scissors. A butcher's boy, whistling tunelessly the whole time he was there, made a delivery. But no man in a turban put in an appearance.

"But where did you get the diamond necklace?" asked Arnold, settling back down at the kitchen table after pouring himself a cup of tea. Bertie looked up from his notebook.

"It's not a real one, Arnold," he said. "That's the whole point. I told Mr. Kaster that it was a family heirloom owned by my sister and that she would like it valued, so he believes they are real diamonds. I knew that he would take the necklace to the man who fences the precious stones he gets at the séances he attends; the ones supposedly asported by the spirits."

"You mean like Miss Fotherington's diamond necklace?"

"Precisely. The supposed medium acquires the jewels and pretends they have been taken by the spirits. Kaster takes the jewelry to this fence – whom we now know to be Mr. Chandra Singh – who removes the real stones and substitutes fake ones. Then Mr. Reinhart Kaster returns the fake version for the medium to produce at the next séance as an apport, and Kaster is there to 'verify' that the stones are real . . . as he did with Miss Fotherington."

"But won't he know that the necklace you gave him is fake?"

"Oh, yes." Bertie nodded. "And when he tells me I'll express great surprise and tell him how upset my sister will be. But the point is, Arnold, that thanks to your smart following of Mr. Kaster, we now know who the fence is. It's this Indian gentleman Mr. Chandra Singh. He's the one who either exchanges the jewels himself or has yet another accomplice who does the actual jewelry work. But we can close in on Singh – we might have to let Campbell in on that – and expose this whole spiritualist confidence-tricking."

"How did you know Kaster was a fake, Bertie?"

"He told me that he worked at Mathesons and to meet him there, presumably so that I would believe him to be authentic. Mathesons is a very high class jeweler with an unblemished reputation. When I made enquiries there, however, they had never heard of Reinhart Kaster. He then pretended to be coming out of the shop, and his office, just as I arrived there and made excuses not to go back inside again, thus giving the impression that he really did have an office there. It was all a bluff on his part."

"So are all these mediums fake, Bertie? All the ones who claim that the spirits take things away and bring things back from the Spirit World?"

Bertie closed up his notebook and tucked it back in his pocket. "No, I don't think all of them are, Arnold. I like to think that there are some honest and honorable mediums 'out there'. The Society for Psychical Research was started a few short years ago. Some really smart people –

professors and the like – have made it their business to investigate many of the mediums. Obviously Madam Stanhope is not on a level to be regarded by them, but others have been very carefully vetted. There is more than one that has been shown to be unequivocally genuine. Madam Stanhope at the moment seems to be under suspicion, in my mind . . . and so too, until I learn otherwise, is Prince Honoré."

*Chapter Fourteen*

Right from the start Bertie felt that it was not going to be a productive, nor even an enjoyable, evening. All of a sudden winter seemed to have descended on London and its environs. As was so often the case, the city was not prepared for it. There was as yet nothing as daunting as snow, but the temperature had plummeted and the crowded streets suddenly seemed even more crowded as pedestrians bundled up in bulging overcoats, capes, shawls, and anything that would give added warmth. Bertie took a closed growler to Kingston House, eschewing the open-fronted hansoms. A thick fog was trying to amass itself and Bertie wondered if that would have any impact on the number of sitters who would be at Lady Marlborough's.

*I should have known better*, Bertie told himself. The spiritualists who comprised this select circle were not to be deterred by weather, least of all cold and fog. As he surrendered his coat, hat and gloves to the taciturn footman, he heard a number of voices coming from the room next to the library.

"Ah! Mr. Hawkins! Now our circle is complete." Lady Marlborough, ever the gracious hostess, acknowledged his entrance.

"I do hope I'm not late," said Bertie.

"Not at all. Do, please, help yourself to refreshment. I will see how it fares with our medium and take him some small repast." She picked up a small bowl of green salad and a goblet of plain water and carried them through to the library.

Bertie nodded to Dr. Price and the professor, who were in conversation by the buffet, and smiled at Miss Dobson and Miss Bell. Maurice Austin detached himself from the other two men and crossed to Bertie, a glass of sherry in one hand and a thin sandwich in the other.

"Good evening, Hawkins. Beastly weather. Best get yourself a glass of something before her ladyship calls us all to heel."

"I see Miss Dobson is with us," said Bertie.

"Yes. Out on bail, I'm told. She and Lady Marlborough have both requested that we make no reference to that whole sorry story this evening. It will work itself out, I'm sure. I think we are all agreed that it is unlikely that Miss Dobson is guilty. Just another example of Scotland Yard's incompetence!"

*I wonder what Campbell would think of that comment*, thought Bertie. "What does our medium have for us this evening?" he asked aloud, as he accepted a glass of sherry from the footman and chose a sandwich of the new Hovis brown-bread, containing a wafer-thin slither of ham.

"I have no idea. I'm hoping he's gone back to using the cabinet. That made for a most interesting evening, don't you think?"

"Indeed I do," responded Bertie. "And I'd like to see it in use again after our visit to Maskelyne's shop."

"My thinking exactly. Might even catch our little turbaned friend in some shenanigans!"

"I wonder if Lady Marlborough's ring will be returned?" Bertie thought of the devious Mr. Kaster and wondered if Prince Honoré was connected to his jewelry ring. *Would they dare to take the gems from her ladyship's ring and replace them with fakes? There was, after all, no Reinhart Kaster here to pretend to authenticate the ring.*

"Ladies! Gentlemen!" Lady Marlborough's voice came from the doorway to the library. They all looked up and then, putting down their glasses and plates, proceeded to the séance room.

There was a general murmur of approval when it was seen that the cabinet was back. It once more stood against the far end of the library, on the only wall without built-in bookcases. Bertie recalled that this had been bare except for a pair of framed oil paintings. Presumably the pictures had been removed so that the cabinet could be placed hard against the wall. He took a moment to ensure that there was no space between the back of the cabinet and the wall, before seating himself with the rest of the group.

Without preamble, Prince Honoré opened the doors at the front of the cabinet and stepped inside, seating himself on the solitary chair there.

This time there was no table holding musical instruments. He closed his eyes and Bertie could see him relax and that his breathing became more pronounced as his head slowly settled onto his chest. Professor Sedgeworth stood up and moved forward. He quietly closed the cabinet doors and returned to his seat, lowering the gas lights as he did so. Lady Marlborough said a short prayer and then led a soft singing of *Till I See Death's Lifted Curtain*.

Their voices faded away and there was silence.

"We invite the spirits to leave the Summerland, that place of joy and delight, and to join with us here in our séance room," said Lady Marlborough. "Come to us through our loved and respected medium Prince Honoré. Speak through him that we may enjoy that rapture which is a part of the Spirit World. Know that we are open and desirous of receiving your teachings."

There was another moment of silence and then Bertie heard a long sigh come from the seated figure within the cabinet.

"My children!"

A bright voice that sounded to Bertie as though it issued from an elderly gentleman, rang out. The others murmured to themselves and Bertie assumed that this was a spirit known to the group.

"Professor Mainwaring! What a delight," cried Lady Marlborough. "It has been a long time since you have graced us with your presence. We welcome you."

The others murmured a greeting.

"Now what's all this I hear about asports?" asked the voice. "Stuff and nonsense to some of you, I know. But pay attention!"

Bertie felt like a child in school again. He could almost imagine this Professor Mainwaring rapping the edge of his desk with a ruler.

"Asports and apports are spirit's way of demonstrating that there can be a connection between our two worlds. A connection that is both spiritual and physical. Objects can be moved between these worlds. Objects and . . ."

There was a pause. Bertie thought it was for dramatic effect, on the part of this spirit professor. The voice continued.

". . . persons!"

"Persons?" It was Dr. Price's hushed voice.

"Ssh!" from Lady Marlborough.

"Think of Mrs. Guppy," said Maurice Austin, *sotto voce*.

"Ssh!" from several of the sitters.

"Persons," repeated the spirit. "I will demonstrate."

Bertie felt a thrill. He didn't know what to expect but it seemed these séances were never dull.

There was a long silence, which dragged on. Bertie felt a sense of anticlimax. After a while he was aware of the others fidgeting.

"Professor Mainwaring?" called Lady Marlborough. There was no reply. Finally, "I think we have lost him," she said. "Professor Sedgeworth, would you be so kind as to see to the gas light? Thank you."

Bertie blinked as the light was turned up. Lady Marlborough stood up. Bertie thought she seemed uncertain as to what to do. Finally she moved forward and tapped on the doors of the cabinet. There was no response.

"Well, open the damn thing!" snapped Maurice Austin.

"Mr. Austin! Please!" Lady Marlborough frowned at the newspaperman. She looked about her as though hoping that something would happen to ease the tension. Then, decided, she moved forward and opened the two doors. The inside of the cabinet held only the empty chair.


The sitters had repaired to the buffet and stood around, sipping sherry, and excitedly discussing the brief séance. Bertie kept hearing the name of Mrs. Guppy mentioned. Apparently her apportation by the mediums Herne and Williams had caused quite a stir in London spiritualist circles. Yet now, here at Lady Marlborough's select séance, much the same phenomenon had been witnessed, with the medium himself literally spirited away. Where had he gone and when would he be back, was the general question?

There was a lot of activity in the house, Bertie noticed, as though even the servants were excited. He observed Lady Marlborough's lady's maid, Lisbeth, come out of the library; the butler hurried in there and then re-emerged, as did a footman; the downstairs maid scurried around.

Professor Sedgeworth, Dr. Price, and Maurice Austin offered possible explanations, none of which made any sense to Bertie.

"What d'you think, Hawkins?" the newspaperman said to Bertie. "Didn't Maskelyne show us how there can be a hiding place at the back of a cabinet?"

"Yes." Bertie nodded his head thoughtfully. "Very true. However, I did take the precaution of checking to ensure that the back of this particular cabinet was tight against the wall. No space for anyone to hide behind it."

Lady Marlborough had bewailed the loss of her ring at the previous séance and now said she hoped that when Prince Honoré eventually returned – as they all seemed to believe he would do – that he would bring her ring with him. Eventually Professor Sedgeworth drew attention to the time and suggested they all go home. It was at that moment that a figure appeared in the doorway out to the hall. It was Prince Honoré.

He wore a pair of gold-rimmed spectacles and leaned nonchalantly against the doorpost, drawing on a thin blue Turkish cigarette. Bertie had not seen him smoking before. Lady Marborough let out a cry. The other two ladies gasped.

"What the . . ?" from Maurice Austin.

"Prince Honoré!" said the professor. "You have returned."

"So it would seem," said the medium. He looked all around the room, studying each of them, and then turned and walked away.

"Well, I'll be . . ." said the newspaperman.

"Yes," said Dr. Price. "For once I think we are all in agreement with you, Austin."

"I don't understand," said Nellie. "How could he just disappear from inside his contraption and then suddenly reappear outside of it?"

"You are not the only one who doesna' understand, Nell," said Inspector Moss, scratching the top of his thinning head. "Was that not the general feeling, Bertram?"

They sat at lunch the day after the séance. Both Arnold and Inspector Moss had appeared at Penny Court – appropriately close to the luncheon hour – to see how Bertie had fared at the previous evening's séance. Nellie had insisted they both stay to eat. Moss no longer made any pretence at protest.

Bertie studied his portion of steak and kidney pudding carefully. It looked to him as though Arnold had managed to acquire far more kidneys than might be considered his fair share. Kidneys – when part of one of Nell's mouth-watering pies – were one of Bertie's favorites. He mentally shrugged and started eating.

"It's like magic," muttered Arnold.

"No. Not magic," said Bertie. "Either a very clever trick, or an amazing example of true Spiritualism."

"And which do you think it is?" asked Nellie.

"Magic!" murmured Isobel, from the foot of the table. "Cor!" They all ignored her.

"I'm going to ask Lady Marlborough if I might have another really close look at that cabinet, next week," said Bertie. "I've been going over the notes I made when Austin and I visited that Maskelyne. There *has* to be some sort of hiding place where Prince Honoré secretes himself."

"But you said he didna' come out from the cabinet again. He suddenly popped up in the next room," said Moss. "How could he do that?"

"Magic," said Isobel again, this time a little louder. Then, "In one of them Penny Dreadfuls, Tommy Turnbull meets a magician 'oo can . . ."

"Enough, Isobel!" Nellie shook her head in despair. "Penny Dreadfuls, indeed! I've told you not to keep buying them for her, Arnold." She looked hard at her brother.

Arnold looked up, his fork full of meat and peas halfway to his mouth. "Me, Nell?"

"No," said Bertie. "No, I don't think it's magic. At least not the Penny Dreadful kind. *Stage* magic, perhaps."

"Presto . . . something, isn't it?" said Moss.

"Prestidigitation. Yes, Campbell." Bertie nodded. "It's all a trick. But a clever trick, I'll grant you that."

"But what is the purpose?" asked Nellie. "Is he just trying to show that Spirits can do these things, and if so why?"

"I can answer that," said Moss, pushing away his now clean plate and settling back in his chair. "It would appear that our Prince does a good bit of side business with private sittings, as Bertram suggested a while back."

"What's that mean?" asked Arnold.

"He will grant a private séance with just one person . . . someone who really wants to contact a particular dead relative. And he charges accordingly."

"That doesn't seem right, somehow," said Nellie.

"It's nay illegal, if that's what you mean. And he can make a nice wee bit of money on the side."

"I'm surprised that Lady Marlborough allows it," said Nellie, signaling for Isobel to start collecting the empty plates.

"I'm sure she turns a blind eye on her guest," said Bertie. "She wouldn't want to lose him."

"Most of them can afford to pay for something like that," said Moss. "They indulge themselves, do that sort."

"Not all of them, I wouldn't think," said Bertie. "Miss Bell, for instance. And Maurice Austin is being financed by his newspaper."

"Aye, well . . . they'll nay be the ones who fall for it." The policeman moved his dessert spoon and fork a fraction, as though to encourage the serving of the gooseberry fool that he knew to be sitting on the sideboard. Almost on cue, Isobel started placing the bowls and passing the whipped cream.

"I'd still like to know how he did it," said Bertie, accepting his dessert and watching his brother-in-law deplete the cream.

Later, Inspector Moss settled into an armchair with a cup of tea on a small table beside him. He had protested that he needed to get back to Scotland Yard and no one had contradicted him, but still he made himself comfortable beside the low burning fire in the fireplace.

"So tell me more about this jewelry ring you've stumbled on, Bertram," he said, peering at Bertie from under his bushy eyebrows. "Is it nay something the Yard should be aware of?"

Bertie sat across from him in another armchair. Arnold had gone out on an errand for Nellie. She and Isobel had cleared away the dishes and taken them down to the kitchen.

"It's as I told you, Campbell. They work with one of the mediums at the Belgravia Spiritualist Association in Belgrave Square. Maybe with more than one, I wouldn't wonder. Through pretense of the spirits taking, or 'borrowing', a piece of jewelry they get possession of it for a week. That gives them time to remove the valuable stones and replace them with fakes. They then return the item at the next séance."

"And you've found the fence; the one who does the actual switch of the valuables?"

"Yes. Arnold managed to track him down. It's a Mr. Chandra Singh, who has a flat at number 15 Grafton Street."

"One of our Indian cousins, is he?" Moss sipped his tea.

Bertie took a drink of his own tea, replaced the cup on its saucer and nodded. "It would seem so. What interested me – and it may be only coincidence – is that the late lamented Captain Grimsby spent a lot of time in India."

Moss tugged at his mustache. "You're saying that there's a connection?"

"I don't know, Campbell. I don't know what the links may be, but remember I told you that Lady Marlborough's ring was spirited away by Prince Honoré?"

"You think he's in cahoots with our Mr. Singh?"

Bertie shook his head and wrinkled his brow. "I just don't know, Campbell. How could he be? Or is there just a lot of this sort of thing going on in spiritualist circles? I just think it's worthy of further investigation and thought you might be able to follow up on Singh while I concentrate on the Prince."

The inspector sighed. "Aye, well . . . we're getting naywhere with that turbaned gentleman. But the Yard has no reason to harass this Singh man without some tangible evidence, as you know, Bertram. However, I'll make it my business to have one of my constables keep an eye on his place and report to me any hanky-panky going on."

"Thank you, Campbell."


"Arnold, we can't rely on Scotland Yard to keep tabs on Mr. Singh. I'd like you to go over to Grafton Street and keep watch." Bertie had said farewell to the inspector, who had reluctantly returned to Scotland Yard, and now greeted his brother-in-law on his return from running Nellie's errand.

"Right now, Bertie?"

"I think so, Arnold. Strike while the iron's hot, and all that."

"What am I looking for?" asked the big man, his brow furrowed.

Bertie pulled his pocket watch out of his waistcoat pocket and studied it. "I'm wondering who else might be involved in this scheme. Why don't you just keep an eye out at his flat till dinner time and then come back and let me know who might have visited the man. If he goes out himself, try to follow and see where he goes. We'll do the same thing tomorrow. I'll take the morning and you can do the afternoon again."

Arnold was sent off in a hansom and Bertie went back into the house and down to the kitchen.

"What do you hope to discover, Bertie?" asked Nellie.

He shook his head. "I don't know, Nell. Perhaps get an idea of how big this jewelry ring is. See who else might be involved."

"Do you really think your Prince Honoré is part of it?"

"Somehow I doubt it." He pulled out a chair at the kitchen table and sat down.

"Don't go getting yourself too comfortable," said Nellie. "Isobel and I have got to start preparing dinner."

He got up again. "Perhaps I'll go and have a chin-wag with Taffy. Get his ideas on things."

# *Chapter Fifteen*

Taffy was very interested in the idea of a jewelry fencing ring but was concerned for Bertie's safety.

"Getting mixed up with a gang of 'high rollers', as the Americans term them, could be dangerous, Bertie. And especially if they are international crooks, as seems likely."

Bertie waved a dismissive hand. "I doubt that it's that big an operation, Taffy. Probably just a few of them working the spiritualist circuit."

"What about the India connection?" Taffy's dark eyebrows knitted over his sharp nose. "You've said that Grimsby spent years in India and this Singh character is definitely Indian. There is, I can tell you, a trade of illegal gems that operates between there and England."

"We'll be careful, Taffy. Thanks for your concern. I've got Arnold watching the Singh flat right now, but he is not to interfere; just to let me know who might go in and out."

The Welshman still was not happy. "There are some things you do have to leave to the police, Bertie."

"I know." Bertie smiled at his friend. "Yes, I really do know that, Taffy. I can do my enquiring and then let Campbell know the results. Don't worry. I won't let anything get out of hand."


Arnold had been standing in the hallway of the Grafton Street flats, leaning against a wall and pretending to read a newspaper while he peered over the top of it and studied the closed door of number 3. He had been doing that for almost half an hour when he realized that he was holding the newspaper upside down. As he corrected that, and turned the paper around, he heard footsteps coming up the stairs from the ground floor. He repositioned himself slightly to get a better view of Chandra Singh's door.

A woman came up the stairs and made her way to Singh's flat. She was well covered against the increasingly colder weather outside, with a black astrakhan cape over a navy cheviot serge skirt. On her head was a dark blue, felt, dress hat trimmed with black taffeta silk. A veil was down over her face, making it impossible for Arnold to make note of any description of the young lady. However, he did observe and make mental note of her auburn hair. She rang the doorbell and stood patiently until the call was answered. Then she slipped inside the only partially opened door as though she had been expected. The woman remained in the flat less than ten minutes, by Arnold's old pocket watch. She came out and made her way rapidly to the staircase without even glancing at Arnold, apparently unaware of his watching her.

The only other visitors that afternoon were to other flats; some on the first floor and some to the floors above. Arnold felt very conspicuous standing with his newspaper but no one seemed to take it amiss that he was there. Eventually the smell of some sort of stew, issuing from one of the flats, started Arnold's mouth watering to the point where he decided that it was time to return to Penny Court and see what Nellie might be preparing for dinner.

Bertie sat at one of the big oak desks in the British Museum Reading Room and studied the open newspaper in front of him. It was *The Calcutta Bugle* of March, 1879. There was a small paragraph on page 7 which read:

*Lucknow: 9 March 1879*
*JEWELRY THIEVES APPREHENDED*
*A gang of thieves responsible for the theft of jewelry from British army personnel at Lucknow has been apprehended and will stand trial in the coming assizes. Led by Aditya Singh and his brother Chandra Singh, the gang includes two junior officers of the 33rd Duke of Wellington's Regiment. A further officer together with his wife are suspected of complicity in the burglaries but they have not yet been apprehended.*

Bertie checked in his notebook and verified that Grimsby had been stationed at Lucknow. In fact, that was where he had married. Could the "officer together with his wife" who were not apprehended have been Cyril and Jessica Grimsby, he wondered? And was it the same Chandra Singh? It seemed that it would be too much of a coincidence for it not to be the same. If so, then there was almost certainly a connection between Singh and the recently deceased Captain Grimsby . . . and what about Grimsby's ex-wife? Was she still in the picture in some way? Perhaps she hadn't disappeared so completely. Bertie tugged thoughtfully at his mustache. He wondered how Arnold was doing at Grafton Street.

"No. Other than the auburn hair I have no idea what she looked like, Bertie," said Arnold.

"How tall was she?"

"Er – medium height. Not too tall and not too short." Arnold looked worried.

Bertie nodded his head. "Average?"

"Yes! Or perhaps just a bit shorter than that?"

"All right, Arnold. You did a good job. You're sure no one else visited Mr. Singh?"

"Quite sure."

"So what does that tell you, Bertie?" asked Nellie. "Perhaps it was his wife, or his sister. It could have been anybody." She was sorting laundry, ready for wash day. "Wash Day" was actually spread over several days, due to the enormity of the project. Nellie's day dresses and Bertie's suits had to be dry-cleaned but virtually everything else was washed by hand, by Nellie and the stalwart Isobel. The laundry was big even though the family was small: shirts, dresses – both Nellie's and Isobel's – petticoats, undergarments, night clothes, table linen, towels both bath and kitchen, bed linen, and more. Once the items had been sorted they were set to soak overnight in large tubs of water.

Bertie nodded. "Yes, it could have been anyone, Nell. And it's not just who she was, but why she was there. I wonder what business she had with Mr. Singh?"

"She wasn't there long," added Arnold.

"So you said. That, I think, is suspicious."

"In what way?" asked Nellie.

"If she was a normal visitor, don't you think she would have spent some time there? But if she was delivering, or picking up, real or false gemstones, then she would have only had to go in for a few minutes." He tugged at his mustache. "I wish I knew what went on in there."

"Per'aps she was a spy, Mr. 'awkins," suggested Isobel, her voice issuing from behind a pile of dirty laundry. She sniffed loudly. "In *Tommy Turnbull's Brush with the Enemy* there was this . . ."

"Get on with the laundry, Isobel," said Nellie, with a sigh. She turned back to her husband. "Do you think this mysterious woman might work with your Mr. Kaster?"

"It's always possible, though he struck me as being more of a loner." Bertie got up from the kitchen table, pushing away his now empty tea cup. Arnold, sensing a return to work, did the same.

"Where are we going, Bertie?"

"I've got something I want to follow up on, Arnold, and you might as well come along with me. Nell, we won't be back for lunch."

"Just as well. Look at this mountain of wash we've got to attack. You go on and do what you have to do. Isobel and I won't miss you, believe me."

"Where are we going, Bertie?"

Bertie led the way across the road and on towards Trafalgar Square. It was an overcast day though so far remaining dry. Bertie hoped the weather wouldn't interfere with Nellie's washing plans.

"It's our good neighbor Herbert Parker, Arnold. It seems that Hattie complained to Nellie that her husband is still somewhat errant."

"Errant?"

"Wandering, Arnold. I thought that if you kept an eye on him at the séances that would be an end of it. I didn't think he'd be able to get into too much mischief."

"And has he?"

Bertie shook his head disbelievingly. "It seems Herbert's need for adventure is insatiable. Come on! Hattie said he accidentally let slip that he was taking off from work this afternoon and she overheard him asking the postman if he knew what hours the National Gallery was open."

"National Gallery? Isn't that all paintings and things, Bertie?"

"Yes."

They crossed Trafalgar Square, around the lions and between the fountains, and then climbed the steps up to the gallery.

"Where to?" asked Arnold, as they entered the vast entrance hall.

"I have no idea," said Bertie looking about him. "I must say, I hadn't really thought about how big this place is. Excuse me!" He waved down an elderly man in uniform, who looked as though he was an employee. The man had tired eyes, Bertie thought, but they seemed to brighten up when he was addressed.

"Yes, sir? May I be of assistance? The Portrait Gallery, if that's what you are a-lookin' for, is set behind this 'ere main National Gallery. People are often confused, I don't mind telling you . . ."

"No, no. Leastwise, I don't know if that's what we want," said Bertie. "We are looking for a gentleman and wondered if you could help us?"

The man smiled and chuckled knowingly. "I am sure I'll do my best sir but . . ." he looked about him. "You might notice that there are any number of gentlemen 'ereabouts . . ."

"Yes. Of course." Bertie tried to be patient. "But this particular gentleman . . . I realize that it is extremely unlikely that you can help me but I must try. This is a gentleman about my own height, though much thinner. He has a straggly mustache – grey in color – and may or may not be wearing spectacles. Er, wire-rimmed spectacles."

"He'd be wearing that old overcoat of his, wouldn't he, Bertie?" put in Arnold.

"Yes. Yes. Very good, Arnold. Yes, he'd be wearing a slightly faded brown topcoat with a black velvet collar. Brown bowler and suit under the coat."

The attendant was standing there sadly shaking his head. "'Tain't no use, sir, if I may say so. We 'ave 'undreds of gentlemen in 'ere who might fit that description. And – if I may say so – even if I recalled such a person, I would 'ave no way of knowing whereabouts in the Gallery 'e might be."

Bertie reflected a moment. "No. No, of course you wouldn't. Silly of me. I'm sorry to trouble you. Come along, Arnold. We'll have to do this the hard way."

They plunged into the many galleries and walked past people standing studying the paintings. There were occasional small groups; one of schoolgirls led by a teacher.

The vestibule of the main staircase was roofed by a glass dome and embellished with marble columns and paneling. Several large paintings of the British School were hung there. Bertie struck off into Room One, with the beginning of the series of Italian works. From there he led Arnold up the staircase to the left and through to the French and Spanish Schools. Suddenly Arnold grabbed Bertie's arm.

"What? What is it, Arnold?"

"Listen, Bertie. Listen."

They stood still. All seemed silent for a while and then Bertie heard a high-pitched, nervous-sounding laugh coming from a nearby room.

"That's Herbert!" said Arnold. "I'd know that laugh anywhere."

"Come on. But go carefully," said Bertie, slipping around the corner.

Ahead, beyond the next two galleries, was the Octagonal Hall, holding paintings of various schools. Standing in front of Paolo Veronese's painting of *Mary Magdalene Laying Aside Her Jewels* was Herbert Parker and a young lady in a too-bright, multi-colored, summer dress of vivid colors. On her blonde head sat a hat trimmed with chiffon, taffeta silk, ostrich plumes, and silk flowers. She pointed her parasol – *an umbrella might be more appropriate in this weather,* thought Bertie – at the painting and made some comment that produced another high-pitched cackle from Herbert.

Bertie kept a tight grip on Arnold and remained back out of sight from the couple. They watched them for several minutes. Herbert and the young lady seemed more intent on conversing than on actually appraising the paintings, thought Bertie. Eventually the young lady said something to which Herbert nodded vigorously, and then she turned and swept away out of the gallery.

"Quickly, Arnold! Follow her. See where she goes and report back to me at the house."

"What are you going to do, Bertie?"

"I'll see if I can have a word with our philandering friend. Now, hurry, Arnold. Don't lose her." The big man scurried away.

Bertie watched Herbert as the little man started walking back towards the main entrance. His gait slowed noticeably as he passed pre-Raphaelite paintings of nymphs and of scantily-draped Greek goddesses, but picked up again as he neared the exit. Bertie stood waiting for him as he emerged at the top of the steps leading down to Trafalgar Square.

"Bertie! Whatever are you doing here?" Herbert didn't seem too pleased to see his neighbor.

Bertie didn't beat about the bush. *Better to have it out and get it over with*, he thought. "Who was the young lady with whom you had your assignation, Herbert?" he asked. He tried not to speak accusingly.

"Wh-what?" Herbert gulped and looked about him as though trying to spy some avenue of escape.

"The young lady you spent time with in the Gallery, Herbert. Don't try to tell me that you took time off from work to study the paintings."

"Bertie!" It was almost pleading.

"Come," said Bertie, softening. "Let's stroll down to the fountains and you can tell me all about it."

"She is the Countess du Bois." Herbert started to sound pleased with himself, having got over the shock of being discovered. "I met her at one of the séances in Belgravia and she is going to take me under her wing, as it were, and make me a medium."

"Make you a medium?"

"Yes!"

It was Bertie's turn to look about him, if only to get things into perspective. He turned back to Herbert. "Let me get this straight. You want to become a spiritualist medium?"

Herbert pulled himself up straight, though he was still a few inches shorter than Bertie. "The Countess said that she thought I would make a very good medium."

"Based on what?"

"On – on – well, she has a *knowledge* of these things. She is able to see 'potential', she said." He looked at his friend defiantly. "You have your Lady Whatever, that you go to, and now I have my Countess!"

Bertie sighed. "Herbert. Lady Marlborough is not 'my' anything. And this isn't a competition. If your young lady is indeed all that she claims to be, and is truly interested in helping you, then I am delighted for you."

"Thank you, Bertie."

"Is she going to charge you money for this?"

"Wh-what? Well, of course there will be expenses . . ."

"How much?"

"F-fifty guineas."

"Fifty guineas!" Bertie was appalled. "Fifty guineas, Herbert? Does Hattie know about this? Does she approve of you spending such a sum? Does she know about this so-called Countess?"

Herbert looked ready to burst into tears. "Now don't go telling Hattie, Bertie. That's not fair."

"Not fair? Is giving that amount of money to some young woman you've only just met, fair?"

"Oh, Bertie!"

Bertie looked at his friend and his heart softened. "Come on, Herbert. Let's go and find a tavern. I think you and I need to sit down and have a drink and a talk. Your wife is very worried about you, you know."


Coming out of the National Gallery, Arnold had been in time to see the mysterious young lady hail a growler and climb into it. He flagged down a hansom and instructed the driver to follow.

They drove to Cranbourn Street, on the corner of Charing Cross Road, to the Hippodrome Music Hall and Burlesque Theatre. London had 50 theatres and 500 music-halls attended by 325,000 people nightly. The Hippodrome was one of the most popular. Arnold had never been there but it was an ambition of his. He watched the young lady enter the stage door of the theatre and, after a few moments, he went to the same door.

"'Old on, sonny!"

Arnold looked down to see a dwarf, wearing a battered top hat and over-large overcoat, holding up his hand to stop his entrance. The diminutive figure had a red face that told of a love of the hops, and a straggly mustache that dribbled down either side of his full red lips to frame a beardless chin. Despite being only a fraction of Arnold's size, he showed no fear, perhaps because of the solid-looking cudgel that he held in his stubby hands.

"Where you fink you're goin' in such a 'urry, sonny?" the dwarf demanded.

Arnold pointed to the dark interior behind the figure. "That young lady that just came in here," he said. "Who is she?"

"'Oo is she? 'Oo is she!" The dwarf laughed and then spat on the floor. "As if you don't know! I get all sorts of you nob sapsculls – usually scammered with ale – all trying to get in 'ere to meet the ladies."

"So who is she?" asked Arnold patiently.

"That's Miss Fanny Camden, that is. The 'Angel of the 'ippodrome', as they call 'er. If you've got a bobstick ready you can nip up to the gods and catch 'er show. That's the only way you gonna get to see 'er while I'm 'ere, sonny."

*Chapter Sixteen*

"Hattie was so pleased," said Nellie. "I think Herbert is going to be spending his evenings at home with his wife and children for a while now."

"Until the next fad strikes him," murmured Bertie, puffing on his pipe and waving his hand to dispel the smoke.

"Well, at least he seems to be over his fascination with spiritualism. And Hattie made a very nice contribution to the coffers of the Penny Court Enquirers."

The two of them sat in front of the fire, Nellie doing some embroidery. To her it seemed to be the first quiet evening alone they had had in a long time. Arnold was back at his rooms in Old Fish Street, trying to fix a malfunctioning mangle for his landlady Mrs. Westbury. Isobel had retired to her room right after her duties so that she could start reading a new Penny Dreadful that Arnold had bought for her.

A piece of coal in the fireplace crumbled and fell. Bertie sat staring into the red glow. As a child he had spent many long evening hours imagining all sorts of scenes in the dying embers of a coal fire. Dragons, he seemed to remember, featured a lot in his childhood fantasies.

"You might put a bit more coal on, I think," said Nellie, bringing him back to reality.

Bertie used the tongs to take two or three pieces from the scuttle and place them carefully on the fire. "Speaking of spiritualism," he said, "this Friday may be the last séance I will be attending at Lady Marlborough's."

Nellie stopped her sewing and looked at him. "Oh? Why is that?"

"It's Campbell having settled on Miss Dobson as Captain Grimsby's murderer. He says that Scotland Yard no longer needs me to be their eyes and ears at the séances."

"But you don't think Miss Dobson did it, do you?"

Bertie shook his head. "No, I don't. But then, I don't know who did do it." He shrugged and looked down at his pipe. He tamped down the tobacco and puffed new life into it. "Well, you never know. Something may pop up this last time; something to clear Miss Dobson and point us at the real murderer."

"What about this Indian gentleman and the jewelry? Where are you with that, Bertie?"

"Again, we've hit a bit of a stone wall, Nell. Everything seems to point to jewels being taken from sitters at the Belgravia séances and switched through the services of that gentleman. But we've no solid proof, so far. I swear that this Chandra Singh is the same person who was involved with jewelry thefts in India, when Grimsby was there.

But again . . . no proof." He leant forward, tapped out his pipe on the grate, and then sat back in his chair and tugged on his mustache. "The Penny Court Enquirers are not getting very far on this one, Nell. Not very far at all."

Friday was cold and windy, with brief showers off and on. Bertie held his wool overcoat close about him as he climbed down out of the growler in front of Kingston House. He hurried up the path and knocked on the door. It was opened almost immediately by the elderly footman who had let him in on his very first visit. Bertie gave up his top hat, coat, gloves, cane, and scarf and then went on through to the now familiar library ante-room.

Alice Bell was there, as was Winifred Dobson – looking to Bertie to be tired and drawn. As usual the two of them were engaged in conversation but each gave a slight smile and brief nod of greeting. Dr. Price was hovering in front of the fireplace, drawing on a cigarette, a glass of white wine in his hand. He looked up when Bertie entered the room and waved him over.

"We're the first, Hawkins. Get some of this wine down you. Keep the cold away."

"Thank you, Dr. Price. I will. The professor not here yet then?"

"Oh, he'll be along. Had some meeting with his psychical research people, I believe. Must have run late, don't you know?"

Bertie wished he could have lit up his pipe but he knew that although Lady Marlborough suffered the occasional cigarette by her sitters, she would be strongly averse to a pipe. He accepted a glass of wine from the footman and selected one of the small salads that were always set out. It was a potato salad and made a nice change, he thought, from the sandwiches, biscuits and small cakes on the sideboard.

They were soon joined by Maurice Austin and, on his heels, Professor Sedgeworth.

"Did you hear the news?" asked Austin, of no one in particular. They all stopped talking and looked at him. He seemed pleased with the attention, thought Bertie.

"What news, Austin?" asked the professor, looking down his nose at the newspaperman.

"You will read it in my column tomorrow," he replied, ignoring the footman and helping himself to a large serving of wine. "The Prime Minister is to attend a séance with the medium William Eglinton in two weeks time, 29 October."

"Are you sure?"

"Really?"

"How exciting!"

"I was not aware that Gladstone was a spiritualist," said Dr. Price.

"He's not," responded the professor. "But he has made overtures to us about becoming a member of the Society for Psychical Research."

There were murmurs from the ladies, and the newspaperman's moment passed.

"Anyone seen her ladyship yet?" asked Austin, looking around. "What sort of a mood is she in?"

"What do you mean, Mr. Austin?" asked Alice.

"Well, last week she seemed positively angry that our esteemed medium had not returned her family ring."

"Oh, I don't know," said the professor. "A little annoyed, perhaps. And understandably so. But I wouldn't have said she was angry."

Bertie agreed with the newspaperman, but refrained from commenting. At that moment the door opened and Lady Marlborough sailed in. She greeted everyone civilly but Bertie noticed that her mouth was set in a thin, tight line. She gathered up a bowl of the salad and a glass of water and hurried out the way she had come in, presumably carrying them to Prince Honoré.

"Better get your refills," said Austin, topping up his own wine glass. "We'll be called to the table in a moment, I'm sure."

"It may be the cabinet again tonight," said Dr. Price.

"I certainly hope so," said Miss Bell.

When they eventually went through to the library Bertie was delighted to see that indeed the cabinet was there. Its doors stood open and a single empty chair sat within. Prince Honoré himself stood in front of the cabinet and bowed to them all as they took their seats. Bertie sat with Maurice Austin on his right and Dr. Price and Professor Sedgeworth on his left, behind the three ladies.

Prince Honoré cleared his throat, which seemed to prompt a coughing spasm. He walked to a small Japan table bearing his water glass and the now-empty salad bowl, and took a long drink. Returning to the center he again bowed.

"This evening, ladies and gentlemen, I have a feeling that the spirits may have yet another surprise in store for us." His normally unemotional face broke into a quick smile which as quickly disappeared. "I think we may dispense with such unnecessary properties as blindfolds and ties. Let the spirits speak for themselves." With a final bow he ascended into the cabinet and took his place on the chair, closing his eyes.

Lady Marlborough started the singing which, this evening, was *Loving Spirit Shine Your Light On Me*. As the song progressed Prince Honoré's head dropped to his chest and his breathing slowed. At the end of the hymn Professor Sedgeworth moved forward and closed the doors to the cabinet, turned down the gaslight, and returned to his seat. Lady Marlborough spoke a short prayer and then there was silence.

The silence was first broken with the sound of a muffled cough from inside the cabinet. Then a voice was heard.

"So you gather once again, my friends?"

Bertie noticed a slight foreign accent, though he was unable to place it. For once Lady Marlborough did not immediately acknowledge the spirit. Hesitantly, she said "Good evening."

"You may not be familiar with my voice. This is the first time I have been allowed to pass through to make contact with you . . ."

The voice was interrupted by another bout of coughing from the medium. Alice Bell and Winifred Dobson whispered together. Lady Marlborough hissed "Sssh!"

From inside the cabinet came "It is . . . I am . . ." Another cough, and then "I beg your forgiveness. This instrument suffers, it seems, from some sudden affliction of the throat. A moment."

There followed a long pause. When the voice continued it seemed to Bertie that it was very strained.

"I am Emmanuel Swedberg, though you may know me as Swedenborg. I was a scientist in Stockholm."

"Swedenborg?" murmured the professor. "He passed to spirit over a hundred years ago."

"Sssh!"

"Some of you may be familiar with my work," the voice continued. "I had my first vision when fifty-six years of age. A vision of my own house threatened by fire . . . and I was more than 400 kilometers way."

Lady Marlborough found her voice. "What brings you here?" she asked.

To Bertie it sounded as though her ladyship's question was a challenge; as though she did not feel that the spirit should have presented itself, though why that would be he couldn't think. He told himself that he must be mistaken.

"What brings me here is that which draws all . . ."

The voice cracked and then dissolved into more coughing. They all heard the scrape of the chair on the floorboards of the cabinet as it was pushed backwards, and then it sounded as though the chair had fallen over. This was followed by what sounded to Bertie like two or three unsteady footsteps. After a moment there was more coughing, though this time it sounded muffled. Then there was silence.

For a long while they all sat waiting. Eventually Professor Sedgeworth spoke.

"I do believe that something is amiss, my lady."

"I must agree," murmured Dr. Price.

"Open the cabinet!" snapped Austin.

Bertie agreed that something was not right. He murmured his assent.

"Very well." Reluctantly, it seemed, Lady Marlborough acquiesced. "Professor, perhaps you would be kind enough to turn up the gas?"

As the light once again flooded the room, Dr. Price moved forward to open the cabinet doors. He paused briefly, looking towards his hostess. She nodded and he pulled open the twin doors. The chair lay on its back where it had fallen. The cabinet was empty.

"And he never did come back?" asked Inspector Moss.

Bertie, Nellie, Arnold and the inspector sat around the Hawkins's breakfast table the morning after the séance. Isobel moved about refilling teacups and listening to what was said.

"Not a sign of him," said Bertie. "Not like last time, when he suddenly popped up again as though nothing had happened."

"How long did you all wait?" asked Nellie, sipping her tea.

"Well over an hour. No one liked to leave. Her ladyship seemed quite disconcerted. The time before, when he disappeared, I almost got the impression that she was expecting him to return. This time she seemed most surprised . . . and not a little over-wrought."

"Did you examine the cabinet?" Moss asked.

Bertie nodded. "As much as we were able. Lady Marlborough didn't want us to interfere with it too much, in case that somehow jeopardized Prince Honoré's reappearance. But the four of us – the gentlemen – did go over it as much as we were able."

"So what are you going to do now, Bertie?" asked Arnold, helping himself to the last slice of toast.

"This afternoon I have to return to Kingston House. Maurice Austin suggested that we get hold of this fellow Maskelyne and prevail upon him to go with us and look at the cabinet."

"Sounds like a good idea," said Nellie.

The inspector nodded. "My sergeant was telling me about this Maskelyne. It seems that

Sergeant Toby Gilmore likes to visit the music halls once in a wee while. He says that he saw this stage performer doing just what your prince was up to, only more so. He'd be tied up and put inside this contraption and then you'd hear music and banging and a guitar playing. Then they'd open the thing and he wasna' there. Completely vanished, according to Gilmore. They closed it again . . . bang, bang, bang on a tambourine and when they opened it again, there he was right as rain! Amazing, according to the sergeant."

"Cor! Magic!"

"I'd like to go with you, Bertram. If I may?" continued the inspector. "We might regard this as a missing person, would you not say – though the police have not yet been notified, if so?"

Bertie nodded. "Good idea, Campbell. Of course, whether or not her ladyship will like that I don't know."

"Well, we'll cross that bridge when we come to it. She's agreed to this Maskelyne person?"

"Reluctantly, it seems to me, but yes. I think the professor pressured her into accepting that something definite had to be done. And she did seem at a loss herself."

At the pre-arranged time two carriages descended upon Kingston House. Professor Sedgeworth and Dr. Price shared a growler while the inspector and Bertie were squeezed into a hansom. Inspector Moss re-introduced himself to the professor and the doctor, but was still reluctant to reveal Bertie as a tool of Scotland Yard.

"I thought we had seen the last of you, inspector, when you arrested our Miss Dobson," said Dr. Price, in none too friendly a fashion.

"Aye, well . . . it seems Lady Marlborough's home is some sort of a magnet for disturbances, would you not say?"

"What brought you into this particular case then?" asked the professor. "If indeed a 'case' it is."

"I heard – indirectly, I might say – of the apparent disappearance of your medium. Since he is one of the witnesses to the murder of Captain Grimsby, I would certainly like to determine what has happened to him."

"I thought Maskelyne was supposed to be here," said Bertie.

"I understand he is being brought by Mr. Austin. I'm sure they will arrive momentarily," said the professor. "Shall we go on in?"

They were greeted at the door by the Parker, Lady Marlborough's butler.

"Her ladyship is indisposed, gentlemen, but she has instructed me to lead you through to the library," he said, as the maid saw to their hats and coats.

They trailed after him, through the ante-room – now devoid of refreshments – and into the library where the cabinet stood as they remembered it.

"Please avail yourself of the . . . of the 'facilities'," said Parker, looking askance at the cabinet. "Should you require any assistance, the bell-pull will immediately bring a footman to you."

"One moment, my man," said the inspector.

The butler drew himself up to his full height – a head taller than Inspector Moss – and looked down on the policeman.

"How did this cabinet get in here? I wouldna' think that our wee medium had it in him to move the thing all by himself."

"A good point, inspector," said Dr. Price. "I hadn't thought about that."

"No, sir," responded the butler. "Two of the below-stairs staff would have seen to that. I believe it was the coachman and the stable-boy, sir,"

"Why them?" asked Bertie.

"This – apparatus – was accommodated in the stables when not in use, sir."

"I see."

"I'd like to have a word with your two lads," said Moss. "Get them up here, if you would."

"Very good, sir."

When the butler had left, the four of them approached the cabinet and appraised it. Professor Sedgeworth moved inside it and studied the side and rear walls, running his hand along them to see if there were any cracks. Bertie went to the back, where it abutted the wall of the library. Dr. Price and the inspector took a slow tour of the outside of the cabinet and looked closely at the doors.

"It's tight against the back wall," said Bertie. "I've always been a little suspicious of that area and have checked it before. But it looks fine to me."

There was a knock at the door and two men came in, respectfully touching their hands to their forelocks.

"George Wilson, coachman, sirs, and this 'ere's Charlie Stubbs, stable-boy. Stand up straight, Charlie! Mr. Parker says as 'ow you wants to ask us questions?" He was a short, burly man with a red face, thin blond hair, and three chins. His eyes darted around the room and wouldn't meet those of the four gentlemen. He shifted uneasily from one foot to the other. The stable boy was tall and skinny and gawked at all four of them. He held a cap squashed in his hands. He quickly ran his sleeve across his nose and then stood slightly behind the coachman.

Bertie let the inspector lead the questioning.

"Aye, lads. As I understand it, you were responsible for building this unit and putting it up here in the library?"

"Yessir."

"What can you tell us about its construction?" asked the professor, not wanting to leave it all to Scotland Yard.

"Beg pardon, sir?"

"The way it was put together," said Bertie. "How did you build it?"

"'twer already built, sir, in a manner o' speaking," put in the stable boy. "Weren't it, Mr. Wilson?"

"Aye." The coachman nodded. "We just brung the sides and things up 'ere from the stables and Miss Drury told us how to join the bits together, like."

"Miss Drury?" asked Moss.

"The lady's maid," said the coachman.

"Ah!" said the professor, as though all was now made clear.

There was a tap on the door, which the two men had left open, and the butler came in.

"Mr. Austin and Mr. Maskelyne, sirs," he announced. Maurice Austin and Nevil Maskelyne came in on the butler's heels.

"Ah! Maskelyne! Am I glad to see you," said the professor. The butler left the room.

"You still need us, sirs?" asked the coachman.

"Oh, aye." The inspector waved them into a corner. "Just hold on there. We'll be getting back to you, never fear."

"So this is the cabinet?" Maskelyne wasted no time on introductions but advanced on the centerpiece. He stood in front of it, one hand cupping his chin, and looked hard at its overall dimensions. "Have we measured it at all?" He didn't wait for an answer but lifted what Bertie had taken to be a cane from his side. It was a folding carpenter's rule. "Does someone have a piece of paper? We need to make a note of what we find."

Dr. Price quickly found a sheet of paper and a pencil and, resting the paper on a book pulled from a library shelf, stood ready to record what was found. Maskelyne measured the outside from the front to where it abutted the library wall and then the inside depth. There was a difference of twenty inches.

"That's . . . that's unbelievable," said the professor. "You can't tell that from simply looking at it."

Dr. Price moved to various positions to observe and compare.

"It's an illusion," explained Maskelyne. "If you as the audience, as it were, look from in front, there is nothing to give you the perspective that would show that small a difference in depth."

"So what does this mean, then?" asked Inspector Moss, his brows knit together.

"I presume it indicates a false back, does it not?" asked Bertie. "Somewhere where the medium could hide."

"A bit cramped," said the inspector.

"But room enough." Maskelyne checked the dimensions across the width of the cabinet and found them normal. "With the front doors closed, the medium can secrete himself behind the false back and to all intents and purposes he has disappeared."

"How does he get behind this false back?" asked Professor Sedgeworth. "I could find no cracks in the middle of that back panel that would indicate a secret door."

"No, you wouldn't." Maskelyne strode to the back of the cabinet and pointed to the two inside corners, where the back met the sides. "There is no door or means of opening in the center. The whole of the back of the cabinet moves as one. It is hinged down one corner and swings open and closed to click together at the other corner. Wait a moment. Let me find the latch."

He ran his hand up and down the inside corner of the cabinet itself, first on one side and then on the other. Bertie suddenly heard the faintest click and the back panel moved out very slightly.

"Well, I'm . . . By Jove!" exclaimed the professor.

The six of them gathered close, with the coachman and stable boy standing up tight against the front of the cabinet and staring in. Maskelyne slipped his hand behind the exposed edge and pulled the panel open.

As the interior was exposed Maurice Austin gave a shout, echoed by Dr. Price. A body, that had been held upright by the close proximity of the rear panel, slid to the floor and rolled onto its back.

"My God! It's a woman!" gasped Dr. Price.

"It's Miss Drury," cried the coachman. "It's Lady Marlborough's lady's maid!"

*Chapter Seventeen*

As Maurice Austin and Nevil Maskelyne drove away in a hansom, a four-wheeler pulled in and came to a stop outside Kingston House. Sergeant Gilmore, an elderly man, and two uniformed constables got out. They hurried up the path to the door which was immediately opened by the butler. The two uniformed men stationed themselves outside the door; Gilmore and the other man went inside.

"Doctor Wright," greeted Inspector Moss, as the gentleman with Sergeant Gilmore entered the library. "We have a possible murder victim for you to look at."

Dr. Wright was not to be hurried. He removed his overcoat and top hat and thrust it at the hovering butler, who stepped back and signaled a similarly hovering maid to take it. She had tried to relieve both men of their outer garments when they first came in but Sergeant Gilmore had barreled his way straight through to the crime scene, refusing to be delayed. He now, also, relinquished his coat and bowler hat. The maid bobbed a curtsey and melted away, followed by the butler.

"What do we have?" asked the doctor, looking about him as though he might find the victim in one of the chairs around the room.

"Here, doctor. In the cabinet," said Dr. Price. "I have ascertained that she is indeed deceased."

Dr. Wright fumbled to extricate his pince-nez from his pocket and clipped them on his nose, studying the tall figure before him. "And who might you be, sir, to presume such a thing?"

"I am a medical man, sir. Dr. William Price of Harley Street."

"Harley Street? Hrmph! You quacks there are all for the golden guinea, if am not mistaken."

Bertie watched the exchange with some amusement but was concerned that Scotland Yard's own doctor had not yet even bothered to look at the victim. He caught the inspector's eye and raised his eyebrows enquiringly. Moss seemed to take the hint.

"The victim is right here, doctor, if you'd be so kind as to take a look."

The white-haired medical man gave Dr. Price a final glare and then at last turned his attention to the lady's maid, still lying on the floor of the cabinet. Dr. Price seemed to Bertie to take no umbrage and, with a slight shrug to the professor, moved away to stand beside the fireplace where he extracted his silver cigarette-case and lit a cigarette.

"Shot? Stabbed? Strangled? What's the story, Moose?"

"That's *Moss*, doctor. Inspector Campbell Moss. We don't know what the story is . . . that's why we called for you." He glanced back at Bertie and raised his own eyebrows, shaking his head.

The old man thrust out his hand for the inspector to steady him, and then slowly lowered himself to kneel beside the corpse.

"No blood, it would seem." He felt for a pulse and then peered at the woman's eyes, pressing back the lids. He drew a pencil out of his pocket and thrust it into the victim's mouth, doing his best to look at her throat. Again sticking out his hand for Moss's help, the doctor pulled himself back up onto his feet, breathing heavily.

"We'll have to get her over to the station. Where are we?" He looked about him as though he might recognize landmarks.

"Kensington, sir," volunteered Sergeant Gilmore. "Nearest station is Division T."

"Thank you, sergeant," said the inspector. "Go and alert those two men you brought with you. Find yourselves a barrow – there's probably one in the stables . . ?" He looked enquiringly at the coachman.

"Yessir. We've got two or three good'uns."

"Then get one of them and take this body over to T Division. And you be careful, Gilmore. This is – was – a young lady. Treat her with respect. Do I make myself clear, sergeant?"

"Oh, yes, sir. Have no fear, sir."

"We do 'ave the trap, sir, if'n that would be more fitting?" the coachman suggested.

"Yes. Good. See to it, Gilmore."

"So what now?" asked the professor, as Sergeant Gilmore hurried out to get his men. Professor Sedgeworth pulled out his pocket watch and studied it. "Now that we have opened the mysterious cabinet, I must be getting back to my study, inspector. The only question that I have is, so where is Prince Honoré? We have discovered Lady Marlborough's maid, who had not disappeared – so far as we knew – but have failed to discover the good prince."

"Yes," agreed Dr. Price. "That's what I was wondering. Where is our turbaned friend? I quite expected to find him hiding in the back of the cabinet."

"You sort this out for yourselves," said Dr. Wright, taking a pinch of snuff and then sneezing. "It has nothing to do with me. I will get on back and examine that young lady. I'll let you know what I find, Ross." He shuffled out of the room, almost bumping into the butler who was hovering outside the door.

Inspector Moss looked at Bertie. "I was wondering about your medium myself," he said.

Bertie tugged at his mustache and looked thoughtful. "I have a theory on that, Campbell," he said. "But we'll have to wait a short while, I think."

"Well, you keep us informed," said Dr. Price, joining with the professor and making for the door. "I have patients to see. I can't waste any more time."

The Sergeant returned with the two constables. The coachman and his assistant had meanwhile removed one of the cabinet doors from its hinges and laid it on the ground. The three policemen lifted the body of the maid onto it and then they followed the coachman and stable-boy out of the room. The inspector called for the butler.

"You rang, sir?"

"I need to speak with Lady Marlborough," he said.

"Her ladyship expressed her regrets, but . . ."

"This is a murder investigation," snapped the inspector. "In fact it now looks as though it has become two murder investigations, together with a disappearance. I think you had better advise her ladyship that she needs to make herself available . . . right away."

Bertie had not seen his friend so forceful before and was duly impressed. The more so when Lady Marlborough rapidly made an appearance.

"Really, inspector, . . ." she started to say.

"May I enquire, where is your personal maid, Lady Marlborough?" he asked, his eyes fixed on her face.

Bertie thought he saw her eyes blink and then narrow very slightly. He wondered if the inspector noticed it and what store he might put by it.

"My maid?"

The inspector said nothing.

"Why – why she is . . . not here."

"And where might she be, my lady?"

Lady Marlborough moved to the fireplace and unnecessarily straightened one or two of the china figures that decorated the mantel. She seemed to straighten her shoulders, as though making up her mind to something, and then turned to again face the policeman.

"As a matter of fact, inspector, I do not know where Lisbeth is. She did not attend on me last night – much to my inconvenience – and has not been seen this morning. I have had to call upon one of my other maids. It is quite unlike Lisbeth. I shall speak sharply to her when she returns." Her eyes lit upon Bertie. "Mr. Hawkins! What, might I ask, are you doing here?"

"Mr. Hawkins is with me, as it were, Lady Marlborough," said Moss, keeping his eyes fixed on her face. "I can vouch for him. Now, to keep to the subject in hand, might I also enquire of your house guest, Prince Honoré? When did you last see him?"

"As I believe you are aware, inspector, it was at last evening's séance. He entered the cabinet, which you see before you, and did not come out. That, I believe, is what brought you here this afternoon."

"Mmm." The inspector nodded and turned back to look at the cabinet and it's open false back. "Has your butler advised you of what we discovered in the back of this cabinet, my lady?"

She looked at him hard, silent for the moment, and then she said "Yes. As you have surmised, Parker apprised me of the situation. I am distraught that Lisbeth was found in such circumstances and am at a loss to understand it."

"As are we, my lady. As are we. I think you might see now why it is important that we speak with your Prince Honoré?"

"Should he return, inspector, I will see that you are informed."


"Are you ready, Bertram?"

Inspector Moss stood just inside the doorway where Isobel had brought him and looked at Bertie, who had come to his feet and was slipping on his jacket. The remains of breakfast were spread across the kitchen table where Nellie still sat nursing her steaming cup.

"Good morning, Campbell," she said. "Can you stop for a cup of tea, at least?"

"Ah, would that I could, Nell, but I'm afraid I dares na' keep old Doctor Wright waiting. He's good enough to come in of a Sunday morning, as it is. I wouldna' want to spoil his day altogether."

"We've got kidneys," cried Isobel, lifting the lid off the dish.

"Isobel! The inspector has said that he cannot stay," admonished Nellie.

Isobel, blushing, replaced the lid and swung away to face the sink.

"Aye! I wish that I could." Inspector Moss dragged his eyes away from the kidneys, scrambled egg, bacon and toast.

Bertie gave Nellie a quick peck on the cheek and then joined the policeman. Together they went up the stairs, where Bertie shrugged into his overcoat.

"I have a cab waiting, Bertram. Doctor Wright did his autopsy at the Kensington station so that's where we'll be going."

"Good of you to let me join you, Campbell," said Bertie, as they went out and climbed into the hansom.

On their way to Kensington they went over the events of the previous day: finding the secret back panel of the cabinet and discovering the body of the lady's maid.

"My thinking is," said Moss, "that it was the prince who stabbed Captain Grimsby and that the lady's maid found out it was him and so she had to be silenced."

Bertie said nothing for a moment. Then, "The motive for the Grimsby murder, Campbell?"

Moss was silent.

"I agree that it would make a nice tidy package," Bertie continued. "Catch the prince and you've got both murders solved. But I have a feeling it's not going to be as easy as that."

"Easy?" Moss laughed. "There isna' anything easy about it, Bertram. We have nay clue as to where this prince character might be. I think we can agree that Lady Marlborough is as much in the dark as we are where our little turbaned friend is concerned."

"Well, I have a theory," said Bertie, hesitantly.

"You have? Aye, you always seem to come up with something, I'll grant you that, Bertram. Well this is no time for holding back, lad! Out with it!"

Bertie shook his head. "Not yet, Campbell. I may well be all wrong. We'll find out soon enough."

They continued in silence, eventually stopping outside the Kensington Police Station, where the blue light shone through the lingering morning mist.

The desk sergeant rang a small handbell to summon a constable, who led the two men back and down a flight of stone steps to the basement.

"In 'ere, inspector," the constable said, tapping on the first door they came to and throwing it open without waiting for a response. He then did a fast turnabout and hurried away back up the stairs.

The room was wide and low ceilinged. White tiles covered the lower four feet of the walls. There was a drain in the middle of the cement floor. Three very large metal sinks stood in a line across the rear half of the room. Worn and stained panels of wood lay across each sink. The far end one bore a sheet-covered body.

Close to the door stood a tall accountant's desk with a stool drawn up to it. Perched on the stool was Doctor Wright. He was studying a thick medical book but looked up when Bertie and Moss entered the room.

"Ah, Ross! There you are. Didn't think you were coming."

"Oh yes, doctor. And it's *Moss*. Inspector Moss."

"Of course it is." The old man eased himself down off the stool and moved towards the covered body. They followed him, though Bertie noticed that the inspector seemed to hang back as the doctor pulled back the sheet.

"Something of a mystery, gentlemen," said the doctor, as though addressing a group of medical students. "No puncture marks. In other words, no stabbing. No signs of strangulation or suffocation of any sort. No trauma. No head wounds or broken limbs. No gunshot wounds. What, then, are we to make of it?" He looked at each of them expectantly.

"All right, doctor," said the inspector. "What are we to make of it?"

"What about poisoning?" asked Bertie, tugging at his mustache.

"Good! Well done . . . what is your name, young man?"

"Hawkins, sir."

"Well done, Hawthorn. Yes. It only leaves poisoning. Or so I believe."

"Poisoning?" Inspector Moss scratched the top of his head. "What sort of poison, doctor?"

"Ah! Now that is the question, Ross. What sort of poison? Well, I can tell you the *type*. Our victim exhibited rawness of the throat. She had slight vomiting and some diarrhea. Almost certainly she sustained abdominal pain. Headache possibly. Then convulsions, almost certainly quickly followed by death."

"And just what would have caused that?"

"What indeed? Whatever it was, it was as toxic as arsenic."

"You mean, you dinna' have any idea just what it was?"

"Oh, I have some idea, all right. A tubor is my guess."

"A tubor?" said Bertie. "What exactly do you mean by that, doctor?"

"I was just looking in the medical pharmacopeia when you came in," said the doctor, pulling the sheet back up over the dead woman's face and then turning to the desk. "They've started labeling things in Latin, if you can believe it? *Solanum tuberoscum* for the good Lord's sake! But we old timers stick to the common names. Not so likely to go amiss then, am I right, Moss?"

"And what is the common name for this tubor?" asked Bertie.

"Oh, didn't I say? Why, potato, young man. Potato!"

"Potato?" The inspector looked as though he couldn't believe it.

Bertie thought about it. "There was a potato salad served at Lady Marlborough's. But *I* had it as did several others."

"How can a potato kill you?" gasped Moss.

"Oh, quite easily," replied Doctor Wright. "Not uncommon in the East End, I might say. They grub up the leftovers from the greengrocer and dig into garbage. If the potatoes are green or full of unripe sprouts, then they can become fatal."

"But Lady Marlborough would never use anything like that," gasped Bertie. "And as I said, I had the potato salad myself."

The doctor shrugged. "Well there you are. Take it or leave it, Floss. That's what is going into my report."

Bertie stood uncertainly for a moment. "Doctor! There is something else I would like to ask you about your report."

The inspector narrowed his eyes and studied Bertie, but said nothing.

"What can you tell us about how the young lady was dressed?" Bertie continued.

"How she was dressed?" spluttered the inspector. "We *know* how she was dressed, Bertram. What are you talking about?"

"I repeat, doctor," insisted Bertie. "Exactly how was she dressed?"

"Well now, young man. That is a good question." He turned to his report, in a green folder on the desk, and thumbed through it. "She was attired somewhat unorthodoxly, even for this modern generation. When I removed her skirt I found that she was wearing a man's trousers underneath it, together with a man's patent pumps."

Inspector Moss pressed forward to see the report. "What are you talking about?"

"Did she, by any chance, have a length of white material about her person anywhere, doctor?" Bertie asked.

"As a matter of fact she did, wound about her waist."

"What are you saying?" Moss was totally at a loss. He looked from Bertie to the doctor and back again. "What is going on here, Bertram?"

Bertie nodded, tugging thoughtfully on his mustache. "It's as I suspected, Campbell. I think we have solved a mystery here . . . the disappearance of Prince Honoré." Moss still looked perplexed so

Bertie continued. "There was no 'Prince Honoré'. It was the lady's maid in disguise."

"You are going to have to spell it out for me, Bertram." Inspector Moss spotted a bench by the wall and sank down on it. He scratched the top of his head and sucked on his mustache, slowly shaking his head in disbelief.

"Prince Honoré and Lisbeth what-ever-her-name-was, the lady's maid, were one and the same," explained Bertie. When the medium – our prince – slipped back into the secret space, he undid his turban and wound the material around his waist. He then dropped the top of his jacket – I wondered why it was so bulky and untailored – and it became a passable skirt. Enough to fit a maid who was moving around. With the turban gone the woman's hair was revealed, again befitting a female and in contrast to the male medium."

"What about the mustache?" asked Moss. "He did have that wee mustache, you remember?"

"Yes. And I wouldn't mind betting that we'll find the false whiskers either on the floor in the cabinet or perhaps even in the trouser pocket?" He looked toward the doctor, who had been listening in fascination. "Perhaps also the green 'jewel' worn at the front of the turban."

"I have not been through any pockets yet. You may look for yourselves, if you wish."

"Now that I think of it," said Bertie, "the evening that the medium first disappeared from his cabinet, I did notice Lady Marlborough's maid come out of the séance room. But then, other servants were about by that time so it didn't really register. He – she – would change in the cabinet and then slip out when no one was looking, to appear again later as the prince. This last time she must have realized that something was wrong and tried to quickly make the change and then hide behind the false back before she collapsed."

## *Chapter Eighteen*

Inspector Moss sat at the Hawkins's lunch table and shook his head.

"I still canna' take it in, Bertram," he said. "How could all of you – all intelligent people, or so I've been led to believe – accept that wee slip of a girl as a man? And a prince, at that?"

"There is quite a movement these days," said Nellie, serving up the Lancashire hot pot and suet dumplings, "for some women to dress themselves like men. I don't understand it myself."

"I think the fact that she presented herself as a somewhat mysterious foreign potentate helped her get away with it," said Bertie. "The turban and the loose fitting clothes all distracted from the details of the person. It was noted that the voice was somewhat high-pitched, but it wasn't that extraordinary."

"Tommy Turnbull . . ." started Isobel, from the foot of the table.

"Isobel!"

"I was just going to say as 'ow 'e once pretended to be a girl, Mrs. 'awkins," the maid's voice trailing off.

"Go on, Bertie," said Nellie.

Arnold, sitting opposite Inspector Moss, leaned over to Isobel and, in a whisper heard clearly by everyone, said "You must tell me later, Isobel. How could he do that, I wonder?"

"As I was saying," continued Bertie, shaking his head as he looked at his brother-in-law, "the voice was accepted by the group. I think, too, that the fact of Lady Marlborough vouching for her medium carried a lot of weight."

"There is another thing." The inspector paused while he chewed on a piece of mutton and then continued. "Did Lady Marlborough know that her maid was also Prince Honoré?"

"Surely she would have to, would she not?" asked Nellie.

"Not necessarily," said Bertie. "It would certainly seem the most likely, but the maid could have got away with it. I imagine that, as the prince, she kept out of the way most of the time. Her ladyship did seem to be somewhat in awe of her medium."

"Well, we'll see what we can find, Bertram," said Moss. "I willna' disturb her ladyship on a Sunday but tomorrow I must go and talk with her staff . . . the cook in particular."

"Her ladyship wouldn't want to risk losing a good cook," commented Nellie. "People kill to get a good . . . Oh! What am I saying?"

Everyone smiled.

"Well anyway, everyone who does any cooking," added Nellie, "knows that green potatoes, and especially those eyes in them, are dangerous."

"Then how could that get into a salad, except through the cook?" asked Arnold, concentrating on his dumpling.

"The thing is," said Bertie, "we may have solved the disappearance of Prince Honoré, but we still have *two* murders to solve. Captain Grimsby and now Prince Honoré, or Lisbeth Drury. We know the murder weapons: a hatpin and a potato." He laughed. "That sounds almost comical, doesn't it?"

The others chuckled. Isobel laughed too loudly.

"There will obviously be no more séances," continued Bertie, "so I can be a little more obvious in my enquiring."

"Me too," added Arnold.

"Aye. Well dinna' forget, Bertram, that this is a Scotland Yard investigation. Much as I appreciate your help, you willna' be getting under foot, I trust?"

Bertie looked surprised. "Under foot, Campbell? Why, of course not." He winked at Nellie. "However, if you are going to question the below stairs staff, I would rather like to go with you."

Moss looked at him sternly. "You mustna' interfere, Bertram. It is my investigation."

"Oh, absolutely."

"Well . . . all right then."

Lady Constance Marlborough was leaving Kingston House in her carriage when Bertie, Inspector Moss and Sergeant Gilmore arrived there on Monday morning. As the growler pulled in front of the house, the brougham pulled out of the driveway and drove away.

"What now, Campbell? Do we still go ahead?"

The inspector tugged on his mustache for a moment and then nodded his head. "Aye. This might be a good thing, Bertram. With her ladyship away, the staff might be more open. As a policeman looking into a murder, they canna' decline to speak with me. Come along. Let's see what we can determine."

The three of them walked around to the kitchen door at the back of the house and, after knocking, opened it and entered.

"What is this then?" demanded Parker, the butler, hurrying forward.

"Inspector Moss, Scotland Yard."

"Yes, I am well aware of who you are. What do you mean by walking in like this?"

"If you recall, my good man, we are investigating a murder. Now then, would you be so kind as to assemble the staff so that I might talk to them? I have some questions to ask."

Bertie thought that Parker looked extremely annoyed but he called to the housekeeper, Mrs. Acton, to gather the staff in the kitchen. There was a lot of running around, with maids and footmen calling on other maids and footmen, but eventually all were assembled standing along one wall of the big kitchen. Sergeant Gilmore stationed himself alongside the kitchen sink, facing the line, and opened his notebook ready to record the proceedings.

"I can't just stop what I'm doing," announced the cook, Mrs. Mayhew, speaking over her shoulder from where she stood at the kitchen range. "I 'ave to 'ave lunch ready for when 'er ladyship returns."

"That's all right," said the inspector. "I can ask you questions from there."

"The coachman has departed," announced the butler. "If you have questions for him then you must await his return."

"Anyone else not accounted for?" asked Bertie.

The butler looked at the housekeeper.

"Young Vicky Braithwaite has her morning off this morning. She will be leaving any minute," said Mrs. Acton. "You can catch her as she goes out. Everyone else is here,"

"Good." The inspector surveyed them all, sweeping his gaze along the line as though they were part of a police identification line-up. "Now then. You are all aware, I'm sure, of the murder of Miss Drury on Friday evening?" They nodded their heads.

"You don't fink we did it, do you?" demanded a sullen-looking chambermaid. The maid next to her dug her with her elbow.

"That is what I am here to determine," said Moss, looking sternly at the girl. "I need to know who, besides Cook here, prepared or laid out the food for Lady Marlborough's guests on Friday evening?"

"Mrs. Mayhew was in charge, of course," responded Mrs. Acton, the housekeeper. The cook waved a wooden spoon and continued with what she was doing. "Two housemaids would have taken up the food and the footmen would have seen to the presentation.  Mr. Parker, of course, would have looked after the wine."

"We are especially interested in the salads," said Bertie.

The cook swung around. "Why? What was wrong with my salads?"

"You prepared those yourself?" Bertie continued.

"Just the first one or two then Milly took over, 'cos I 'ad other things to prepare." The cook dismissed him and went back to her work on the stove.

"Which of you is Milly?" asked the inspector.

A frail-looking girl with a slight cast to her eyes stepped forward uncertainly. She was biting her lip, Bertie noticed. Sergeant Gilmore made a note of her name.

"Don't be afraid, Millie," Bertie said. "We just need you to answer the inspector's questions."

"I just did what I was told, sir," she said, her voice barely above a whisper.

"I'm sure you did."

"Who decided on potato salad?" asked the inspector, directing his question at the broad back of the cook.

"Her ladyship always draws up the menus," said the housekeeper, "especially for her Friday night gatherings." The sergeant scribbled.

"And who prepared the potatoes?"

"Cook," said Millie, her eyes wide.

Mrs. Mayhew, the cook, turned to face the inspector once again, waving the wooden spoon and using it to emphasize what she was saying. "There ain't nothin' wrong with my 'taters! I'm very careful with 'em, as Mrs. Acton 'ere will tell you. There is certain fings you do need to watch – like watercress. 'Oo would 'ave thought that watercress could do for you? But when 'er ladyship asks for them little watercress sandwiches, I tells 'er: 'that stuff comes from Camden Town, my lady, and 'oo knows 'ow much sewage has made 'em so green.' No. I am very partic'lar about my veggies, I am."

It was a big speech for Mrs. Mayhew and having delivered it she swung back to the stove and started banging lids on pots with great ferocity.

Just then the door from the back stairs opened and a plump young woman muffled up in a lamb's-wool cape with a well-worn rabbit-fur collar, appeared. On her head was an overlarge fur-felt walking hat secured with hatpins. She hesitated and looked at the assemblage before starting towards the outside door.

"One moment, Vicky," said Mrs. Acton. "Inspector, this is another of our housemaids, Vicky Braithwaite."

"Did you have anything to do with the food preparation on Friday evening?" asked Moss. The girl shook her head, looking frightened. "All right.

No questions for you then." The inspector waved her on.

Bertie stepped forward and opened the outside door. "I'll be right back, Campbell," he said and followed the maid out.

"'Ere! What you want?" Vicky the maid looked suspiciously at Bertie as he fell into step beside her, leaving the house.

"Don't be afraid," said Bertie. "My name is Mr. Hawkins and I am working with Inspector Moss on this murder case."

"You a policeman, then?"

"No. No, Vicky, I am not. I am a private enquiry agent. That means that I do not work for Scotland Yard but I do my own investigating and, if I turn up anything worthwhile, I then share it with the inspector."

"So what you want wif me?"

Bertie indicated her voluminous hat. "I was intrigued by your hatpin, Vicky. That's a very fine one for a young housemaid to sport, wouldn't you say?"

She stopped and turned to face him. She glanced quickly left and right, as though to ascertain that they were alone, and then looked him in the eye. "Why shouldn't I 'ave a nice 'atpin?" She tipped her head up defiantly.

"No reason at all," said Bertie, quietly. "I wonder if I might have a look at it?"

Reluctantly she reached up and, steadying her hat with one hand, pulled out the largest of the pins securing it to her hair. She didn't say anything.

Bertie took it and studied it. It was in the form of a beautiful ivory teardrop-pearl nestled in an elongated silver-filigree cone, atop an eight inch, gold-plated, brass hat pin. He turned it around and around and then looked at the girl.

Bertie didn't say anything but Vicky finally blurted out "All right! So I found it! But I didn't steal it!" She was most vehement. "I *found* it . . . so why shouldn't I 'ave it?"

"Where did you find it?"

"It was thrown away . . . laying in the grate of the fireplace. I could 'ave swept it up with the cinders, but I spotted it and thought as 'ow I'd like it . . . so I took it." She remained defiant.

"When and where was this, Vicky? What room was it in? Do you remember when?"

"It was after one of 'er ladyship's see-ances; a Friday. About four weeks ago now, I fink. This is the first time as I've worn it."

"So it was in the library?"

"Yeh! Yeh, now I fink about it, it was the night that military gentleman 'ad 'is 'eart attack."

"Captain Grimsby?"

"Yeh."

Bertie turned the hatpin over and over in his hand, looking at all parts of it. "Vicky, I'm afraid I am going to have to take this. It may turn out to be a murder weapon. It's possible you may be allowed to have it back after . . ."

"Murder? Ew! No fanks! I don't fink so. You keep the bloody fing!" She turned and stamped away. Bertie let her go.

"So what makes you so certain that this is the hatpin that was used to kill Captain Grimsby?"

Inspector Moss sat, with his sergeant at his side, facing Bertie as the growler trundled along Knightsbridge on its way back to Scotland Yard.

"There were one or two things that struck me," said Bertie. "First, of course, was noticing such a fine, obviously expensive, hatpin on the head of a lowly housemaid."

Moss grunted and nodded. Sergeant Gilmore looked sharply at his superior.

"After I came to examine it, I think I can tell you exactly what happened . . . and who killed Captain Grimsby."

"Sergeant!" said Moss, sharply. "Your notebook, if you please."

Gilmore had it out and began scribbling in it as soon as Bertie continued speaking.

"It was when I asked Vicky – the housemaid – to let me see the hatpin that I got my first clue. She reached up and steadied her hat with one hand while she withdrew the pin with the other."

"So what is so extraordinary about that?" asked Moss.

"Nothing," replied Bertie. "And that is the point. If Miss Dobson was the murderer, as you charged, then she would have taken out her own hatpin and would probably have used two hands to do it . . ."

"Not necessarily."

"No, not necessarily. But if she wanted to replace it in her hat, after stabbing Grimsby, she would *definitely* have needed two hands – one to steady the hat and the other to place the pin. This she could have done easily and almost automatically, since it would be a normal, regular action. She would not have thrown it away."

"Go on."

"If someone else was the murderer, they would have been able to reach up, even in the darkness, and grasp the pearl end of the pin and draw it out, without disturbing the hat, but it would have been extremely difficult to replace the pin. In trying to do so, they might have stabbed Miss Dobson in the face, the head, the ear . . ."

"Go on."

"So they drew it out, stabbed their victim, and then tossed the hatpin in the general direction of the fireplace, where it landed in the gate and where Vicky found it next morning."

"Anything else?"

"If you examine the hatpin where the ferrule, the filigree, meets the shaft of the pin, you can make out a dark stain that might well be dried blood."

"So who was this mysterious murderer, Bertram? Who took Miss Dobson's hatpin and then cast it aside?"

"I would suggest that it had to be someone sitting directly across the table from the Captain, which really rules out Miss Dobson and Miss Bell. I think it was the medium Prince Honoré, and I may know why. A couple of people said that they heard the trumpet fall over. I think that our medium, while pretending to be in a trance, reached across the table, knocking over the trumpet in the dark, drew out the hatpin, stabbed Captain Grimsby, and then threw away the murder weapon."

There was silence for some minutes as the inspector digested what Bertie had proposed.

"If . . . and I do say 'if', Bertram . . . that is what happened, then we are still left with our most recent murder. Who, in turn, poisoned Prince Honoré?"

"I have an inkling about that," said Bertie. "And also about the motive for the Grimsby murder. But I need to do a little more enquiring." He smiled at his friend. "I'm sure you can understand that, Campbell."


Snooky Thompson was laying-out the colonel's evening clothes when Bertie again found him at the Army and Navy Club. The batman hardly looked up when Bertie tapped on the open door and peered in.

"'Allo, my old son! I rather thought you'd be back."

"May I come in?"

Snooky waved an expansive hand. "Be my guest. 'is nibs the colonel is still 'olding up the bar downstairs, so we've got a few minutes. Take the weight off your plates." He moved a pile of crisp white, folded shirts from a chair and set them on the bed. Bertie closed the door behind him and sat down.

"What can I do you for? 'Awkins, wasn't it?"

"Yes, that's right. Good memory," said Bertie.

"Oh, in my line of work, as it were, I gotta keep the old memory cells working. What was it you wanted? More on Cyril?"

"Indirectly, yes. And I hope your memory is as sharp as you suggest. Tell me, did you ever meet Grimsby's wife, or see a photograph of her?"

"See 'er? Nar! Was before my time, as it were. But a picture, yes, now I put's my mind to it." He sucked on his stringy mustache and gazed off into space, balancing a winged collar in his hand. "Old Cyril did 'ave a photo of 'er 'e once showed me. Real stunner, she was. A dazzler, according to Cyril. Pretty face, I thought. 'e said that she 'ad that deep red 'air – not ginger nor nothing, but the darker sort."

"Auburn?" asked Bertie.

"Yeah! Yeah, I think that's what they calls it. Real stunner. Don't know 'ow Cyril could knock 'er about like 'e did." He returned to setting out the clothes.

"Any idea of her height?"

He shook his head.

"Slim? Heavy set?"

"Oh, slim I'd say. Cyril never went for the meaty ones."

Bertie got up. "Thank you, Mr. Thompson. I thank you very much. That is a great help."

Inspector Moss moved some papers about on his desk, for no apparent purpose that Bertie could see, and then settled back in his chair.

"So you have pieced together more of the puzzle, Bertram?"

"I think so." Bertie moved a pile of *Police Gazette* magazines off the only other chair, set them on the floor, and sat down.

"Well, the first thing I want to know is the same thing you kept asking me – what was the motive? *Why* did the prince kill Grimsby?"

"Do you have that marriage certificate we found in Grimsby's flat?" Bertie asked.

Moss dug into the pile of paperwork on his desk and located a faded blue folder. Opening it, he searched through and extracted a document. "Here it is. Now what?"

"What does it say?"

The inspector pulled out his wire-rimmed spectacles, put them on, and then held the paper almost at arm's length. He frowned at it as he read: "*Marriage Certificate No. 127; When Married: Ten April 1876; Cyril Harold Grimsby, Bachelor, to Jessica Elisabeth Drury, Spinster; Residence at time of Marriage: Machi Bhawan Fort, Lucknow, Awadh Region, India* . . . What do you need to know, Bertram?"

"Does it give a father's name for Jessica?"

The inspector moved the paper back and forth as though to focus on the script. "Father's name for Cyril is Arthur Buchanan Grimsby, listed as a merchant, and for Jessica it's R. Drury, listed as deceased."

Bertie nodded thoughtfully. Moss removed his spectacles and studied his friend.

"What are you thinking, Bertram?"

"Did you notice the girl's name, Campbell?"

He glanced back at the paper. "Jessica Elisabeth Drury . . ." He sat up straight. "Wait a minute! Wait a minute! Elisabeth Drury . . . Lisbeth Drury the lady's maid!"

Bertie nodded. "Exactly. Now do you see why she – as Prince Honoré – would want to kill Grimsby? She was Grimsby's ex-wife. She was suddenly faced with the man who had abused her for years. There he sat, facing her in the dark and not knowing that it was her. I seriously doubt that she set out to kill him; probably just wanted to inflict some very real pain."

The inspector nodded. "I think I can understand that. But tell me, Bertram, what was she doing at Lady Marlborough's in the first place? Why was she dressed as a man and playing the part of a spiritualist medium?"

"Ah!" Bertie gazed up at the portrait of Queen Victoria, gazing unsmilingly down on Inspector Moss's domain. His face grew serious to match hers. "I do have one or two theories, Campbell. I intend to pursue them and, as ever, I will let you know what transpires."

"You are not going to tell me anything now?" Moss looked like a small boy denied his toys.

Bertie shook his head. "Better that I get things as accurately as I can, rather than shoot off in the wrong direction and mislead you . . . and Scotland Yard. No. Have no fear, Campbell. You will be the first to know."

*Chapter Nineteen*

"I think I'm beginning to get to know this place," said Arnold, gazing around at the interior of the Reading Room at the British Museum. "What are we looking for this time, Bertie?"

Bertie lowered a stack of old magazines on to the big oak table and divided them into two piles.

"These are old copies of *The Graphic Times Gazette*. It was only in print for a few years before the *London Illustrated News* started up and out-sold it. But *The Gazette* was the only one at the time that we are interested in."

"And what time would that be, Bertie?"

"I'm guessing about 1840 or 1842 . . . that's when – so far as I can determine – Lady Marlborough was coming out."

Arnold digested this information for a moment before asking, "And why are we interested in her coming out?"

"One step at a time, Arnold." Bertie looked at the dates on the magazines lying on top of the piles. "Now you start with this set for 1839 and I'll start with these for 1840. It was a weekly so there are fifty-two for each year. A lot to look through.

We're looking for any mention of Lady Constance, daughter of the Earl of Marlborough."

They settled down to read, turning pages quickly as they looked through the contents.

"Here's a mention," said Bertie. Arnold stopped what he was looking at and leaned over towards his brother-in-law. Bertie pointed to a picture of three young girls in elaborate crinoline dresses and wide white hats. They all wore white gloves and carried matching parasols. Bertie read the caption: *"Often referred to as 'The Three Graces', inseparable friends Lady Marcia Effington, Lady Sarah Duberin and Lady Constance Marlborough are seen at Kew Gardens, taking the springtime air.* Hmm, that's interesting. There were three close friends." Bertie took his notebook and wrote down the names. "The young ladies usually come out at eighteen years of age. This must be about the year before."

"Is this important, Bertie?"

"I don't know yet, Arnold. But it could be."

They went back to perusing the periodicals. They found a number of mentions and photographs of the three young ladies, always together. Then, in the early spring editions of 1840 there was talk of "The Season" for that year and the preparations of "The Three Graces".

"It seems that they spent a lot of time together at Marston Keep, the ancestral home of the Marlboroughs," Bertie commented. "That's in Wiltshire. Lady Marlborough's older brother is the present Earl."

"Look at this Bertie." Arnold slid an open copy of the magazine across the table. "See? It's the 9 May, 1840, issue,"

"What about it, Arnold?"

"There's mention of two of the ladies – Lady Effington and Lady Duberin – but not of Lady Marlborough."

"Let me see that. Hmm. Now that is strange. Well done, Arnold."

The big man grinned.

"Why do you think that is, Bertie? I thought it said they were always together."

"So it did. Keep looking. See if any mentions after that date are only for those two or if the three are back together again."

But from then on the only mention of the two ladies did not include reference to Lady Marlborough nor give any indication as to why she had disappeared from the social scene.

It probably wasn't a good time to discuss things with Nellie, thought Bertie, as he stood just inside the steam-filled laundry room and watched his wife and the carrot-topped maid-of-all-work manhandle wet sheets and tablecloths and crank them through the mangle. Big pots of water steamed on the nearby kitchen range and flat irons stood ready on the hot plates.

The previous day the two women had laboriously scrubbed the sheets, together with all the clothes and towels, using the well-worn corrugated scrubbing boards. They had exerted their energy on the washing dolly and then further soaked everything overnight. Now they gave the clothes multiple rinsing and ended with the trip through the mangle. Nellie, her blonde ringlets escaping her lace-trimmed cap, used both hands on the wringer handle while Isobel wrestled the linen through the rollers.

They had been blessed with a sunny, if chilly, October day enabling them to hang out the washing on the lines in the back garden. The final step would be the ironing and folding.

"What is it, Bertie?" Nellie kept her eyes on the passage of linen through rollers. "You've been hovering there for half an hour. If you've got something to tell me then please get on with it, otherwise Isobel and I have plenty to keep ourselves occupied."

"No. I was just wondering if you had any opinion, Nell," said Bertie, nervously watching Isobel's fingers come close to the turning rollers.

"On what, Bertie?"

"Last night I told you what we found in the old magazines," he said. "Why would an aristocratic young lady suddenly disappear from the coming out scene; especially after preparing for it so assiduously?"

"What's she coming out off, Mrs. 'awkins?" asked Isobel.

"It's what all the society young ladies do, Isobel. Watch that sheet! Don't let it bunch up."

"How do they do that?"

"They get to meet the Queen. They go to Buckingham Palace, to the Throne Room, and are acknowledged by Her Majesty. They get to wear beautiful gowns and three white ostrich feathers in their hair and . . ."

"Feathers! Cor, I wouldn't like that!"

"Then be thankful that you're not coming out," said Bertie. "Nell, what do you think?"

"It certainly seems strange. Obviously something happened; something came up that meant that she couldn't go through with the ritual."

"Like what?"

Nellie paused in cranking the mangle while Isobel dragged another sheet across to the machine, dripping water all over the floor.

"She wasn't engaged, was she?"

"What? Engaged? What would that have to do with it?"

Nellie started turning the handle again. "Just a thought, Bertram. If she had a gentleman friend, perhaps . . . but no, I'm sure there was nothing like that."

Bertie turned away, his face thoughtful. He had seen no reference to any young man or men in *The Gazette*, and such a magazine ran on gossip. He needed to do some more digging. Waving to his wife – who was too busy to acknowledge him – he went in search of Arnold.

Inspector Moss nudged Sergeant Gilmore. They were standing on the corner of Old Bond Street, across the road from the building on Grafton Street which housed the flat of Chandra Singh. Sergeant Gilmore had been absorbed in studying the toes of his boots. He had never really noticed it before but it seemed to him that the toe of the right boot was a lot more pointed than that of the left boot. Now that he had observed it, he was fascinated by it. When his superior suddenly nudged him with his elbow, Sergeant Gilmore jumped and grunted.

"What?" Moss looked at him, surprised. "You falling asleep standing up now, Gilmore? Come on! Looks like that Kaster fellow Bertram alerted us to is about to pay a visit to our Indian friend."

Gilmore was just in time to see a figure in a fur-collared coat and beaver hat disappear into the front entrance. The sergeant followed the inspector across the road, hopping over a large pile of horse manure as he did so.

As they entered the building they heard the door of the flat on the floor above close.

"Look lively now," said the inspector, starting up the stairs.

They turned right at the landing and proceeded along to the door to Chandra Singh's flat. Guessing that the door would not be locked, since it had just been opened to admit Kaster, Moss turned the handle and flung it back.

"What the . . . ?"

They found themselves in a small room, sparsely furnished. A well worn, scarred table faced the door with a large and seemingly incongruous Wooton desk open against the far wall. There was a fireplace on the adjacent wall. Beyond the table a heavy curtain hung covering a doorway. A worn carpet was on the floor. On the walls were prints and water-color paintings of scenes from India. A poorly executed painting of the Taj Mahal had pride of place over the fireplace.

Chandra Singh – a dark-skinned man in western dress – sat at the table and as the door was thrown back he quickly spread a piece of green velvet cloth over whatever was lying on the table in front of him.

"Who the hell are you to come forcing your way in here?" he cried, coming to his feet.

"I didna' force my way," snapped Moss. "The door was nay locked."

Reinhart Kaster had been sitting in a wooden chair facing Singh. He now also came to his feet.

"Sit yourself down again, Mr. Kaster," said the inspector. "You are part of the reason I am here." He looked at Singh. "You too can sit down, Mr. Sing. Inspector Campbell Moss of Scotland Yard, at your service. Now then." He advanced to the table.

Singh sat down and placed his hands on top of the square of velvet, in what might have been taken for a casual posture. Moss noted the several diamond rings on his fingers. "And what possible reason could Scotland Yard have for bursting into my humble flat, sir?" Singh asked, eyes wide in innocence. "I am but a humble person who does a little harmless trading out of his own home. There is no law against that, now is there inspector?" His heavily macassar-oiled black hair flopped down on one side of his face. With a quick and vigorous shake of the head, he sent it back into place.

"No, indeed." Moss nodded. "Now, what do we have here, I wonder?"

He reached towards the cloth on the table but Singh held up his hands to ward him off.

"You have no right to go through my things! Do you have a search warrant, inspector?"

"Nay, I do not. I would just like to ask you a few questions is all, Mr. Singh. I give you my word I willna' attempt to lift yon wee bit of velvet that you seem to feel is so important."

"You will not attempt to lift this?" Singh sounded doubtful.

"Nay. I will not."

A large hand suddenly reached around from behind Singh, grasped the edge of the velvet and pulled it away, disclosing a display of brilliant diamonds and other precious stones. Singh cried out in dismay.

"Of course, I canna' speak for my good sergeant there," said Moss.

Kaster again came to his feet.

"Sit down, Mr. Kaster, or I will have my sergeant take care of you." The portly figure again sat, his monocle gleaming in the light of the gasolier.

"A little harmless trading, is it? And what, might I ask, are these baubles?"

"They are not real," said Kaster. "They – they are traveler's samples."

"Is that right?" asked Moss. "And so it wouldna' matter to you if we were to confiscate these, then?"

"Be quiet, you fool!" Singh snapped at Kaster. "They can easily find out if they are real."

"Oh, I believe they are real," said Moss. "Only too real. Just ask some of the ladies who allowed the 'spirits' to take them away for a wee while."

"You know about that?" gasped Kaster.

"Oh, aye. That is what brought me here."

"There is no way you can tell ownership of these stones," said Singh, looking smug. "Oh, yes. You can tell that they are genuine, but one diamond looks pretty much like another, I think you will agree. How can you tell where it came from? You cannot prove that they are not mine."

"Oh, I think we can, Mr. Singh." Moss moved around the table to the Wooton desk. It stood open, revealing its one hundred and ten compartments. Moss couldn't help thinking of the advertisements he had seen for such a desk: *A place for everything and everything in its place*. It had a bird's-eye maple interior with decorative gallery and carving. It was said that Her Majesty herself owned one. He wondered how Singh had acquired such a valuable piece.

"You should really keep this thing closed up when you're not using it," Moss said.

"But I was . . . I mean . . ."

The inspector reached down and picked up an item lying out on the lowered desk flap. It was a ring. "Now if I am not mistaken this ring is very much like one that is missing from Lady Constance Marlborough, would you not say, sergeant?"

Sergeant Gilmore had not the slightest idea what his superior meant but was smart enough to nod vigorously and mumble acquiescence.

Singh threw up his hands in surrender. "I told that woman I would need a lot of time to work on that," he muttered.

"That woman?"

"Lady Marlborough's personal maid," admitted Singh. "I had done business with her many years ago, back in India, but I should not have worked with her now."

"No, you should not. Sergeant Gilmore! I think we need your derbies for these gentlemen."


"Why are you investigating Lady Marlborough, Bertie?" Taffy Lloyd thumbed through the *Debrett's Peerage* that his friend had returned, before placing it back on his reference bookshelf.

Bertie sat in Taffy's office and glanced out of the windows at the reporters and columnists busily working in the crowded office. He recalled the many times he had sat there in the past, absorbing Taffy's advice and learning the ropes of being a newspaperman.

"We seem to have exhausted everyone else, Taffy. Either Inspector Moss or myself have looked into all of the other members of Lady Marlborough's séance circle and come up empty. We were surprised when it turned out that the medium was actually a woman and had, almost certainly, been the one who murdered Captain Grimsby. But now, of course, we need to find who murdered the medium . . . and Lady Marlborough herself has to be considered."

"Do you really think it's her, boyo?"

Bertie slowly shook his head. "I think it's highly improbable but, as I said, we have to consider everyone."

"So what did you need Debrett's for?"

Bertie told his friend of his discovery of the close friendship of the three young women, in their early years. "Lady Marlborough seemed to suddenly disappear," he concluded. "There just ceased to be any reference to her in 1842 or from then on. She wasn't mentioned in the society pages for many more years. Obviously something drastic happened at that time to stop her from coming out. I'm hoping that I might be able to trace Lady Marcia Effington or Lady Sarah Duberin and to see if either one of them is willing to open up to me."

"If they were as close as you're suggesting, Bertie, I doubt that they would divulge any great secrets."

Bertie nodded. "I'm sure you're right, but I can at least try."

The Welshman tapped the spine of the reference book. "So what did you learn from this?"

"Lady Marcia was the daughter of the Marquis of Dawnton. Apparently she married William 'Willy' Struthers, Viscount Plumley, and so is now Lady Marcia Struthers, Viscountess Plumley. They live at Seven Cedars in Sussex. I think it might be worth a trip out to Seven Cedars to see what I can see."

East Sussex is on the South Downs; a line of chalk hills that run across the southern part of the county. Seven Cedars was located close to the tiny town of Battle, almost fifty miles from London and the site of the Battle of Hastings in 1066. The town was built around Battle Abbey, located at the opposite end of the town from Seven Cedars. Bertie had written to the Viscountess, requesting an interview and – somewhat to his surprise – had been granted one. When he arrived at the stately home he was shown into the drawing room by the butler.

The room was papered in light blue velvet flocking. Heavy dark blue drapes framed the large windows. The room was crowded with miscellaneous tables and chairs; the furniture all very dark but highly polished. Bertie noticed whatnots, console tables, sofa tables, and other occasional tables. Many were covered with *objets d'art* and knick-knacks. Jardinières were about the room, displaying fresh flowers and trailing ferns. Just inside the entranceway stood a pedestal bearing a stuffed toucan under a glass dome. The room was dominated by an elaborate Carrara white marble fireplace which had the arms of the Plumley family carved into it. A large oil portrait of the first Viscount Plumley hung over the fireplace.

"Mr. Bertram Hawkins, is it?"

Lady Struthers languished on a deep blue, velvet couch, a long ivory cigarette-holder held in her bejeweled fingers. She wore an elegant tea gown of pale violet Sicilienne trimmed with velvet, which set off her coiffured silver-grey hair.

Bertie was surprised to find a second lady also there; a grim-faced woman with a mouth set in a determined straight line. She was dressed in a black and dark-green bombazine gown with a necklace of onyx beads at her neck and a matching bracelet over her dark green gloves. She sat straight-backed on the edge of a lady's parlor chair.

Lady Struthers waved a hand nonchalantly towards her companion. "My dear friend, Lady Duberin," she said.

Bertie was thrilled to find that both the ladies of the original Three Graces were there together.

"Now what is it that you think I can do for you, Mr. Hawkins? Are you sure that it isn't my husband you wish to see?"

"No, my lady. It is definitely yourself. And might I say that I am delighted to find you in the company of Lady Duberin. It is my understanding that you two ladies have been good, close friends for many years."

"You intrigue me, Mr. Hawkins." Lady Struthers drew on her Egyptian cigarette as she studied him. "You know far more of us than we do of you. You mentioned Scotland Yard, in your correspondence. What, pray, does that estimable establishment want with two elderly ladies?"

"I am not an official member of Scotland Yard," explained Bertie. "I have the privilege of working with their Inspector Moss from time to time but I am here today on my own volition."

"In your *prise de contact* you mentioned a murder." She flicked ash into a jade ash tray on the sofa table beside her. "That is the only reason I agreed to see you." She glanced at her companion. "It sounded so intriguing Sarah. Don't you think?"

Lady Duberin shrugged and said nothing.

"The murder occurred at the home of a lady whom I believe was once a close friend of the two of you," said Bertie, wondering if he should advance and sit down uninvited or should just stand there while they eyed him up and down.

"Even more intriguing!" cried Lady Struthers. "Do tell."

"Lady Constance Marlborough . . ." began Bertie.

"Enough!" It was the dark clad figure on the chair. Lady Duberin stamped her foot; a sound that would have been resonating, thought Bertie, had it not been for the thick Turkey carpet that covered the floor. "I will not listen to that woman's name."

"Now Sarah," soothed Lady Struthers. "Let us hear out Mr. Hawkins. It has been many years – far too many years, if you want my honest opinion – since we were in contact. Just because of Rich. . ."

"Stop, Marcia!" Lady Duberin came to her feet, her eyes flashing.

Lady Struthers looked down at her lap and murmured "Sorry, Sarah."

There was a moment of silence and then Lady Duberin resumed her seat. Lady Struthers looked up at Bertie. "I am afraid this interview is at an end, Mr. Hawkins."

"But . . ."

"At an end."

"Yes. Yes, of course." Bertie realized it would be useless to argue. "I thank you for your time, Lady Struthers."

She inclined her head very slightly, in acknowledgement. Bertie turned back to the door and was a little surprised to see it opened, in anticipation, by the butler.

# Chapter Twenty

The Earl of Marlborough's estate was located in Wiltshire, on the main London-Bath highway. Marston Keep, the ancestral home, stood on the chalk downs overlooking the Vale of Pewsey and on the edge of the historic Savernake Forest established by William the Conqueror.

"Tell me again why we're going to this castle," said Arnold, gazing out of the railway-carriage windows at the passing scenery. The Great Western Railway line left London's Paddington Station and went, by way of Reading, out to the West Country and on to Exeter. Bertie and Arnold were due to change trains at Savernake and there take the smaller branch line north to Marlborough.

"It's not a castle, Arnold. Just a very large manor house, so far as I know, though I've never actually seen it. But we are going there to see if we can learn a little more about those missing years of Lady Marlborough."

"Missing years?"

"Yes. Why it was that she suddenly disappeared from the most important episode in the life of an aristocratic young lady . . . the coming

out. We know that just months before the start of
the season, Lady Marlborough dropped out of sight.
Her lifetime friends were left alone and, in fact, she
never did return to them. It looks as though it was
more than three years before she was again
mentioned in any magazine. I'm hoping to find out
what happened."

The train chugged across the plains of
Berkshire and into the high downland and wide
valleys of Wiltshire. At Savernake they
disembarked and waited on the little station
platform for the local train coming up from
Andover and going to Marlborough, Swindon and
Cirencester. When it arrived it was a short, two-car
train with a small but energetic engine seemingly
anxious to keep going. It was a little over five miles
to Marlborough and when they arrived the time was
close to noon.

The village consisted of no more than a half
dozen cottages, a church, and the inevitable public
house: *The Shepherdess*. Bertie led the way to the
latter.

"I think we might as well fortify ourselves
before we approach our goal, Arnold. Let's see if
their ploughman's platter is as good at the ones in
London."

They quickly determined that it was every
bit as good as any they had tasted. They washed it
down with some of the excellent local hard cider
and sat back contented.

The pub was old and for generations had
been the regular evening gathering-place for the
adult population. With its red curtains, low beamed

ceiling, blazing fire in the wide fireplace, worn and
polished oak tables and benches, it was seductively
inviting and to many of the locals must have been a
true home from home.

"What's the plan, Bertie? What do you want
me to do?"

"Just stay close to me and listen to anything
and everything," said Bertie. "When I spoke with
the two ladies, Lady Struthers started to say what
sounded like the name Richard, but Lady Duberin
cut her off. Whenever you can, write down what is
said in your notebook, but don't be too obvious
about it."

"Who are these people we are going to see,
Bertie?"

Bertie got up and stretched. The day was
warm for late October, yet not warm enough to go
without a top coat. He took his down from the peg
on the wall and shrugged into it as Arnold did the
same.

"It seems that Earl Marlborough – Lady
Marlborough's brother – is away in Scotland for
this month and next, so we don't have to try to see
him. What I want to do is to speak with a Mrs.
Mortimer. My information is that Mrs. Clara
Mortimer was the cook in the old earl's day, when
Lady Marlborough was growing up here. Mrs.
Mortimer is long since retired and now lives in one
of the cottages on the estate, with a sister. I don't
think the sister was a servant here at that time, but
I'm not certain about that."

"And this Mrs. Mortimer can tell you
what?"

"Ah!" said Bertie enigmatically.

The landlord of the tavern, in answer to Bertie's enquiries, summoned a pony and trap.

"Take these two Lond'un gentlemen up to the big 'ouse, 'enry," he said to the driver, an old man in a leather surcoat, wearing a battered bowler hat and leather gaiters.

The driver watched Bertie and Arnold climb into the trap and then cracked his whip and started off along the road leading out of the village.

"Actually I'd like to go directly to see Mrs. Mortimer. I have the name Rose Cottage," said Bertie to their driver. "You know that?"

The man nodded but said nothing.

"Mrs. Clara Mortimer?" further queried Bertie.

Again he nodded and gazed steadily out over the pony's back. They drove on for several miles. Bertie and Arnold exchanged glances. After taking a winding side lane, their driver brought the trap to a halt outside an ancient thatched-roof cottage. It had white-washed outer walls and diamond-paned windows. The little garden about the house had obviously been a profusion of flowers earlier in the year but now looked sadly neglected. Bertie asked the driver to come back in an hour and, climbing down, led the way up to the low, red-painted, front door. He knocked on the polished brass knocker.

The old lady who answered the door was surprised to see visitors, but listened patiently to Bertie's explanation of why they were there and then opened the door wide to allow them access.

"My elder sister is the one what you want," she said. "She is Mrs. Mortimer, as was one time cook to 'is lordship.'"

She led them through the small outer room to the cozier inner room. A second elderly woman sat there in front of the fire, darning a woolen cardigan and straining to see in the dim light from the fire and what little came through the one small, begrimed window. She peered up at the two men through steel-rimmed spectacles, one lens of which Bertie noticed to be cracked.

"These 'ere two gen'lemen 'as come down from Lond'un to talk to you, Clara. Somethin' about your days up at the big 'ouse."

Clara Mortimer studied Bertie and Arnold but made no move to invite them farther into her cottage.

The sister fussed around and cleared knitting and sewing materials off a settle. She indicated it to the visitors and went to sit down in her own chair, opposite her sister. "You must take no notice of me," she said. "I'm Marjory. It's Clara as is the one."

"Thank you, Marjory. Thank you, Mrs. Mortimer," said Bertie, smiling at the older woman as he and Arnold sat down on the settle.

"Would you be wantin' a cup o' tea?" asked Marjory, but made no attempt to get up again.

"Oh, no. No, thank you," said Bertie. He turned to Clara. "Mrs. Mortimer, I understand that you were the cook at the time that Lady Marlborough – Lady Constance Marlborough, that is – was growing up here at Marston Keep?"

Clara Mortimer seemed to think for a moment before nodding. "That were Miss Constance."

"Right." Bertie glanced at Arnold before continuing. "I understand that she spent a lot of time with two friends who would visit here."

"That'd be Miss Marcia and Miss Sarah," put in Marjory.

"I know that!" snapped Clara. "Of course it was Miss Marcia and Miss Sarah. Wasn't they always 'ere? Stayed 'ere at the big 'ouse all summer; every summer."

"Couldn't separate 'em with a bucket o' water," said Marjory. "Close as . . ."

"I know that!" said Clara. "The Three Somethings they used to call them."

"Graces. Three Graces."

"I know that!"

Bertie sighed. "I wonder if you can recall the time leading up to Lady Constance's coming out?" he said. "I understand . . ."

"Never did," said Mrs. Mortimer.

"No. Never did," echoed her sister.

"Why was that?" Bertie persisted.

The two sisters looked at one another for a long moment.

"It was all a very long time ago," continued Bertie, hoping to get them to continue.

"It were for the best," said Mrs. Mortimer, concentrating on her darning.

"For the best," came the echo.

"Could you – would you be good enough to explain?" Bertie smiled his friendliest smile but neither woman was looking at him.

"A bundle of joy was them three ladies," said Mrs. Mortimer, after a moment.

"Bundle of joy."

"They used to love to sneak down to my kitchen. O' course, 'is lordship didn't know. 'e wouldn't 'ave been 'appy."

"Not 'appy at all, *I'm* sure."

"Liked Miss Constance to know 'er place, 'e did. But she – and them other two – they just loved sneaking down to my kitchen."

"And what did they do there, in your kitchen?" asked Bertie, hoping to get where he wanted to go indirectly if necessary.

"I teached 'em to cook," said Mrs. Mortimer proudly. "Them young things didn't know an egg from a 'tater till I showed 'em."

"Clara showed 'em all right."

"Mind you, there were nothin' fancy. Just simple things like how to prepare a salad and stuff like that."

As Bertie looked about the small room he noticed a faded photograph on a dresser, half hidden behind some cups and saucers.

"Might I ask?" he said. "Is that a photograph of the staff that worked here?" He pointed.

Marjory leaned forward to see where he was pointing. Clara peered over the rims of her spectacles.

"Oh, yes!" cried Marjory. She got up and retrieved the picture, reseating herself and studying it. "I almost forgot we got this, Clara. Look! 'ere's you an' them all. Right in front of the kitchen door. Remember?"

She passed the photograph across to her sister, who laid down her cardigan and took it in both hands. She pushed her glasses up on her nose and looked hard at it.

"I was fat in them days," she said, and chuckled; the first time Bertie had seen her smile. "I remember when this was took. Old Wilfred Jenkins, the under butler, was 'aving a snoodge and missed it. 'e was fair took for missing 'is only chance to be photo-pictured." She cackled.

"May I see?" asked Bertie. It was handed to him. The servants stood rigidly in three rows, the well-endowed figure of Mrs. Mortimer in the center. Bertie happened to turn the picture and saw a list of names written on the back. "Ah! I see here the names of everyone." He studied them. "By any chance, was there a Richard among the staff? I don't see . . ."

"Richard . . . no. Oh! Richmond, you must mean!" cried Marjory. "Richmond Drury. Yes. Poor Richmond. 'e was – what was 'e, Clara?"

"Footman," said her sister, suddenly serious again. "Poor Richmond."

"What happened to him?" Arnold couldn't contain himself.

"Nothing . . ." began Mrs. Mortimer.

"Died. Poisoned," said Marjory, speaking at the same time.

"Poisoned?" It was Arnold again.

The two elderly ladies looked at one another and then it all came pouring out. Bertie realized that they must have kept it bottled up for so many years and now, looking at the photograph again and talking about the old days, it had to be spoken of.

"We was all flummoxed."

"Such a 'andsome boy."

"Poor Miss Constance and Miss Sarah."

"That was the end for both of 'em."

"That is the Lord's truth!"

"Never the same again."

"Never!"

"Miss Sarah was took 'ard."

"Well, they both was, but Miss Constance . . . well, no one can say she didn't bring it on 'erself!"

It took Bertie a lot of questioning to sort out everything. Arnold got out his notebook and scribbled. It was more than an hour later that the two men finally left the cottage; Bertie with a satisfied look on his face. They found the trap waiting and their driver lying across the seat with his hat over his face, snoring.

"Lady Marlborough sent us a very large sum in gratitude for you getting back her missing ring," said Nellie.

"That's nice," said Arnold. "I wouldn't be surprised if Miss Fotherington will feel the same way about her necklace."

"Lady Marlborough may not feel quite so generous in a day or so," said Bertie, his face serious.

"What do you mean?"

"I'll explain it all very soon," said Bertie. "First, I need to get together with Campbell and then go with him to talk to Lady Marlborough."

"Again?"

"Yes, Nell. Again," said her husband. "Though I somehow think that this may be the last time we visit Kingston House."

The hansom cab moved along Grosvenor Place towards Hyde Park Corner.

"You are sure about all this then, Bertram?" asked Inspector Moss, a deep frown on his already lined face.

"Just one or two small details that I'm hoping her ladyship can fill-in for us," replied Bertie. "But yes, I got the main outline from Mrs. Clara Mortimer and her sister. I think that, if you need to, you can verify the major points with the Swindon police. Marlborough falls under their jurisdiction I believe."

Moss grunted agreement. "And this Richard Drury was a footman for the earl?" he asked.

"Richmond, not Richard. Yes. This was where all Lady Marlborough's troubles began. It seems the young Drury was a handsome devil who drew the attention of both the young Lady

Marlborough and her close friend Lady Sarah Duberin."

The inspector sighed. "Ah, so many problems come about when the upper class and the lower class don't keep to their appointed places."

Bertie pursed his lips. "Well, it's my belief that young love is a poor acknowledger of place and time."

The hansom turned onto Knightsbridge where it was briefly delayed in traffic. A horse-drawn omnibus and a brewer's dray seemed determined to hog the road, side by side, before the omnibus finally stopped to discharge some passengers.

"Lady Duberin was especially smitten with Drury, it seems," Bertie elaborated. "The young lothario played the girls one against the other, eventually seducing Lady Constance Marlborough and thereby breaking the friendship and love the two young ladies had for each other."

"Where did this third lady fit into all this?"

"She really didn't. It seems that she was not quite the looker that the other two were and so did not draw Drury with the same energy."

The cab came to a halt in front of Kingston House and the two men got out.

"I take it there is a lot more to the story," said Moss, as he lifted the brass door-knocker and allowed it to drop.

The butler, Parker, escorted them into the library where they were shortly joined by Lady Marlborough.

"Have you come to tell me who was the murderer of my maid . . . and my medium?" she asked, settling herself in a high-backed rosewood armchair close to the fireplace.

Bertie noticed that the cabinet had been removed and the room returned to its original function. He and the inspector remained standing.

"In a sense yes, my lady," responded Moss. "Though we do have to beg your indulgence and clear up one or two points, if we may?"

She inclined her head and then fixed her gaze on Bertie.

"So, Mr. Hawkins, you are now displayed in your true colors, apparently. The eyes and ears of Scotland Yard in my sacred circle, it would seem."

Inspector Moss attempted a smile which did not quite succeed. "We were, at that time, doing all that we could to determine who had murdered one of your sitters, my lady. Your Captain Grimsby."

"Not exactly *my* Captain Grimsby," she replied. "But I would have thought that you might have consulted me before infiltrating what was a very private group of people . . . unless, of course, *I* was one of your suspects?" She appraised the inspector from head to foot.

Moss shifted uneasily and quickly ran a finger around his collar. "To the matter in hand, Lady Marlborough," he said, in what Bertie had come to think of as his 'official' voice. "Mr. Hawkins has indeed done some highly valuable work for the Yard – bringing about the return of your heirloom ring, which I believe you have already acknowledged?"

She had the grace to again incline her head, this time in Bertie's direction.

"So," Moss continued, "I was not unhappy to learn that he had taken matters into his own hands in verifying certain points about your ladyship's own background."

"Oh?" She sat up straighter and now fixed a steely look on Bertie.

"Yes, my lady." Bertie was not to be browbeaten. He slipped a notebook – Arnold's – out of his pocket and referred to it as he spoke. "I know it was many years ago but I understand that there was a certain 'incident', if I may refer to it as such, involving your ladyship and one Richmond Drury, one time footman to your father the earl." He was aware of a sharp intake of breath from her ladyship but he continued. "This footman apparently died under unusual circumstances."

"It was ruled accidental!"

"An accidental poisoning?" said Bertie. "And by ingesting the poisonous part of a potato?"

"What?" The inspector took a step forward. He had not heard this from Bertie prior to now. "Did you say a potato? Like our friend the medium, Prince whatshisname?"

"Prince        Honoré,"        snapped        Lady Marlborough. She returned her attention to Bertie. "What, pray, Mr. Hawkins, does this event from so many years ago have to do with me?"

"I understand that the death was ruled accidental," said Bertie, "though after the earl, your father – who was also the local magistrate – ruled it so."

Lady Marlborough remained stoic. "And whatever would induce anyone to murder Richmond . . . Mr. Drury?"

Bertie took a deep breath and glanced at the inspector. He seemed caught up in the whole dénouement, so Bertie plunged ahead. "Because you had found yourself pregnant, my lady."

## *Chapter Twenty-One*

There was complete and utter silence, finally broken by the sound of a coal tumbling in the fireplace. The fire flared briefly.

"Go on, Bertram," said Inspector Moss quietly. Lady Marlborough said nothing.

"Your life seemed ruined," continued Bertie. "Indeed in many ways it was. There would be no coming out. You would be shunned by society. No man would look at you let alone consider marriage." He paused. "There was but one possible course of action."

"What was that?" The inspector's voice was hoarse; his eyes large.

"You were sent off to Europe to have your child, which was then placed with foster parents . . . a Mr. and Mrs. Shepperton, I believe. After a reasonable amount of time – a few years – you were able to return to England and very gradually return to some sort of a place in society with no one any the wiser. No one other than your two childhood friends, that is."

Lady Marlborough came to her feet and moved across to stand in front of the fireplace, staring down into the coals.

"You are very clever, Mr. Hawkins," she said finally, her voice soft and subdued. The inspector turned a little so that his good ear was towards her. "That is exactly what happened. Oh, I am not admitting to poisoning Richmond; I'm not fool enough to say that. But Mrs. Mortimer had taught me to cook and had warned me to be very careful with potatoes – to make sure that I did not use any that were green or that had large eyes to them." She turned away and looked at Bertie. "But I did make the potato salad that day, so long ago, and who can say whether or not – somehow, without anyone's knowledge – some of that poisoning got into it?"

"Like with your medium?" Moss couldn't help asking. She ignored him.

"Sarah was madly in love with Richmond," continued Lady Marlborough. "Not I. I only flirted with him . . . but he took me too seriously. Sarah held his death against me." She took a deep breath and then seemed to resume her superior manner. "But why do you drag up all of this nonsense from the past, Mr. Hawkins. Of what use can it possibly be to you now?" She returned to her chair and sat. She pointed to two other chairs. "Why don't you two gentlemen seat yourselves? You're standing there like . . . like policemen!"

Bertie and the inspector moved to the pair of walnut Rococo Revival gentlemen's chairs indicated and sat.

"What happened to the child, Bertram?" Moss couldn't help asking.

"Ah! An important point, Campbell . . . as it happens." Bertie glanced again at the notebook before continuing. "The Sheppertons took good care of her – it was a girl – as I'm sure they had been well paid to do. Mr. Shepperton later held a commission in the Royal Engineers and the family eventually found themselves in India."

"But wasn't . . ?" The inspector started to speak but then stopped and waved Bertie to continue.

"The girl, Jessica Elisabeth, remained unmarried until she was thirty-four, at which time she finally became betrothed to one Cyril Harold Grimsby, just four years her senior."

"I blame him for what followed," said Lady Marlborough.

"Yes," agreed Bertie. "He did abuse his wife, terribly. They eventually left India and returned to England in 1884 and she – unable to take further abuse – left him the following year."

"I can continue your story there, Mr. Hawkins," said Lady Marlborough. She sat up straight in her chair and fixed her eyes on the dying fire. Her face was pale and drawn. She shook her head slightly from side to side, as though rejecting thoughts. "Shepperton had died some years before Lisbeth married Grimsby. Apparently, on his death bed, he told the girl who her mother was . . . is. Myself." She was silent for a long moment and Bertie wondered whether he should speak, but eventually she picked up the narrative. "When the girl left Grimsby she had nowhere to go; she knew no one in England. So she found her way to me."

"That must have been a shock," murmured the inspector.

"To put it mildly," said Lady Marlborough. "I had no time for the girl. I – my father – had settled the affair, and paid handsomely for it, many long years ago. I felt no obligation to her."

"Your own flesh and . . ." began Bertie.

"Spare me!" she snapped. "No! I had no obligation to her." She looked hard at Bertie and then equally at Moss. "Would you believe that the hussy came to me and, when I rejected her, had the temerity to attempt to blackmail me into taking her in."

"Attempted to?" asked Moss.

"Threatened, if you prefer. Yes, inspector. And, like a fool, I gave in. I allowed her to reside here as my personal maid. I hadn't gone through all of that turmoil so many years ago to now have it all brought out into the open."

"Where did the spiritualist nonsense come from?" asked Moss.

"Not nonsense, inspector, I beg you. Oh yes, there are charlatans – any number of them, I regret to say – but that does not negate the work of many more fine, upstanding mediums."

Lady Marlborough reached behind her to where a gold cigarette box rested on an onyx-surfaced lamp stand. She opened it. A long, ivory cigarette holder lay beside the box. She took a cigarette, fitted it into the holder, and then put it to her lips. Bertie rose and took a lucifer from beside the box and held the flame as she blew smoke into the air.

Bertie sat down again. "You were explaining about how spiritualism entered the picture," he said.

Lady Marlborough nodded. "That was Lisbeth's idea. She knew of my interest in the subject and she had some small ability herself, in that direction. She did connect me with my mother."

"Whose idea to dress as a man and claim to be a prince?" asked Moss.

"Again, Lisbeth's." She lowered the cigarette holder and sighed before continuing. "The way she suggested it, it seemed like an interesting experiment. Foreign royalty is always fascinating, especially so when connected to spirit communication. Look at that Russian woman, what's her name?"

"Madam Blavatsky?" asked Bertie.

"Yes. I understand she went to Germany earlier his year. Anyway, her cousin was Count Witte and her grandmother was Princess Helene Dolgoruki. She has been exhibiting her mediumship all over Europe and has gained a tremendous following."

"But why as a man?" persisted Moss.

"Apparently Lisbeth found it helpful to gather information about her clients while dressed as a woman, then to dispense that knowledge as a male medium. No one, she assured me, would connect the two of them."

"She had clients?"

"She honed her skills with my special group, but then acquired large fees for private sittings." Lady Marlborough drew on her cigarette then, suddenly tiring of it, snatched it from the holder and flung it into the fire. "The Devil take her! She went too far!"

Bertie looked at the inspector, who gave the briefest of shrugs and tugged on his mustache.

"Went too far?" Bertie queried.

"When she started stealing my jewelry. When she took my mother's diamond and ruby ring. She had no intention of returning that, I can tell you!"

Bertie looked hard at Lady Marlborough. He glanced at the inspector then turned to face her ladyship directly.

"Is that when you determined to kill her?" he asked.


"What is this, again, Nell?" asked Arnold, studying the dish that his sister was serving. The aroma was mouth-watering and Arnold had his eating utensils in his hands ready to do battle.

"My mother called it Galantine of Pork," said Nellie. "Breast of pork, nicely seasoned. And I'm serving it with beef tongue stuffing, peas – Bertie's favorite – carrots, and potato cakes. Dessert will be rhubarb pie with custard."

"Mmm!" Isobel, standing by to pass around the plates, made loud sounds of appreciation until she caught Nellie's eye.

"I think I've gained a few pounds weight since I started enjoying your dinners, Nellie," said Inspector Moss, spreading his napkin across his knees and fastening his eyes on the pork.

"So, is Lady Marlborough in custody?" asked Bertie. "Not to detract from Nell's dinner, but I was wondering."

"Not in custody, on Detective Chief Inspector Villiers's orders," said Moss. "I don't think she is likely to try to run away. She has her cousin Sir Mortimer Long, the QC, who is going to handle her case. Not that I can see him doing her any good, but you never know."

"Exactly how did she poison the medium?" asked Nellie, passing the plates to Isobel, who ran around the table serving everyone. "I know Bertie said something about a potato salad but he also said that he ate it and so did some of the others. How could that be, Campbell?"

Moss took a moment to heap stuffing, peas and carrots on to his plate. "It seems that on her way to delivering one of those salads to the prince she took a quick side trip to the kitchen, where she had hidden away some shredded potato of the green, toxic variety to sprinkle on it – Doctor Wright assures me it can act just as lethally as arsenic or foxglove or any one of a dozen poisons."

"How terrible!"

"We don't know about the episode in the days of her youth, with the footman, but it seems that is where she found the potency of the potato. Probably she only wanted to hurt the footman but it did kill him."

"Can this be brought up in any trial?" asked Bertie.

Moss shook his head. "I've applied to Swindon to get their records of that case, if they can find them. These country stations are not too reliable, you know."

"So your days of going to séances are over, Bertie?" said Arnold, waving his fork in the air and scattering peas across the table. He hurried to pick them up, looking through lowered brows at his sister.

"At least for the time being," said Bertie. "I did find the whole subject fascinating and I do believe there are some good, authentic mediums out there, but I think I'll let the subject sit for a while."

"I do have one question," said Nellie, thoughtfully. "When the medium was tied to the chair and yet the musical instruments were heard playing? How was that done?"

"Yes, Bertram," said the inspector. "I'd be interested to know that."

Bertie helped himself to a little more pork and then looked at the others. "It was Mr. Maskelyne who explained that to me. It seems that the arms of the chair, to which the medium was tied, were loose in the sockets where they fitted into the back of the chair. The medium could pull out the arms and, although they would still be fastened to his own arms, he would then be free to stand and move away from the chair. He could then go to the false back of the cabinet where he had placed duplicate musical instruments. Playing on those, we sitters would assume that we were hearing the instruments under the cloth on the table. He would then close the back of the cabinet and sit down again, fitting the chair arms into their sockets. When we opened the cabinet, we would find the musical instruments all on the table and still covered by the cloth and the medium still apparently secure in the chair."

"Well I'm . . . well, who would have thought!" said Moss.

"Cor!"

"Isobel," said Nellie. "You don't have any of the potato cakes."

Isobel shook her head with a shudder. "No, Mrs. 'awkins. I ain't taking no chances on them 'taters!"

Everyone laughed. The red-headed maid blushed and then joined in the laughter. But she didn't try the potato cakes.

**RAYMOND BUCKLAND** is a prolific prize-winning author of both fiction and non-fiction. His books have been translated into seventeen foreign languages. Born and raised in England, he is fascinated by the Victorian age and loves to set his mysteries in that era.

Visit www.raymondbucklandbooks.com